LIES BETWEEN US

ALSO BY JESSICA GOODMAN

They Wish They Were Us

They'll Never Catch Us

The Counselors

The Legacies

The Meadowbrook Murders

LIES BETWEEN US

JESSICA GOODMAN

putnam

G. P. PUTNAM'S SONS

G. P. PUTNAM'S SONS
An imprint of Penguin Random House LLC
1745 Broadway, New York, NY 10019
penguinrandomhouse.com

Design by Rebecca Aidlin
Text set in Granjon LT Std

Library of Congress Cataloging-in-Publication Data
Names: Goodman, Jessica, 1990– author
Title: Lies between us / Jessica Goodman.
Description: New York : G.P. Putnam's Sons, 2026. | Audience: Ages 14 years and up | Summary: "A murder-mystery set during the summer after a local teen is found dead in the water, exposing the devastating secrets three sisters keep"—Provided by publisher.
Identifiers: LCCN 2025029538 (print) | LCCN 2025029539 (ebook) | ISBN 9798217005239 hardcover | ISBN 9798217005253 trade paperback | ISBN 9798217005246 epub
Subjects: CYAC: Murder—Fiction | Secrets—Fiction | Sisters—Fiction | Mystery and detective stories | LCGFT: Detective and mystery fiction | Novels
Classification: LCC PZ7.1.G6542 Tg 2026 (print) | LCC PZ7.1.G6542 (ebook)
LC record available at https://lccn.loc.gov/2025029538
LC ebook record available at https://lccn.loc.gov/2025029539

First published in the United States of America by G. P. Putnam's Sons, 2026

Manufactured in the United States of America
BVG

ISBN 9798217005239 (hardcover)
ISBN 9798217005253 (paperback)
2nd Printing

The authorized representative in the EU for product safety and compliance is Penguin Random House Ireland, Morrison Chambers, 32 Nassau Street, Dublin D02 YH68, Ireland, https://eu-contact.penguin.ie.

To Rūta and Simone,
for making this one (all of them) sing

MILLIE

I did not plan to start the summer by dangling out of a second-story window. But on this breezy night, all that separates me from plunging to my death and living to see my eighteenth birthday is the grip my older sister, Lucy, has on my wrists from inside my bedroom. Frankie, the youngest, suggested this was the best way to sneak out of our house. Maybe for her.

"It's easy!" Frankie calls from fifteen feet below. "Swing your foot over to the ladder thingy and hold on."

"It's called a trellis," Lucy says above me.

"Whatever." Frankie blows a raspberry, clearly not caring a bit about our safety.

"She's insane," I say through gritted teeth as Lucy readjusts her clutch on my wrists, inching her fingers down to get a better hold. "Don't you dare let go." I kick my feet back and forth, hitting nothing but wind.

I make the mistake of glancing down and suck in a big breath of air. *Crap.* The ground is very, very far away. "I can't do this."

"Why did we let Frankie go down first again?" Lucy says, her breath heavy above me.

"Because I was the only one who volunteered." Frankie laughs and plops down on the grass.

I shake my head. "Unbelievable."

Lucy knits her brow together in determination. "I won't let you fall, Millie. Just get it over with."

"Easy for you to say." I grunt and fix my gaze on the trellis beside me. "You're not the one who's half-in, half-out." I swing my leg with as much strength as I can muster, and with a rush of relief and a small miracle, my foot latches on to a section of wood. "I got it!"

"I'm gonna let go," Lucy says.

"Wait! Let me get my grip." I release one of her hands and grab a slat of wood, then redistribute all my weight and scamper down to the earth, wisteria and ivy crunching underfoot as I leap off onto the grass and roll over to Frankie.

"Oh my god," I say, pressing my cheek to the cool ground. "Never again."

Frankie leans back on her elbows, and we both look up to see Lucy crawling on the roof on her hands and knees, securing herself to the same pathway I took with what looks like no effort at all.

"Why is that so easy for you?" I ask.

Lucy looks back over her shoulder at me, and her lips spread into a smile.

"Wait a second. She's done this before." Frankie smacks the backside of her hand against my shoulder.

"Gotta get to Ethan somehow," Lucy says as she hops off the framework, landing on the grass on one dainty foot.

Of course. Lucy sneaks out to see him without us. I tuck a stray curl behind my ear. "Mom and Dad don't even care." I glance up to our parents' bedroom window and see their light still on, the silhouette of Mom reading in bed dark against the linen curtains. "It's practically sanctioned."

"Zip it!" Lucy says. "Don't ruin it for Frankie."

"Are you serious? They really know?" Frankie asks, turning to me.

"But that doesn't make it any less fun," I say. "I promise."

Lucy skips ahead toward the hedge that separates our home from the Silvers' property next door and waves her arm for us to follow. I grab Frankie's hand and pull her with me as we take off after Lucy through the grass. The stars are bright, illuminating us against the dark sky. When we get to the archway, I pause and close my eyes, inhaling.

Summer nights always smell the same: of sea salt and burnt driftwood, cut grass and lingering barbecue. Of beginnings. When I blink my eyes open, I see the moon glinting off the Long Island Sound, right over the boardwalk that leads to the beach. The bonfire we made only hours before is gone, but a tiny plume of smoke drifts into the air. We'd left a few blankets out there, rocks stationed at the corners to keep them secured, and I wonder who forgot to clean up. Alex, maybe. Probably Frankie. Goose pimples rise on my arms, and I shiver even though it's warm out, the breeze only a gentle suggestion.

Everything about this moment is perfect. I wish I could bottle up this feeling—the humming in my stomach, the fluttering in my heart. Every little indicator that reminds me *this* is what's important in life. My sisters, the beach, and the boys who live next door.

"Millie, let's go," Lucy whispers, and I follow my sisters through the archway that connects us to our next-door neighbors, a label that's never felt quite right. *Friends* doesn't feel intimate enough. And yet the Silvers aren't *family* either.

There is no word in the English language to describe the connection between our two households—whose last names are conveniently (and ridiculously) the Golds and the Silvers—whose members spend every Friday Shabbat dinner together, have open invitations to each other's snack pantries and sports equipment and first aid kits. Whose lives mirror one another's in peculiar and almost cosmic ways.

The Silvers are as much a part of my life as the cicadas that sound right after Memorial Day or my membership to the Pelican Island Tennis and Beach Club.

Lucy leads us to the pool house at the far end of their property, past the newly lined pickleball court, the crystal-clear infinity pool, and the tiny putting green Gil installed last spring when he and my dad decided their short games needed work.

"So, Mom and Dad *let* us come over here this late?" Frankie says. "We've been sneaking out after Shabbat every year for . . . ever."

"They think it's cute," Lucy says. Her voluminous hair falls down her back as she stands up straight, facing the side of the pool house. "Besides, it's not like they have anything to worry about. When was the last time something bad happened here?" We don't answer because the answer is *never.*

Lucy raises a fist and knocks three times, then waits. The lights are off inside, and the only sound comes from the tiny waves lapping at the shore. I shiver in my oversize T-shirt and sleep boxers, the unofficial uniform of Friday nights, when the six of us meet here. Tonight, my top says I BELIEVE IN HAPPILY EVER AFTER, a merch tee I snagged at the romance bookstore in Brooklyn the last time we schlepped into the city.

"Why do the boys insist on all this hoopla?" Frankie says. Her corkscrew curls are tied into a bun on the top of her head, sticking out every which way, and she fiddles with one, pulling a tendril from its secure station until it springs back into place.

"Because it's *fun*," Lucy says, knocking her with an elbow. "We get to pretend like we're in a secret club."

"We *are* in a secret club," I respond, though I flush when I hear desperation in my voice.

Shit, it's happening again. The wetness in my eyes, the soreness in my throat. The sentimentality I can usually push down has been rising to the surface so often, ever since Lucy and Ethan's graduation last week. The countdown to their departure has begun, and I hate that it's all I can think about. I've never known life without Lucy sleeping on the other side of my bedroom wall and I don't want to. When I think too hard about what it will be like without her asking me if I want to take a bike ride, singing Taylor Swift in the car, or communicating with me using just her eyes from across the dinner table, my brain gets hazy, like I can't quite picture that version of reality. If I had it my way, we'd stay these exact ages forever: Lucy, eighteen. Me, seventeen. Frankie, fifteen.

We had one perfect school year, when we all went to Pelican Island Academy's high school at the same time. Lucy drove us every morning, dropping Frankie off at the freshman circle before we parked in the senior lot, separating only when I had to go off to junior assembly. We saw each other in the halls, the bathrooms, at homecoming and pep rallies. I got to play on Lucy's varsity tennis team, and though Frankie sulked about being on JV, we all got to wear those uniforms together. And now it's over.

Lucy knocks again. "Let us in!"

Finally, a voice rings out from inside the pool house. "What's the password?"

"Oh my god, Alex, who cares?" Frankie steps forward and presses her face to the window.

"Nuh-uh, the password," says a different voice.

I can't fight the smile forming on my face. "Pennywise."

Lucy groans. "You used that one already, Trevor."

Laughter erupts inside the pool house and then finally the lights switch on and the door swings open, revealing all three Silver boys in various states of repose around the small room.

Alex, the youngest, is perched on top of the counter in the kitchenette, kicking his socked feet against the cabinets, twisting a Rubik's Cube around in his hands, even though he's crossing his vivid blue eyes at Frankie. Like Frankie, he's the physical outlier of his family: He's got the same features as his brothers—a round chin, sharp cheekbones, a nose that makes a near-perfect forty-five-degree angle—but he's the one who towers over the others, whose light eyes are so bright they seem to pierce your skin.

Trevor's laid out on the couch, my copy of the first Bridgerton novel in his hands. He pushes himself to sit up, his mouth forming a lazy smile. "Catch, Millie!" He tries to fling the book to me, but his face contorts into a wince as it falls to the floor at his feet. Ethan, the oldest boy, who's leaning against the doorframe, rushes to scoop it up.

"Dude, careful," Ethan says.

Ever since Trevor messed up his shoulder in a bike accident a few months ago, he's been itching to heal faster than he should, tossing balls and books and all sorts of stuff his physical therapist says he shouldn't. The only person he'll listen to is Ethan, who's giving him a stern look, a whole conversation passing between them.

"I know," Trevor says, sulking, and Ethan's face relaxes.

It's always jarring to look at them side by side. To everyone else, they're nearly identical, with their dark curls and broad shoulders. But when you know them as well as we do, it's obvious they couldn't be more different. That if I was faced with the question *Which one would you give your heart to?* there was only one answer.

Heat flames up my cheeks, down my neck, and there's a flicker in my core as I watch Ethan flip through the book—*my* book. The pages make a pleasant *whoosh*ing sound when they move through space. He looks up at me and smiles, a dark lock of hair flopping down to cover one of his eyes. When he pushes it back, his T-shirt rides up a little, revealing a sliver of skin, and a lightning bolt strikes my stomach. He extends his arm to me, the book in his hand. "Here you go."

I take it from him and hug the copy to my chest. "Thanks." The word comes out chalky, like all my words do when I'm talking to Ethan.

It's a sickness, I know. One I've tried to rid myself of for the past five years. But I can't help it.

I'm desperately in love with my sister's boyfriend.

LUCY

I lock eyes with Ethan, and that sweet, sloping grin spreads across his face. "Hey." His voice is low, and he leans in for a kiss, chaste by our measures, but even so Frankie makes a retching noise.

"Get a room!" she calls.

"Kissing is a totally normal greeting, Frankie." I sit down beside her and bump her shoulder with mine. "You'll have to try it sometime."

"Barf. At least next year, you guys can do that away from us."

"Knowing you two, you're going to have dorm rooms right next to each other," Alex teases.

Ethan squeezes my thigh, and I know what he's thinking. *I can't wait.* But my stomach seizes, and I desperately want to change the subject.

"Let's deal," I say. "Who's up?" Trevor pulls out a deck of cards from under the coffee table and starts shuffling. We've been doing this exact Friday-night ritual for years, since Frankie and Alex were old enough to understand the rules.

"Mills, hearts or what? It's your turn to choose." Trevor nudges Millie with his socked foot, but she's got her eyes on me, that bottom lip wobbling. *Oh no.* I hate when she gets like this.

"What are we going to do on Friday nights in the fall?" she asks, her voice strained. "When you're gone?"

A hush falls over the room, and while I used to think her sentimentality was sweet, I wish she'd stop making such a big deal about next year. The whole shtick has started to bug me and makes it so I can't focus on my emotions, only hers. I'd never say that to her face, though. My oldest-sister brain kicks on, and I reach my hand to hers and squeeze. "You'll do the same things, and it'll be fun. I promise."

My phone buzzes beside me, and Frankie swipes it before I can see. "Speaking of fun," Frankie says, "looks like Billy is having a throw down tonight."

I cringe. That's a party I have no intention of attending.

"Please say you're not going," Millie says. "We only have eight Fridays left."

"We're not going," I say, and elbow Ethan. "Right?"

"No way. I don't want to be hungover for work tomorrow." Ethan flashes a grin at Millie. "See you on the lifeguard stand."

"It's almost midnight," I say, not even trying to suppress a yawn. "Time to call it."

Everyone rises from their seats, yawning and rubbing their eyes. These nights usually go late like this, but over the past few weeks, Millie has been stretching them longer and longer, like she's desperate to make time stand still. Ethan's always telling me that I can't keep worrying about her like she's my kid or something, but that's impossible.

Mom says that having children is like having a piece of your heart walk around outside your body—that's how I feel about my sisters. Millie and Frankie are small slices of me, toddling out in the world on their own, and I'll always want to protect them.

As everyone makes their way to the door, Ethan grabs my hand and holds me back so we're the last ones in the pool house. "Wanna go down to the bonfire?" he asks, his breath soft on my ear. "I left some blankets down there."

"Okay," I say, even though the promise of sleep sounds better. "For a little."

When we get outside, Millie and Frankie are about to disappear through the archway between our properties, and Trevor and Alex are racing back to their house. Millie turns around, and I wave at her. "Go on without me," I say. "It's okay."

She nods once, her brows pinching, and then disappears behind the hedges.

Ethan slips his hand into mine, his touch as familiar as if it were my own. Together, we trod over the wooden walkway, beyond the dune, and drop down onto the blankets spread around the firepit. Only a few hours earlier, we were here with both sets of parents, roasting marshmallows, assembling s'mores, the air heavy with heat and humidity. But now the wind has picked up, whipping my hair across my face, and the darkness above is an inky black dotted with stars.

Ethan leans forward and blows on some of the embers that have stayed lit. I lay a few pieces of kindling on top, then stack driftwood like a Jenga tower. It doesn't take long for the splintered edges of wood to catch fire.

"How many hours do you think we've spent on this beach?" Ethan asks, leaning back to rest on his elbow.

"Months." I sit cross-legged and warm my hands against the flames. Ethan wraps his arm around my back, his fingers light on my side.

"Years," he says. "By the time we're our parents' age, how long do you think it'll be?"

Something inside my brain zaps like it does every time Ethan brings up our future. These big assumptions that he and I will live exactly like our parents do, that perhaps we'll inhabit this very same stretch of Pelican Island Road and send our children to Pelican Island Academy and find a family to live next door who can produce a child the very same age as ours, which will result in an inevitable best friendship, or perhaps a new generation of Gold-Silvers, though we'd probably have to choose one last name because together they sound absurd.

At some point over the last two years, Ethan assumed we had our lives planned out together, on one single track, even though I have no recollection of ever agreeing to such a thing. When Ethan talks like this it has a dizzying effect, like my head is a Mylar balloon being pumped full of helium and it might soon float away on its own.

"I don't know," I say, and scoot closer to the fire.

"Everything okay?" Ethan asks. "Are you nervous about work?"

I shake my head. Interning at Mayor Cho's office has been the only thing I've been thinking about since graduation, even while all Ethan wants to do is play tennis and go to Billy's parties and fool around in the pool house.

"Everything's fine," I say.

Ethan raises his eyebrows. "You're going to act like I can't read every single one of your facial expressions?"

I look at him, his angled features shadowed by the firelight, the tiny gold hoop in his earlobe vibrating with the wind. He's concerned, flexing his fingers in the sand, and I can tell his heart rate has picked up from how quickly his chest is rising beneath his shirt. Here is a boy who knows every single part of me, even the awful parts like how I cried hysterically in my car when Erica got a higher score than I did on the AP Gov final or how I ruined Millie's favorite sweater with black cherries last summer or that all dairy makes me gassy and yet I still can't stay away from the chocolate flavors at Scoop DeVille. All that and he loves me still.

Now. Now is the time to tell him the truth.

It would be so easy, in theory, to say the words. *I'm not going to Cornell with you.* I could tell him in one breath—that I got off the waitlist at Penn last week. That he *knows* how much I want to go there and study in the political communications school. That, sure, Ithaca is far from Philadelphia, but we would find a way to work it out if we wanted to.

But I can't say that because he would hang on to that one word. *If.*

He would know immediately what I've been trying to hide for months: that I'm not sure I *do* want to find a way to make our relationship work come September.

I raise my hand to his cheek, feeling the familiar fuzz of his face, the hint of stubble on the bottom of his chin. He turns his lips to my hand, kissing my palm, then looks up at me.

"Whatever's going on, you can tell me."

I open my mouth, believing him. He's never given me any reason not to. But when I think about what his face will look like when I *do* tell the truth—*I'm scared; I don't know if I want to keep this going in college; I don't know who I am without you, and that's not a good thing*—I press my lips into a smile.

"You're right," I lie. "I'm nervous about my internship. First summer not working at the Club. And I want to do a good job for Mayor Cho."

Ethan's face brightens. "You're going to be *amazing*. Lucy, you planned a mock election when we were in kindergarten."

"Herbert the Toad was robbed."

"You were built for the role. There's a reason she picked you and only you out of a hundred applicants."

I nod, hoping he believes he's comforting me when, in truth, I know all those things myself. Have never doubted that I would be an excellent intern with Mayor Cho.

Ethan's phone buzzes, and he looks down at the screen where I see Billy's texted again. Ethan's gaze lingers, and he presses his lips together.

"You wanna go?" I ask, trying not to make a face. Billy's always felt like an ear infection I can't get rid of. He's been Ethan's best friend since we were born, more because of the fact they rolled into each other at a Mommy and Me class rather than because they actually like each other. Billy's the guy who takes a joke too far, whose sole focus is riling everyone up as much as possible, who needles you and then calls you "uptight" when you tell him to quit it.

He only became tolerable when he started dating my best friend, Erica, who insisted that he was different behind closed doors. But ever since they broke up after prom, it's been a relief to have an excuse to pass on hanging with Billy.

"Maybe for a little," Ethan says. "Is that terrible?"

I glance at my own phone and see a text from Erica. Oops I ended up at Billy's party. Come?? Please???

I turn the phone around so Ethan can see the message. "Looks like tonight is going to get messy." I scrunch up my face. "No thank you."

Ethan nods, and I let him pull me in for a hug, as he's done so many times, enjoy the warmth of his lips pressing down on my head. His heart rate steadies, and I calm, too, knowing I've played my part well enough for him not to worry. There will be no tears tonight. No conversation about my betrayal. No desperate pleas for me to change my mind. No bike rides to Billy Godwin's party.

"You're right," Ethan says. "Let's just enjoy this."

I close my eyes and try to be *present*. The summer is long, stretched out, and we have, like Millie said, eight more Fridays together, just the six of us. Eight more weeks of bike rides down the boardwalk and ice cream cones at Scoop DeVille. We have the summer solstice party at the Club, the Fourth of July parade on Main Street, the tennis tournament where Ethan and I will crush our competitors at mixed doubles, and so many lazy days of swimming in the Sound and snuggling up in sweatshirts to search for shooting stars as they flicker over the sand.

But tonight, I can sit by the fire with Ethan and forget about what comes next. What lies I've already told. The ones I'm still plotting out. Tonight, I can let myself be loved for a little longer.

Sometime during all the sparklers and the buttered cobs of corn, and the parties at Billy's house and the kegs Erica pays for with her parents' credit card, there will be a discussion about our future. There will be unrelenting tears and cracked voices, pleading. Because this summer, I am going to break Ethan's heart.

THE PARTY

Midnight

Billy Godwin had thrown a lot of parties throughout his high school career, and they always started the same way: with a keg and a dream. Tonight's keg was courtesy of Erica Richardson, the girl Billy wished he were still dating. And the dream was a new one. An ambitious one.

Tonight was the night he would get Erica back.

Billy plopped down in an Adirondack chair and surveyed the party, even though it looked like every other one he had ever thrown. There were a few dozen kids from Pelican Island Academy dancing on his brick patio by the pool. Most everyone was in a bathing suit, though the bikini tops seemed to ride up by the minute as his friends grinded with one another to the beat of some bad EDM song.

Billy wondered who'd stolen the aux cord and changed up his carefully curated playlist, but he didn't have the energy to get up from his chair, to actually give a shit. As long as the music was thumping, he didn't care.

He swiveled his head and saw his cousin Olivia perched on the stone ledge overlooking the water. When her gaze met his, she rolled her eyes at him, like she couldn't believe she was back here at a party with these people. But she had nowhere else to go. She had arrived from the city a few hours ago, dumped on his doorstep by her totally negligent parents—and coming from Billy, that certainly said a lot. It's not like Sally and Reid Godwin were about to win any awards in the parenting department. Hell, his mom had taken a handful of pills a few hours ago and told him to only wake her if someone set the place on fire. He hadn't seen his dad since midafternoon, when they played nine holes at the Club.

But for the most part, Billy didn't mind. They left him alone as long as he got good grades, which he did, and they had good enough manners to scream at each other when they thought he was out of earshot, though he rarely was. But Olivia's parents . . . They didn't give a shit about her. That's what his mom insinuated while Olivia was unpacking in the pool house. "At least we never ditched you and went to Europe."

Olivia looked as she always did—tan, blond, preppy, basically the female version of Billy—and when he told her she was right in time for the party, she asked exactly only one question: "Will Lucy be there?"

Billy had shrugged. "Probably not." It was a Friday, after all, and you never could count on seeing any of the Silvers or the Golds on Fridays. Olivia seemed disappointed, but Billy reminded her that Lucy and Ethan were basically married, and that was lame as hell.

Secretly, Billy didn't think their love was lame. In fact, he was a little envious. For a while, he thought he and Erica had that kind of relationship, too. He even entertained the idea that they might stay together freshman year when she was at NYU and he went off to Boston College. Not the whole year. A semester. Maybe until Thanksgiving. At least until he could find his footing in a new place, see if there was anyone else out there better suited for him.

That plan got royally fucked when Erica dumped him right after prom. Said she didn't like who she was around him. That she wanted a summer on her own to find herself before school.

Billy suspected Lucy had something to do with it. He saw the way she looked at him.

Like he was a pity hang. Like he wasn't good enough for Erica. Like Ethan was wasting his time hanging around Billy. Man, she was so stuck-up.

It's good to be honest about the people you know the best. Billy was sure of that.

Anyway.

Tonight he would prove Erica wrong. He could show her that he really was a good guy! Billy scanned the crowd and saw her huddled with a group of girls by the firepit. Her long dark hair was tied up in a cute, messy bun on top of her head and she wore a bright pink bikini top and jean shorts. He smiled. She was so pretty. So fun. She tossed her head back and laughed, placing a hand on her chest. Billy wanted to be *that hand. He wanted to kiss that bare skin.*

But he stayed in his seat, sipped whatever was in his red cup. It tasted like ass, but it was doing the trick.

He needed to wait a little while before approaching her. She might be more amendable if she had a few drinks, if her guard was down. But Billy needed some backup. Dylan was here, obviously, but he really needed Ethan. He'd texted him a little while ago, but there was no response. Not yet.

Ah, screw it. No time to waste, really. In June, summer seemed endless, but by August, you'd slap yourself, shocked that you wasted so much time. Billy would not waste a single second of summer. Not this year.

"Erica!" he started to call, but the syllables came out mushy, bleeding together. That's not a good look, he realized. He should find Justin. That kid always had a stash of something that would wake him up.

He started walking the perimeter of his property, nodding at his guests, holding his cup up as a greeting. Without him, his friends would have no parties, no fun, no excitement. He *made the magic happen on Pelican Island.*

Someone called Billy's name, and he blinked, looking up.

"My man," he said, his face splitting into a smile. "There you are."

FRANKIE

"I can't believe this is an actual job," Alex says, bouncing his knee up and down.

I shield my eyes from the sun, which slices through the small wooden welcome hut at the Pelican Island Tennis and Beach Club. "Kind of crazy they let the babies have the best gig." I elbow him in the ribs and reach for a salt-and-vinegar chip from the bag in front of us.

Millie and Lucy complained about being on welcome-hut duty during the summers between their freshman and sophomore years. I can't really see why. We're only a few hours into our first shift, and I can already tell it's going to be the easiest job of all time.

All we have to do is say hi to our neighbors as they stop by to pick up free sunscreen and fresh fluffy towels, tell people where to go for their tennis lessons, and make sure visiting relatives have guest passes. Besides that, we can basically do whatever we want. For Alex and me, that means working through the hardest level of logic puzzles from the big book I found in my dad's office around the holidays. It's as heavy as my world history textbook, but it's ten years old, marketed as a study guide for law school hopefuls taking the LSAT, and when I asked Dad about the book, he waved his hand. "I do them for fun. They keep you sharp."

Dad handed it over, then bought me a few more books for Hanukkah, each one leveling up in difficulty. "The associates at my firm can barely get to level ten," he said. "But you will."

I'm *almost* there, but really only with Alex's help. I find them relaxing and Alex's competitive streak makes him to want to solve them as fast as I do. He's the perfect partner for this kind of thing.

I extend my long legs beneath the desk, wincing as my joints ache. My doctor called the consistent pangs growing pains, but I don't totally understand why reaching my full height has to cause such distress. Especially when both of my sisters remain at a very average and nonpainful five-foot-four.

"Want some ice?" Alex asks, motioning to my knee, which I'm bending back and forth. "I can grab you a bag from the Snack Shack?"

I swat at him. "You want to go over there because Rishi is working today."

Alex blushes but doesn't deny it. He's had a crush on that kid for months, and even though Rishi sometimes flirts back, we've never been able to confirm if he might be into Alex.

"You're so annoying when you're right," Alex says with a grin.

I flip open the thick book and find a puzzle we haven't yet done. "This one's a grid murder mystery." I start to scan the clues, but before I can read the puzzle aloud, a short woman wearing tennis whites rushes up to the check-in hut. She's clutching a tote bag, and her brow is knit into a deep, worried V shape. A thick gold bracelet catches the sun.

"Hi, Mrs. Godwin," I say. "Are you here for your court assignment?" I page through the tennis sign-ups. "Looks like the Ladies Clinic is on court four. Mitch is the pro over there today."

I smile wide and wait for Alex to do the same, but suddenly he turns his attention to the corkboard on the wall.

Mrs. Godwin waves her hand. "No, no," she said. "I'm wondering if you've seen Billy."

Alex snaps his eyes to me, and I know it's my job to give her an answer.

I flip to the staff sign-in sheet and scan the list of names, but it looks like Billy hasn't checked in yet. "Sorry, he's not here."

Mrs. Godwin's mouth turns into a frown. "Let me see that." She grabs the book from my hands and mutters something under her breath before dropping it on the counter. I look at Alex and turn my mouth into a straight line, but he shakes his head. He has no idea what's going on either.

"Do you want me to radio down to the courts and see if he showed up early?" I ask. "Forgot to sign in?" Based on the fact that Ethan said he threw a party last night, my guess is that he woke up naked on the beach half a mile down the sand.

Mrs. Godwin lets out a frustrated sigh, but before she can respond, someone calls behind her, "Sally, hello!"

My spine stiffens as my mother approaches, kissing Mrs. Godwin on the cheek. Beside her is Mrs. Vreeland, another woman in their doubles group. She's got dark hair tied up in a bun, beaded bracelets that make clanking noises when she raises her hand to wave at us. "Hope these kids aren't giving you too much trouble," Mom says.

Mrs. Godwin offers a weak smile. "Looking for Billy, that's all."

"Well, the search party will have to wait, because Mitch is ready to whip us into shape so we'll be prepared for the tournament," Mrs. Vreeland says, swinging her racket.

Mom readjusts her tennis visor. "Hopefully we won't have to play each other until the semifinals."

"You'll crush it, Debbie," Alex says.

Anyone else's obvious sucking-up-ness would bother me, but Alex is the best when it comes to my mom. He knows it's easier to deal with Debbie Gold when she doesn't suspect you of anything, and she's *always* on my case about something.

"Thanks, Alex." Mom winks at him, which is honestly mortifying.

"If you see Billy, tell him his mother is looking for him. Okay?" Mrs. Godwin says. Her voice is shaky, and Mrs. Vreeland pats her on the arm.

"Sure, Mrs. Godwin," I say.

Mom's eyes travel to the top of my head. "You really should tie your hair up while you work, hon," she says as she starts to walk away. "And at least wear some mascara. It's not like it'll *hurt*."

My cheeks burn, and I press my lips together.

Mom has no idea how to deal with a daughter like me. She's always nitpicking about stuff I can't control, like how my uniform skirts are too short (I grew six inches in a year!) or how my hair is a frizzy mess (I don't want to spend an hour fighting with a diffuser!) or how I should be more like Millie and Lucy when it comes to my "overall appearance" (can't a girl *not* be interested in makeup?). Alex once suggested I talk to her about this stuff and tell her how much it bothers me when she critiques me like that, but the idea of confronting my mother is as appealing as swimming in the Sound on New Year's Day.

An idea reserved for sociopaths. No thank you.

Alex nudges my foot with his, checking in.

"I'm good," I say, and focus my attention on the logic book in front of me, not even reading the clues. Having my mom speak to me like that in public was like being seen right when you come out of the shower, flushed and naked with your hair flat, stuck to your scalp.

"Liar. Doesn't matter, though. I like your curls like this." He pulls at a ringlet and lets it spring back into place.

"Thanks," I say softly, warmth filling my fingertips.

For a moment, we're both quiet, listening to the sounds of the toddlers behind us splashing in the shallow end, the thwacking of distant tennis balls, the gentle crashing of tiny waves from the Long Island Sound.

I inhale and take a whiff of sweaty sunscreen and fried food from the Snack Shack. I roll my shoulders down my back and point to the book. "Here's the first clue," I say, and start to read aloud to Alex.

MILLIE

The backs of my thighs stick to the lifeguarding stand, and sweat drips down my legs. I've been up here for hours in the sun, the heat already oppressive, even though it's not even noon.

"You good?" Ethan calls below me from the sand. He's wearing red swimming trunks and Ray-Bans, no shirt. I avert my eyes. "That wood'll do a number on your tush."

A flush spreads across my neck at the very mention of *my tush* from Ethan's mouth. "Yep!" I eke out.

He laughs and tosses up a bottle of sunscreen.

"Thanks," I say, catching it with both hands, and watch as he climbs up the chair. My stomach fizzles like a popped can of seltzer as he settles in next to me, and for a brief moment as he readjusts, the edge of his thigh, hot and sticky, grazes mine.

I push my sunglasses high up on the bridge of my nose so he can't see my eyes.

"Want some help?" Ethan doesn't wait for an answer and instead takes the bottle from my hands. He squirts some into his palms before motioning for me to turn around so my back is to him.

"Um . . ." I start to say, though it's probably best to say nothing at all. I twist my spine and squeeze my eyes shut, bracing for his touch.

Nothing prepares me for the burn of Ethan's palms resting on my shoulders, nudging lotion under the straps of my bathing suit.

"Gotta be careful on days like this," he says. "All you Gold girls burn like crazy."

"It usually turns into a tan," I say, my voice quiet. "With some mild agony and peeling along the way."

Ethan laughs. "Lucy burned so bad when we all went to Anguilla. Remember that?"

I swallow. "Mm-hmm."

Ethan drums his fingers on my shoulder. "Your turn."

Shit. I didn't realize that now I would be expected to rest *my* hands on Ethan's back, rubbing lotion onto *his* skin. My chest tightens.

"I—"

Thankfully, someone interrupts us down below. "Silver! Yo!"

Ethan leans over and a smile spreads across his face as Dylan Fisher runs up to the tower wearing his Beach Club tennis pro uniform, holding his sneakers in his hands. "What's up, my man?" Ethan asks.

Dylan shields his eyes and nods at me. "Hey, Luce."

I let out a small sigh. This *always* happens. I hate that when people see me, the first thing they think of is my sister, and it makes me wonder what it would take for them to look at me and see *me.*

"That's Millie," Ethan corrects Dylan before I have to say something.

Dylan squints up at us. "Ah, sorry. You guys look like twins."

"We get that a lot," I manage.

He moves his gaze back to Ethan. "You seen Godwin?"

Ethan leans forward and rests his elbows on his knees. "No. Have you?"

Dylan laughs. "Nope. I bet he's still wrecked from last night. That was a wild one, right?"

Huh. I guess he *did* go to Billy's party. Ethan shifts in his seat but doesn't look at me. "He's probably still passed out waiting for a bacon-egg-and-cheese to be hand-delivered to him in bed," Ethan says.

"Honestly, that sounds dank right now." Dylan holds up his tennis racket. "Wanna rally later? Free court at four."

"In this weather?" Ethan says. "As if I have a death wish."

"Fair, bro. Tomorrow a.m.?"

"You got it."

Dylan jogs toward the tennis courts, and Ethan and I lean back, gazing out at the water. "Here," Ethan says, handing me a Diet Coke from a mini cooler. The aluminum is frosty against my skin, a momentary reprieve.

"Oh, thanks." I close my eyes and take a sip, trying to cool down, savor the bubbles and calm my nerves. Even though it's our first day, I can't believe it's taken me this many summers to finally make it up here on the tower.

Everyone on Pelican Island gets access to the Tennis and Beach Club, and applying for a summer gig at the Club is basically a nonnegotiable for all the teenagers on the island, unless you're like Lucy and score some sort of prestigious internship. But *which* Club job you get greatly determines the trajectory of your summer.

Last year, I was stuck as a day camp counselor four days a week, hanging out with six-year-olds as they skipped around the property moving from the arts-and-crafts station to instructional tennis. But this year, I finally passed my lifeguarding test after Trevor coached me through the drills all winter.

Trev and I were so excited to line up our shifts, but then he tore his rotator cuff while riding his bike home from baseball practice. Still, his injury did make it so I get to work with Ethan every day instead. Though I'm not sure that's such a good thing.

I blink open my eyes and try to sneak a peek at Ethan in my periphery without being obvious. But he's not as relaxed as I am. He's leaning forward, squinting at the water. A bead of sweat slides into his eyebrow.

"What are you looking at?" I ask.

He extends his arm and points at the sea, and when I turn to follow his finger, I see what he sees—something bobbing in the water fifty yards from the beach.

"Is that a buoy?" he asks.

The answer flashes in my brain. *No.*

What's floating out there in the water is not a buoy nor a lost noodle nor a boogie board. As the waves crest, pushing whatever *it* is closer to the beach, the shape becomes obvious. Four limbs. A torso. A head.

"Millie . . ." Ethan says, his voice trembling.

A jolt shoots through my body, and I move on autopilot, reaching for my radio. "Lifeguard A to Clubhouse. Code forty-five. Call 911. Now."

"Millie . . ." Ethan says again, but I don't hear what comes next because in a split second, my feet hit the sand and I'm sprinting toward the water with the red flotation device slung over my back. Behind me, there's a commotion—voices rising. A stray shriek. One word: *Help.*

I dive into the water, the cold a welcome shock. My cupped fingers slice through the waves and the sounds of the sea fill my ears, drowning out the noises on the beach—the screams, the harrowing realization that a perfect Saturday morning has been upended.

I pop my head up out of the water and realize I'm right where I need to be, the person in distress only a few yards away.

At first, I see feet. Bare: no shoes, no socks. He's wearing jeans and a white T-shirt, floating face down. I can't tell how old he is, though he has pale skin that's now nearly blue. Translucent.

I do what I was trained to do, sliding my flotation device under his stomach, maneuvering it so I can turn the person over while calling out, "Can you hear me? Can you hear me?"

There's no response, and when I flip him over, I take in his features. A bow-shaped mouth. Thick eyebrows. A Roman nose and freckles scattered across his cheeks. Light hair, stuck to his forehead. I'd know him anywhere. Ethan's best friend, the guy Lucy calls a loser behind his back, the kid who throws the parties.

Billy Godwin.

I push all emotions away as best I can and hook my arms under his, positioning the flotation device between us so I can swim back to shore. There's still time to save him. I don't know when he turned over, if he only recently became unconscious. But as my skin touches his, even in the water, I gasp at how cold he is.

A crowd has formed on the beach. Ethan stands there with the walkie-talkie in his hand crackling. Children circle around the kayak stand, shielding their eyes, and then I see my mother standing next to Billy's, Mrs. Vreeland behind them. They're all dressed in tennis whites, visors obscuring their faces. I want to tell

Mrs. Godwin to run. That she shouldn't see this. But as I get closer, she crumples to the sand, her hand over her mouth.

Suddenly, I can stand. I'm nearing shore, and Ethan is by my side, helping me drag Billy up the beach. "I don't know . . ." I start to say, out of breath as I wade through the shallow water. "I don't . . ." The air is still and heavy, the unyielding sun pounding down on my scalp, and as soon as I stumble onto the sand, I wonder if the heat can warm Billy fast enough to save him.

"The paramedics are coming," Ethan says, his voice quavering, then drowned out by the sound of sirens wailing and a beach buggy cruising down the sand. EMTs push us aside, and I stagger back, nearly falling into a pile of beach toys and plastic shovels.

Something inside me takes charge, and I begin to corral the children. "Over here," I say, and realize my voice is still wavering. "Come on. Come this way."

Just then, the sky darkens all at once. A crack of lightning shatters the sky and a rumble of thunder growls in the distance. I look up and see an army of gray clouds moving toward us, a summer storm rolling through. They'll dump rain on us any moment. But I have to keep my attention on what's happening, on Billy.

Maybe the EMTs can revive him. They're crowded over his body, taking his pulse, checking his breath. The air fills with sounds of medical equipment—beeping and electrical currents and metal hitting metal—and then . . . nothing.

One of the first responders flicks her eyes to another with a silent message: *There is no hope.*

I run a hand over my face and find my fingers wet. From tears or the Sound, I don't know.

"Head wound on the left side," mutters one of the EMTs. "We gotta take him in."

Ethan's mouth is open, and his gaze is fixed on Billy while Mrs. Godwin shudders in my mother's arms.

My vision blurs as I look at Billy's body, see a gash on his skull. His clothes torn and stained with red smudges. His arms, covered in bruises. I blink, trying to see more, but before I can take him in again, one EMT drapes a white cloth over his body and lets out a *whoosh* of breath like he's trying to steady himself.

The EMT rocks back on his heels and wipes his arm over his sweaty face. "Call the morgue."

LUCY

A roar of thunder echoes in the sky. "Quick," I say. "We have approximately fifteen minutes before we're gonna be drenched."

"I refuse to rush ice cream time." Erica digs into her cup of mint chocolate chip. "Besides, stop avoiding the question."

"What was it again?" I play dumb, dragging my spoon through a scoop of fudge brownie.

"Why haven't you told Ethan yet?"

"Ugh," I say. "Because I'm a scaredy-cat."

Erica sets her cup down on the table. "He's going to find out somehow. You don't think your parents are gonna spill the beans to Gil and Paula? They're like . . . incestuous."

"Ew." I wrinkle my nose. There's truth in what Erica's saying, obviously, but not even my best friend in the world's urging can convince me to tell Ethan about my college plans before I'm ready. "Mom said they would keep it quiet. And the girls don't know yet. There's no way they'd be able to keep their mouths shut."

We're sitting at a picnic table on Main Street outside Scoop DeVille, smack-dab in the middle of downtown Pelican Island, though there's not *that* much here. To our left is the Book Bonanza, and to the right is Hot Diggity, which smells like chicken tenders and French fries no matter the time of day or season. Even though it's early, the street is buzzing with people passing by in their swimsuits and jean shorts, beach bags, and sandy feet as they all make their way to the Beach Club at the end of the block. No one seems that preoccupied with the summer storm swirling above.

Erica rolls her eyes. "Your mom is obsessed with you. You've gotta harness that power."

I hold up my phone, which currently has three missed calls from her, all from the last ten minutes, though that's pretty par for the course on Saturday, when she's trying to get me to play tennis with her. "I know."

She points her spoon at me. "You know that telling him the truth doesn't mean you guys are gonna break up, right?"

"I know," I say, looking down.

"Oh shit."

"What?"

"You *want* to break up."

"I don't—"

"Don't even try lying to me about this."

"It's just . . ." I start. "How did you know it was over with Billy?"

Erica hunches over the table and lowers her voice. Her eyes flick to the garbage can, where flies circle, surrounding the dregs of discarded sticky paper cups. I catch a whiff of the rankness as the breeze picks up. "There were a million little things. But the biggest one was I realized I had more fun without him. I was more relaxed when he wasn't around. I wanted to spend my time with other people, people who made me feel . . . I don't know, like I'm a good person."

"You're the *best* person."

"You have to say that."

"A boyfriend should say that, too."

"And that's exactly why I broke up with Billy. He made me feel like I was an accessory."

"Well, single looks good on you."

She takes another bite of her ice cream but then scrunches up her nose and pushes away her cup, looking like she's about to be sick.

"You okay?" I ask.

Erica swallows slowly and presses her fingers to her mouth. After a beat, she nods. "Yeah. Sorry, I think I'm hungover from last night."

"Another reason why I'm glad I didn't go," I say. I expect her to roll her eyes at me or make a jab about how I am so uncool these days, but a dark cloud rolls through the sky, and all the sunlight disappears.

"Yikes," Erica says. "Apocalypse weather incoming."

A juicy raindrop plops on my head, and I brace for a downpour, but nothing comes, the clouds lingering above.

Erica reaches into her tote bag, retrieving the digital camera she's been carrying around all year. "Want to see pictures from last night?" she asks. "Make you feel like you were part of the chaos?"

"Oh my god, I thought you were done with that dinosaur." She'd spent the whole year documenting little moments on the camera for the yearbook, swearing it captured more *real* experiences than our phones. Though I had to admit the yearbook looked amazing thanks to her.

"I'm good," I say. "I can picture it—red plastic cups and keg stands! How exciting."

Erica doesn't laugh and her face pinches for a moment, like she might be gearing up to tell me something. Right as I'm about to ask what's up, the bell chimes on the front door of Scoop DeVille, and I turn to see the back of a tall girl about our age wearing a pretty lavender minidress and platform sandals. Her long blond hair is held in place by a thick gingham headband. A fly lands on her shoulder and when she turns to swat it away, I get a look at her face. My core tenses, and I drop my plastic spoon as the girl heads inside the shop.

"What the hell is Olivia doing here?" I hiss, trying to keep my voice down. I crane my neck to see her through the window, tasting different flavors and laughing with the kids behind the counter. She looks the same as she did when I saw her last, when she broke my heart.

"Oh my god, I can't believe I forgot to tell you," Erica says. "She's back. Apparently, she's staying in Billy's pool house all summer while her parents are in . . . Switzerland? Maybe France? I'm surprised Ethan didn't tell you he saw her at Billy's last night." Erica picks up both of our empty cups, tossing them in the trash.

"Ethan didn't go to the party."

Erica cocks her head. "Yes, he did."

I peek at my phone and see another missed call from my mom, which I ignore, and head over to my text messages, pulling up Ethan's thread. Maybe he mentioned the party last night after I'd gone to bed, and I missed it. But when I read our texts, I only see our standard back-and-forth. The good-morning messages exchanged at seven a.m. A question from him ninety minutes later: do you think mango is a morning fruit or an afternoon fruit? His reminder to wear sunscreen (50 spf, Luce!!!) at 10:45 a.m., and my most recent question: What was that flavor I liked last time at Scoop DeVille? to which he responded, You thought the choc brownie crumble was way too sweet!! Get chocolate moose tracks.

But nothing about the party.

"Anyway, yeah." Erica leans in. "Olivia was there, and she'll be here all summer. Are you okay? Now you look like you're the one who's gonna puke."

"I'm fine." I push back my hair, smoothing the flyaways down over my scalp.

"Please don't tell me you're still hung up on her, Luce. That was like two years ago."

I force a smile on my face and shake my head. "Of course not," I say so forcefully, I almost believe it.

The door swings open, and Erica looks back at me. "Here she comes."

I sit up straight and roll my shoulders back. The last time I saw Olivia was at our stepping-up ceremony, an end-of-year tradition at Pelican Island Academy that marks each class's ascension to the next grade level. She wore a white lace dress and had tied her hair back with a long matching ribbon. I can still remember the breeze winding through her hair, the tail of the fabric floating in the sky, as I wondered if she would come over and say goodbye. She never did, and I spent the whole afternoon trying not to cry, wondering what it was about me that made Olivia not care.

Ethan told me Olivia was a fool for letting me go and promised me he would be by my side that summer. By the start of junior year, when he and I were officially a couple, I realized Olivia's decision had actually been a blessing, even though her rejection made me feel like my chest was collapsing for two whole months.

Now I remind myself of all the things that have happened since then: I've been crowned valedictorian *and* prom queen of Pelican Island Academy, been named to the all-county tennis team, chaired the mock-trial team, landed a plum and totally impressive internship, *and* gotten accepted to my dream school. I'm Lucy Fucking Gold, and I refuse to let Olivia Godwin make me feel unworthy after all this time.

Olivia steps through the door, and Erica stands up, waving at her. "Hey, Liv. What's—" But when Olivia faces us, Erica stops talking. Olivia's dark brown eyes are wide, and she's clutching her phone so hard, her knuckles are white.

She looks at Erica, then her gaze shifts to me, a flash of recognition crossing her face.

I want to say something—*anything*—to show her how wildly *over* her I am, how much I truly do not care that she's in my presence. But before I can, Olivia flings her arms around my shoulders, nearly collapsing on top of me.

Erica mouths the words *what the fuck?* in my direction. I shake my head and, in the process, get a whiff of Olivia's hair, smelling notes of jasmine and linen.

"Is everything all right?" I ask. Though the answer is obviously no, because there's no reason I can think of for my ex-girlfriend to literally throw herself at me.

Suddenly, my phone buzzes. At first, I assume it's my mom again, but Erica's dings at the same time. Olivia doesn't let me go, and so I look to Erica as she glances at her screen, her eyes widening in shock. "Oh my god."

"What?" I ask as Olivia's grip gets tighter, her nose pressed against my chest.

"We need to go to the Club now," Erica says.

"What's going on?" I ask.

"Billy's dead."

FRANKIE

"Holy shit, holy shit, holy shit." The words slip out of my mouth before I can stop them. A few minutes ago, it was just another Saturday at the Beach Club, a storm about to roll in. But when Millie's voice came in over the staff walkies calling a Code 45—*emergency*—nearly everyone stopped what they were doing and rushed down to the beach.

By the time Alex and I get to the waterfront, the EMTs are already loading Billy's body, covered by a sheet, onto a gurney. Without saying a word, they slide him inside the back of the ambulance and shut the door. I can't tear my eyes away from the back window and my whole body has turned wobbly, like I might fall over at any minute. Alex grabs my hand and jerks me toward him.

"You gotta calm down, Frankie," he whispers. "People are staring."

"The last thing people are looking at right now is *me*." I'm right, too. The beach is full of people—our staff supervisor, Jordan Grover; Club president Lowell McIntosh; head of maintenance Freddy Barnes; forty-five second graders who were preparing for instructional swim; Dylan, quietly crying into his hands; and my own mother, carefully guiding Mrs. Godwin toward the ambulance so she can ride with her son.

Millie stands off to the side, a towel wrapped around her shoulders, as she talks to one of the EMTs. Her back is straight, like she's trying to channel Lucy's poise, but her shoulders shake, and she fidgets with the corners of the terry cloth. Seeing Millie there all alone makes me inch forward.

"I should go to her," I say, and Alex nods.

But before I stride over, someone zooms down the beach past me, flying right through the caution tape, snapping it in half. Lucy. Millie turns around and when she sees our sister, she gasps.

Lucy envelops Millie, wrapping her up tight. She's kicked up sand that sticks to her legs and the back pockets of her denim shorts.

"Oh, Millie." She rocks her back and forth as Millie starts to cry into Lucy's chest, gripping her back with her fingers.

When they stand like that, so close together, it's like they become one person, with their similar hair and builds and mannerisms. If I were there, I'd tower over them. The odd one with the messy bun and the lanky limbs. The one with bare nails and picked-over cuticles. The one who doesn't belong.

I hang back and clasp my hands together, squeezing tight. The sun beats down on my scalp, the tender skin on my arms already burning from being outside the welcome hut. Behind me, Erica watches the ambulance drive down the beach, crying into the arms of a blond girl who looks so much like Lucy's ex. I look closer, and, holy shit, it *is* Olivia Godwin. There's no time to dwell on that, though, and I refocus my attention on my sisters, who are still huddled close. Despite the fact that Millie found a *dead body*, a wave of jealousy hits me square in the chest. I want to be inside that hug, with them, a part of this.

Being the youngest of three means all of the good stuff has already happened to your family. You were in utero for that one trip to Maine. You don't remember the Thanksgiving where Aunt Trish fell asleep in the pumpkin pie. You were too young to understand the overheard conversations your parents had behind closed doors during Grandpa's shiva. You arrived too late to be in on the jokes, the secrets, the stories.

I clench my jaw and watch them together, Lucy's hand on Millie's head, pushing away her damp hair. But then Millie's eyes flash open, and she sees me. Her mouth crumples yet again.

"Frankie!" she calls, and as quickly as my envy appeared, it dissolves with the reminder *I'm one of you, and you know that, too.* There are three of us, and we are never whole unless we are together.

Lucy turns around and extends an arm to me, and I fold inside their hug, ducking down as Lucy whispers to us both, "I got you guys. I got you."

Safe in my sisters' arms, with Millie crying softly, I believe Lucy.

We break apart, and Lucy's gaze flits over to Ethan, who's sitting by the shoreline, tears streaked down his face as he looks out at the water.

I turn back to Alex, who's walking over to Ethan with Trevor, and see the two brothers sit down on either side of Ethan, the three of them pulled together.

"I should probably . . ." Lucy says, and nods toward the boys.

"Right," Millie says, and we watch her bend down and take Ethan in her arms. Trevor and Alex back away to let them have their space.

I've asked myself what it must be like to be Lucy many, many times, especially when she aces a test or earns an award. Life has come so easily to her, like the world bends to her will, like people turn to her and smile, happy to be in her presence. But looking at her now, watching her navigate one group, then the next, comforting them with her soft voice, her knowing gaze, her soothing hands, I wonder if she views her gifts as a power or a burden.

"Millie Gold?" I turn to see a woman with a dark bob approaching Millie with a little notebook in her hand.

"That's me."

"Detective Hampton," the woman says, shielding her eyes from the sun. "You found Billy, yes?"

"Yes."

"We'd like you to come down to the station. You and"—she looks at her notebook—"Ethan Silver. Just answer a few questions."

"Okay," Millie says quietly.

At that moment, Mom rushes up, gripping Millie to her. "Oh my god, I can't believe you pulled him *out*."

Hampton clears her throat, and Mom looks up. "Is she yours?" Hampton asks.

Mom nods, then grabs my hand, too. "They both are."

"Millie's going to have to come with us for questioning."

Mom's mouth forms an O shape, and she looks to Millie.

"It's okay, Mom. They just want some details."

"Maybe you should call Dad?" I ask.

Millie's gaze shifts to me, her eyes wide. "Why?"

It takes a ridiculous amount of effort not to roll my eyes, but sometimes I think Millie lives on a different planet—or has at least never seen a true-crime documentary. "He's a lawyer."

"Dad does real estate law."

Mom's brow knits, and she nods vehemently. "That's an excellent idea, Frankie." Pride builds in my chest. "I'll call him before I head to the hospital to meet Sally. She needs all the support she can get right now."

Detective Hampton makes a coughing sound. "Do you need a ride?"

Mom shakes her head. "Her sister Lucy will drive her."

Lucy's head pops up from where she sits with Ethan. "Yes, of course," she says. "We'll be right behind you."

Millie starts to follow Lucy and Ethan up the beach, but as they disappear, my heart rate picks up, like I need them to be closer. "Wait!" I say, but they're already gone. "Mom?" I turn to where she was standing, but she's already rushing toward the parking lot. I realize I'm alone, a creeping sense of dread spreading through my stomach.

My hands are clammy, and I wipe my palms on my shorts, leaving sweat stains on the cotton. The beach has cleared, and the only people still here are the ones in Pelican Island PD polo shirts and latex gloves. One of them pulls out a camera and starts taking photos, as if to document evidence, as if this beach were a crime scene.

But that's when reality hits me.

Oh my god.

The beach *is* a crime scene.

MILLIE

Ethan hunches over in the passenger seat of his jeep, his head resting in his hands as Lucy drives us to the police station. From my place in the back seat, I watch her reach for him, flutter her fingertips from his his neck to his thigh like she's trying to find a landing place. Every few moments he lets out a sob, then a whimper, and Lucy clucks her tongue. Her eyes meet mine in the rearview mirror, and she shakes her head to the right once. *I'm scared.* I lift my left hand to my right ear. *I love you.*

This silent communication comes naturally to us, an unspoken language Lucy and I developed when we were little, before Frankie could talk or walk or do anything more interesting than coo and wrinkle her nose as she fussed in her bouncer. When she turned six and could finally understand that we were speaking without her—raising our hands to our hair, twitching our mouths in specific directions, looking up at the sky for two seconds exactly—Frankie threw a fit, nearly kicking a hole through Lucy's bedroom door.

Lucy rolled her eyes and called Frankie dramatic, but I couldn't bear to see Frankie like that. Instead, I led her into my bedroom, and we sat on my shag carpet until she calmed down.

"Why don't you include me?" she asked, her voice warbling.

Even with Frankie crying in front of me, I didn't want to tell her that I hoped by keeping this secret between us, it meant Lucy loved me most of all. Being older meant being wiser and cooler and smarter and braver. As the youngest, Frankie was malleable and easy to influence, a little doll that I could protect and fawn over but not someone I could learn from or treasure in the same exact way.

But if I felt that way about Lucy—like she hung the moon, the stars, the sky—there was a chance Frankie felt that way about both of her older sisters, one of whom was me.

"It's important for sisters to have secrets with each other." I stood up and walked to my desk, pulling out a small pad of purple paper and a pen.

"But it makes me feel bad," Frankie said.

"Yes, well, that's okay, actually," I said. "Because you and I can have a secret, too. Something Lucy will never know. Just for us."

Frankie's eyes widened as she realized that we could splinter off and have our own relationships. Because that's how it is with sisters, especially three of them. We're never three separate circles, forming perfect Venn diagrams, with overlapping sections equaling the same size. Instead, our intersections morph and twist and sometimes disappear depending on the time of year or month—who's busy with midterms or bat mitzvah preparation. Who needs help. Who thinks they don't.

"What should our secret be?" Frankie asked.

I looked down at the pen and paper in my hand and drew a heart, then divided it into three sections, lines shooting off from the bottom point. "How about this?" I said, turning it to face her. "Whenever we see this symbol, we know the other needs us, and we drop everything to go help each other."

We practiced drawing the heart over and over in my room for an hour, and when Lucy finally came around to see what we were up to, Frankie hid the paper behind her back, elbowing me in the ribs.

It's stuck over the years, like when Frankie got detention for her too-short skirt, when Dad learned I spent $150 at the Book Bonanza without his permission—but we never discussed it out loud again. I never learned if Frankie ended up having a secret with Lucy, though I always wondered if they found a way to create a bond that didn't include me.

"Come on," Lucy says as we pull into the police station parking lot. "It's time, Ethan."

"I can't go in there. I can't." He's shaking his head now, his arms folded over his stomach.

Ethan whimpers beside her as Lucy turns around and plays with the ends of her hair. *Help me.*

I reach out my hand and graze his shoulder, feeling him stiff beneath my touch. "We're going to tell them what we saw," I say. "That's it. My dad's already in there. Frankie texted me."

Lucy nods. "Everything's going to be all right. It's just a few questions."

Ethan sniffles and turns his head to face me. "Stay with me?" he asks. "I can't do it alone."

A rock sinks to the bottom of my stomach. How has this dead body, *Billy's dead body*, forced those words out of Ethan's lips?

"Of course," I say, and mean it.

ETHAN AND I sit side by side in uncomfortable metal chairs behind a table as my dad paces the room, waiting for the detective to take a seat. When she finally does, she flips open a manila folder, and her perfect red manicure is stark against the white papers.

"Thanks for coming in, kids," Detective Hampton says. "We need some more information on what happened."

My dad stops pacing behind us and rests a hand on my shoulder. "These two have been through a lot today," he says. "Let's keep this as short as we can?"

Hampton flicks her eyes to him but then turns her gaze back to me.

"Can you walk me through the events that led up to you swimming out to the body?" she says. "To Billy?"

I knit my hands together in my lap and recount the morning step-by-step. But I don't know how to explain to her how cold Billy was. How his skin was tinted blue, how obvious it was there was nothing left to save. My breathing grows ragged, and I'm suddenly dizzy, air coming to me in gasps.

When I finally finish speaking, I'm left with only this understanding: Billy Godwin is *dead*, and I held his lifeless body in my arms.

"She was amazing," Ethan says quietly. "I . . . I couldn't do anything."

"You were in shock. We both were." I swallow and force out the words. "Was there a chance I could have . . . we could have . . ."

"He'd been dead for hours by the time you found him," she says, her voice kinder than it was a few minutes before. "There was no way you could have saved him."

"Oh." I clench my hands into fists and glance at my dad, whose arms are crossed over his chest.

"Billy had some marks on his body," she says, her voice still kind but affirmative, like she has a plan. "Did you see them?"

I squeeze my eyes shut. *The ripped jeans. His bruised torso. Scratches up and down his arms. A wound on his scalp. Slashes on his cheeks.* I blink, desperate to rid the images from my mind.

I nod at the same time Ethan says, "No. Not at all." I turn to him and wonder how he could have missed them. "I don't understand," Ethan says. "I thought he drowned."

"We don't have a cause of death right now," Hampton says. "It could take weeks before we have answers."

Dad rests a hand on my shoulder. "I think that may be enough for today," he says. "These kids have been through hell, and I'd like to get them home."

Hampton's mouth spreads into a thin line as she looks back and forth between Ethan and me. Ethan's chest begins to rise and fall quickly, so noticeable I can see his torso move out of the corner of my eye.

"I'd really like to ask a few more questions," she says. "Especially of Mr. Silver. We're hoping to learn more information about Billy's movements last night. We heard he threw a party."

Ethan looks to my dad, communicating something I can't quite understand, and my dad shakes his head. "We're leaving. But if you'd like to ask them anything else again, you can call me, their lawyer. Understand?"

Detective Hampton makes a sucking noise, then stands, grabbing the folder in front of her.

The hallway is so quiet I can hear our shoes squeak against the tiled floor as we walk to the lobby.

"What did she mean by—" I start, but Dad shakes his head quickly.

"Honey, would you wait by the car for Lucy?" he says. "She'll take you home."

I remember the words Ethan said to me: *Stay with me.* "Ethan, are you . . ." I ask.

But he won't meet my gaze. His hands are by his sides, his thumbs flexing back and forth. He nods once, and Dad leads Ethan to his black SUV parked next to Lucy's. Together they get inside, and I watch them drive away.

LUCY

A heel juts into my stomach, hard and swift from my left, and I wake with a start, popping up in bed. But when I sit up, my foot extends, colliding with a meaty thigh on my right, and the person that thigh belongs to grunts.

"Shh," the body on the other side says, and I rub my eyes, realizing I'm smushed between Frankie and Millie, who seem to be taking up most of my mattress, leaving only a sliver of space in the middle for me.

"What are you guys doing here?" I climb over Millie, and when I get out, she and Frankie fill the extra space easily, spreading out under my quilt.

"It's too freaky to be alone," Frankie says, mumbling into the pillow.

Millie nods her agreement, her face hidden beneath the sheets.

My stomach drops, and I remember what happened yesterday. Billy, dead in the water. The crowd on the beach. The tears in Millie's eyes. The fear on Frankie's face. The terror shuddering through Ethan, the way he shivered when we got to the police station, how my dad took him home, kept him in his study for hours, so late that I didn't see him before I fell asleep in a fit. It's enough to remind me that everything on Pelican Island has changed in an instant. Nothing will ever be the same as it was.

I squeeze my eyes shut and see Billy as I knew him, smiling and laughing, crossing his eyes, chugging a beer, throwing Ethan in a headlock, kissing Erica, his fingers pressed against her neck. I never liked him, not even when he was at his best. But the loss of him is staggering, so swift, so complete, it nearly takes my breath away. Even if he wasn't perfect, even if he wasn't *nice* or *kind*, he should still be alive. He should still have the chance to change.

All I want to do is slip back under the covers and shut my eyes, wish to rewind twenty-four hours before any of this happened.

But I look at my two sisters, still and intertwined, and I know I have to set the example. Move forward. Be strong. Show them how to *be* after witnessing something like that.

"You guys rest up, okay?" I dip down and drum my fingers on Millie's shoulder before I reach for my phone. I expect to see a text from Ethan. But there's no word from him, not even *good night*, which he usually sends every evening. Nor a good-morning message, which always comes in before I wake up. I call him, but it goes right to voicemail, so I send him a text: lmk when you're up. Worried about you.

I splash some water on my face and brush my teeth, then hear the sound of the coffee grinder in the kitchen, and soon the smell of a fresh pot lures me downstairs. Dad is already standing at the kitchen counter, dressed in his tennis clothes, his brows narrowed as he stares at the percolator.

"Hey," I say.

"Oh, hi, hun-bun." Dad moves toward me and plants a kiss on

my forehead, but he's still tense, his shoulders up around his ears and his voice strained. "You're up early for a Sunday."

I shrug and slide onto a seat at the counter. "Not a normal Sunday."

"No," he says. "No, it's not." The coffee machine beeps, and Dad pulls down two mugs and retrieves the milk from the fridge.

"Thanks," I say as he slides mine over. When it reaches me, liquid sloshes over the side, scalding my fingers, and I yank them away, shaking them in the air to cool.

"Ah, sorry, Luce." Dad reaches for a rag and dabs at my hand. "You okay?"

"Fine," I say, though my skin burns. "It wasn't even that hot."

"Run it under cold water," he says, and I follow his lead, let him get the tap just right. "I'm sorry," he says again. "Preoccupied. As are you, I'm sure."

"Yeah," I say softly. Dad's focused on my hand even though my skin has returned to its regular shade. "Can I ask you something?"

"Sure," he says. "But you know the rule."

"You might not always answer."

"Perks of being a lawyer." One corner of his mouth twitches.

"What did you talk about with Ethan last night?" I ask. "He never responded to me, and I'm getting nervous."

Dad shuts off the water and positions himself on the stool at the island. "Luce," he says like I'm a child. "I can't tell you that."

"So, he's a client now?"

"He is," Dad says. "There's a confidentiality agreement."

Nerves flutter in my stomach, but I push them away. As soon as I talk to Ethan, he'll tell me what's going on. He's never kept anything from me, and now's not the time to start.

"But I wanted to talk to you about something," Dad says. He presses his lips together then lets out a big exhale. "You haven't told Ethan about Penn yet."

My head snaps up. "*That's* what you want to talk about right now?"

He pauses, thinking through his words. "Ethan's going to be going through a lot over the next few weeks, and I want you to be mindful of how you speak to him, okay? I also want to make sure you've thought this through."

"Thought what through?"

"That Penn really is the perfect place for you." Dad raises his hands like he's trying to preemptively calm me down, which is annoying because his instincts are right. My heart rate picks up, and I'm crafting my retort in my mind. *Yes, obviously. I've done the research and—*"Your mother and I had such formative experiences at Cornell. Gil and Paula, too. I was so looking forward to you going, for us having something else we can share." His phone buzzes, and he grabs it, covering the screen. "I've got to take this. I'm sorry I upset you, Luce."

Dad takes his coffee and slips into his study, closing the door behind him. I clench my hands into fists, notice the tension in my shoulders, the square set of my jaw. Dad's not-so-subtle attempt at pressuring me has only made me surer that I need to go to Penn and carve my own path. I look down at my phone to see a text from Erica.

> Can you come to Dylan's? He's having people over soon so no one has to be alone. Little vigil-type thing. I need you there.

I respond right away. Of course.

I'm freaking out, she texts.

Do you want me to pick you up? I ask.

No. I'm going to ride my bike. Just meet me there.

In the bathroom, I run through my everyday makeup routine, the familiar steps comforting as I swipe blush on my cheeks, mascara on my lashes. I've long known that feeling put-together is the first step toward *being* put-together, and today is no exception. I purse my lips and smooth out my hair, watching my waves bounce into place. Whatever today brings, I will be ready.

Pretty soon I'm at the Silvers' back door, knocking on the glass, trying to get Paula's attention while she flips French toast in the kitchen. As soon as she sees me, her mouth puckers, and she rushes over to slide open the door. "Lucy," she says, running a hand over her hair. "How're you doing, sweetie?"

"Holding up," I say, and Paula clutches her spatula to her chest. "Is Ethan ready? Everyone is gathering at Dylan's, and I thought we'd go together." Best not to let her know I haven't heard from him yet.

Paula's eyes flit to the staircase leading upstairs and then back to me. "He's still sleeping. I think we should let him rest."

"Of course," I say, lingering.

"I'll have him call you. Breakfast before you go?" she asks, waving her spatula in the air, but I shake my head and get back on my bike.

As I turn onto Pelican Island Road, it's impossible to shake the strange feeling churning in my stomach. There's something *off* about Ethan's behavior. How he went to the party without telling me, knew Olivia was in town and didn't warn me, and also failed to text me after he left the police station. I've never known him to lie to me or to withhold information, and it seems like this weekend, he's done *both*. Obviously, there are reasonable explanations for all of these things, but I wish I could get him alone so I could hear them and stop worrying.

Because what I'm really worried about is this: What if he's acting weird because he knows I'm lying?

I blow a puff of air out of my mouth. That's not possible. Erica wouldn't have told him and neither would my parents.

Ridiculous. I'm being ridiculous.

I have to focus on the road and get to Dylan's. That's all.

TODAY IS ANOTHER perfect day on Pelican Island with a clear blue sky and a gentle breeze. Sweatshirt-and-shorts weather, toes-in-the-sand weather. But not even the high sun or the smell of sea salt can make us forget that Billy's dead.

Dylan and his mom moved into one of the old Colonials, all red brick and stately, after his father passed away, and it's one of my favorites on the island. From the front, it's an old East Coast manse, but as soon as you follow the pebblestone walkway, you're greeted with an unobstructed view of the beach, the deck lined with reedy seagrass.

On Dylan's patio, my classmates are huddled around a barely lit firepit, speaking closely, passing around tissues. Someone set out a paper sack of bagels on the stone wall, and a few flies circle untouched tubs of cream cheese.

"There you are." Erica rushes toward me. Deep circles have formed under her eyes since I saw her yesterday, and her cheeks are swollen.

"Oh, Erica."

"I can't believe it . . ." She shakes her head, then looks up at me, gripping my arms. But before she can say anything else, the sound of clattering metal rings in the air, and I spin around to see Justin Vreeland with his hands up, his eyes wide.

Dylan lunges toward him, his index finger pointed at his chest. "You shouldn't be here," Dylan says, spit flying from his mouth.

"What are you—" Justin starts to say, but Dylan shakes his head.

"No one wants you here. Get out." Dylan moves forward until Justin backs up, nearly tripping over the raised patio stairs.

Justin's brows narrow, and he throws up a middle finger before turning around and running back to the street. Everyone else starts murmuring to one another, wrapping their arms around one another, and I grip Erica's elbow.

"What the hell was that?" I ask.

Erica shakes her head. "He and Billy got into a fight on Friday. Like, blood-and-guts fight. I wouldn't be surprised if they brought him in for questioning."

"Questioning?" A tingling sensation spreads from the top of my head.

"You don't know?" Erica says. "They're saying it was murder."

THE PARTY

12:45 A.M.

"You showed." Billy's face split into a smile and he threw his arms around Ethan.

"Couldn't miss the first party of the summer. Last party of the school year? How are we framing this thing?"

Billy bowled over laughing, clutching his stomach. This dude still had the power to make him giggle like a kid. He knew there was a reason they stayed such good friends, even when Ethan spent all his time with Lucy.

"No girlfriend tonight?" Billy asked.

"She's tired. It's late."

"Classic."

Ethan didn't say anything, which was strange. He always stood up for Lucy even though she was so freaking annoying. Whipped. That's what Ethan was. Totally and completely whipped.

Ethan surveyed the party and squinted. "Is that Olivia?"

"Yeah. She's here for the summer. Her parents shipped her to my house while they went off to Switzerland. Or France. I can't remember."

"Maybe I should talk to her," Ethan said, his eyes focused on her.

It was so funny that Ethan cared about Olivia. It's not like he could bang her. She was gay. Much to the frustration of half the guys on

Pelican Island, though the thought of anyone getting with his cousin made Billy want to barf.

Billy shrugged. "I mean you kinda stole her girl. Not sure she's down to be best friends, bud."

Ethan made some sort of sound. A grunt.

"Oh, wait, was that the story? Or . . ."

"Old news." Ethan shook his head, but his eyes were roaming the lawn like he was looking for something. Someone.

Which made Billy remember his dream. The whole point of the night. "Hey," Billy said, leaning toward Ethan. "You think I can get Erica back?"

"Seriously?"

"I mean, why not? Final summer. Feel like she might still want to—"

"I don't think so."

"Aw, come on." Billy was wounded. Ethan always had the best advice when it came to Erica. That's when being in such a boring relationship came in handy. But tonight Ethan seemed distracted. Billy should go talk to Erica by himself.

He looked over to the firepit where he had seen her last, laughing in that adorable bathing suit, her hair tied up off her face but coming loose thanks to the mist from the Sound. She looked like she did when Billy brought her on his family's boat, the Sea Witch. *When they went snorkeling and fishing, then lazed on the sun deck for hours.*

Billy swung his whole body around as he looked across the lawn, but he couldn't find her. "You see Erica anywhere?" Billy asked. He drained the contents of his cup. "Did she leave?"

"Come on, man. Forget about her." Ethan shook his head. "Let's hang with the boys." He pointed toward the keg where Dylan was currently being held upside down with the spout in his mouth.

Billy's face looped into a smile. Ethan was right. Tonight could also be about the boys. "Dog out?" he asked.

Ethan tilted his head up and opened his mouth, letting out a loud and blunt "Woof, woof!"

From his place at the keg, Dylan landed back on his feet and stood at attention, hearing the call. "Arf, arf!" he barked across the lawn.

"My boys!" Billy yelled, his voice echoing in the night. That's what it was all about, he decided. His buds. His guys. They wouldn't have these moments come September, and if he could spend another night howling at the moon with his bros, he would do just that.

FRANKIE

"Hot, hot, hot!" I spit out a bite of chicken finger into the red plastic basket between us as Alex starts laughing so hard, I worry Diet Coke's going to shoot out of his nose.

"That's what you get for not being patient," he says, blowing on his French fries.

"If you wait too long, they taste like garbage. Everyone knows that." I lean back and cross my arms over my chest, tapping my foot up and down. Alex and I are sitting outside Hot Diggity after work, our first shift back since they found Billy. The whole day had been weird and creepy, like everyone who came through the Club gates was looking over their shoulder, waiting for a masked man with a knife to burst out from behind a sand dune.

All anyone can talk about is how the police think that Billy's death wasn't an accident. Millie said as much when she got home from the police station the day she found him, and Mom made us turn on location sharing yesterday, started locking the doors and insisting we use the alarm system, even though I'd never seen her turn it on.

But it's hard to imagine that something actually bad could happen here on Pelican Island, where the police are basically glorified traffic cops and the last *real* crime was insider trading, though I'm pretty sure the Vreelands only paid a fine for that one. Everyone's imaginations are running wild because it's easier to think Billy was killed by someone else rather than admit he was an idiot and made some stupid mistake in the same water we've all spent our entire lives enjoying.

"What do you want to do for the rest of the day?" Alex asks, crumpling his garbage into a ball.

"I dunno." I lean my elbows on the picnic table, my gaze settling on the building across the street. It's a little white-brick structure with wide windows and flower pots outside. The only way you'd know it was the police department was the massive shield on the sign out front, the few cop cars parked around the corner. "We could take your kayak out?"

Alex shakes his head. "Nah, I think I'd rather do pool time."

"Fine by me." We stand and head for the bike rack, but I don't look where I'm going and walk right into something tall and hard, slamming to a stop. "Owww," I whine, gripping my shoulder. "What . . ."

"Watch where you're going." I jerk my head back and realize I've walked right into Justin Vreeland as he exited Hot Diggity. He's staring at me with his mouth pinched and a baseball cap casting a shadow over half his face. Even though he's wearing navy shorts with whales embroidered on them, which is definitely the least threatening item of clothing on the planet, a nervous hum begins in my stomach. I take a step back, bumping into Alex.

"Sorry," I mumble.

"You should be." Justin scowls at me, then hurries across the street.

"God, he's creepy," I say.

Alex winces. "I can't believe his family owns this place." He throws his thumb back at the hot dog stand.

"Oh, please. It's probably a tax front."

"You don't even know what a tax front is!"

"Didn't his grandparents just open the place for fun?"

"I am so not debating the ethics of owning the establishment that makes my favorite French fries in the world." Alex rolls his eyes. "Come on."

We pick up our bikes, but before we take off, I twist my head over my shoulder. Justin's standing in front of the police station, and a tall Black woman walks toward him. She's wearing a well-tailored suit and has a briefcase in her hand. Standing next to her is Justin's mom, Mrs. Vreeland, who I last saw at the Club on Saturday. She grips Justin's arm and practically drags him through the door, disappearing inside the station.

"Did you see that?" I ask.

"See what?" Alex says, buckling his helmet.

"Justin. Police station. Looking suspicious."

Alex glances back, and his eyes flick wide for just a moment. "Ethan said they're talking to everyone who was at the party. He was probably there." He waves his hand toward the bike lane.

I follow Alex all the way back to our side-by-side homes in silence, not really listening as he explains the rules to the new board game he got for his birthday. All I can think about is the fact that if Billy was murdered, then there has to be a reason—a person—behind what happened. Basically, there has to be an *answer*.

Just like our logic puzzles.

When we reach his driveway, I'm practically buzzing.

"Pool?" Alex drops his bike and tosses his helmet into the grass.

"Better idea," I say. "Hear me out."

"Okay?"

"You know how our logic puzzles start with clues that hint toward the answer?" I say. "Like the one we finished this morning."

It was about flight delays at an airport, and we had to figure out which plane took off first. The clue that nearly stumped us turned out to be the easy one once I realized what it was really saying. That was the key with these types of puzzles—to search for hidden meanings.

"Duh," Alex says, reaching for the side door to his house. "That's the whole point."

"What if Billy's death is like a logic puzzle?"

Alex stops in his tracks and shakes his head. "I don't like this."

"Yeah, well, I don't think anyone likes *murder*. But if something sus is going on, what if *we're* the people to find out what happened?"

"We don't know it was murder, Franks. Besides, even if it was, the last thing anyone needs is two freshmen trying to figure out what happened."

"We're going to be *sophomores*," I say. "There's a difference." Alex scoffs, but I persist. "You really don't want to?" Alex has never once said no to any type of game or puzzle, is *always* down to solve any sort of teaser.

He pauses but then starts up the stairs. "We don't have the clues. We don't have suspects. We don't have anything that could help us solve something like this."

I take that as a maybe.

"You guys smell like Hot Diggity." Trevor's leaving his room, a duffel bag over his shoulder. "What'd you bring back for me?"

"Nada," I say, stopping on the landing.

"Where're you going?" Alex asks.

"PT appointment," Trevor says, his hand moving to his shoulder absentmindedly.

"You good?" Alex asks, his voice dropping.

I glance between them, an invisible string connecting their gaze, and for a moment they remind me of Millie and Lucy, speaking in their annoying silent language. At least with them, I've decoded some of it by now. But the boys . . . they might as well have ESP.

"Yeah, just overdue," Trevor says, moving past me. "What're you guys up to?"

"Solving a murder," I say.

Trevor spins around. "Excuse me?"

"Don't mind her." Alex moves in front of me and gently shoves me inside his room. "Ever."

"Hey!" I say, craning my neck so I can see Trevor shake his head as he takes the stairs two at a time.

"Stay out of trouble, you two," he calls, then heads out the front door.

Alex follows me inside his room and flops down on his bed, but I make a beeline for his closet where he keeps the erasable markers. "What are you even doing?" Alex asks.

I move to the whiteboard hanging on his wall. "I'm laying out the facts."

"I thought we were going swimming."

Outside, the wind picks up, batting a branch against the window, and the natural light in Alex's room grows a shade darker, the weather taking a sharp turn. "Mother Earth has other plans," I say. "Come on. You know you want to."

Alex sighs behind me, but he doesn't protest.

My heart rate picks up as I start constructing a story, writing the words down as they come to me, speaking them out loud. "Billy Godwin was found dead in the Long Island Sound on Saturday."

I tap the marker cap against my chin and stare at the board. A tiny *zing* shoots through my limbs, the same one that starts when I'm faced with a problem to solve, when that problem actually has a solution that can be figured out with a little brainpower. "We need clues."

"This is pointless," Alex says. "We are *not* detectives."

"But we could be." I boop his nose, and he frowns, swatting my hand away. "Let's use our powers for good."

"When have we ever used them for evil?" he mumbles, annoyed, but I power through.

"Who else was at the party? That's our list of witnesses. And suspects."

Alex falls back against the bed, bouncing slightly.

"What is it?" I ask.

"I don't want to tell you."

"Now you have to. Was Ethan there or something?"

Alex rests a hand over his face but speaks through his muffled fingers. "Yes."

"Well. Yeah. Shit." I push my curls off my forehead. "He's not a suspect. I mean, it's *Ethan*."

"Obviously."

"Who else was also there? Not Lucy. I was still awake when she came home and heard her close the door to her bedroom. But I'm gonna guess Justin Vreeland was there since we literally saw him walk into the police station," I say. "If Ethan was there, Dylan definitely was too. Probably the usual party crowd. Like Erica—"

I stop, an idea forming quickly. *Erica.*

"She was on yearbook with you, right?" I ask Alex.

"She was the *editor* of the yearbook. You know this. That's why she was always carrying around that digital camera, taking photos of everything."

I point finger guns at Alex, waiting for him to realize what we have to do. It takes a minute, but then his eyes go wide. "You think she took photos of the party on that thing? Yearbook's over."

"I mean, *everyone* took photos of the party, I assume. But they're all on their phones. Erica's might be on that camera. Which would be much easier to—"

"Steal?" Alex's voice rises one octave.

"I was going to say *borrow.* Don't you think she'd want to document every party just for herself? That thing was practically glued to her face all second semester."

Alex considers this. "I don't know. Maybe. But if she did, she probably deleted them by now." He sucks on the inside of his cheek, which he only does when he's trying to tamp down his frustrations.

"You okay?" I ask, perching on the bed beside him.

"Yep. Just thinking about how a lot of people didn't really like Billy."

"Well, he was kind of a douche," I say.

"Also means a lot of people may have wanted him gone."

"That's true. But only one person actually did it. And I want to find out who."

MILLIE

"Holy moly, it's packed," Trevor whispers as we walk through the foyer of the Godwin home to sit shiva. The space is filled with people standing shoulder to shoulder, speaking in hushed tones, their faces red, from the summer heat or their own grief, I'm not sure. Trevor fiddles with the collar on his button-down, and I pull at the hem of my black skirt. Usually, it's my most comfortable piece of clothing, but today the fabric is scratchy against my thighs, and my whole body is on fire, itchy like it's rebelling against this entire day.

It's been four days since Billy died, and if this were a *normal* death, Billy's funeral would have taken place as soon as possible, as per the Jewish tradition. But because the police needed to do all of their forensic tests and analyses and whatever else happens in a murder investigation—honestly, thinking about all the details makes me want to vomit—there hasn't been an official funeral. Not yet. Instead, we've all gathered at the Godwin house for the first day of shiva. By the look of it, everyone who lives on the island seems to have come to comfort the Godwins as well as eat the copious amounts of food spread out on every surface in the house.

I follow Trevor through the throngs of people until we get to the back patio. Everywhere I look, there are buffets—enormous tables full of sushi, a carving station where meat sits under a heat lamp, a make-your-own-pasta station—but the sight of everything turns my stomach.

"What do we do now?" I ask Trevor. Practically everyone we've ever known is here, and I can feel people staring, their eyes darting toward me as they whisper behind cupped hands. I can only imagine what they're saying. *That's the girl who found him. Lucy's sister. Debbie's daughter. She should have saved him.*

"I don't know." He shrugs. "Act normal?" Then he shakes his head. "Dumb idea. What's normal, anyway?"

"I don't know," I say. "Everyone keeps staring at me."

Trevor glances around the patio, then ducks his head toward me. "Don't you think it's kind of weird that so many people are here when no one really liked Billy, anyway?"

"He's *dead*, Trevor."

His neck grows pink, and his jaw tightens a bit. "I know," he says. "I'm just saying . . . he was a jerk. That's all."

Before I can respond, my parents appear, and Mom places her hand on my elbow. "Did you pay your respects yet?" she asks.

"We just got here, Mom."

"Go on now," Dad says, nudging me. "You can do it."

Trevor whispers in my ear, "I'll come, too. Get it over with."

Mom pretends not to hear him as she guides us over to the Godwins, who are standing in the threshold of the French doors with somber faces. Billy's mother has a pretty blond bob and is wearing a lace black dress that covers her shoulders and flares at her hips. She looks so put-together, except her chin wobbles and she sways from side to side as if she's not quite rooted to the ground. Beside her, Mr. Godwin shakes hands and has a determined look on his face, like he's steeling for *something*.

"We are so, *so* sorry," Mom says, leaning over to give Mrs. Godwin a kiss on her cheek. "You know how much we loved Billy."

Trevor's elbow digs into my ribs, but I barely notice the pressure because suddenly all I can think about is the fact that I held Billy's lifeless body in my hands. That his parents are looking at me expectantly like I might say something to comfort them, like I might *know* something.

But all I can muster is "I'm so sorry."

Disappointment flashes across Mrs. Godwin's face, and I'm thankful that Dad sticks out his hand to Mr. Godwin. "Reid," he says, as if by saying his name, he has just uttered an entire monologue. But then he bows his head and steps back. "If you'll excuse me."

Mom leans forward as if that weren't weird. "You know we and the Silvers are here for you no matter what."

"Of course," Mrs. Godwin says, clasping my mother's hands in hers. "We are so lucky to have friends like you." She then turns her gaze to me. "We know you did all you could, Millie."

"Thank you," I say, though no response would have felt right, and a few moments later, Trevor and I are back by the buffets, my heart starting to return to a normal rate.

"That was awful," I say. "I wish we could just get out of here."

Trevor turns to me and wiggles his eyebrows. "Book Bonanza?"

My shoulders relax, and I place a hand over my heart, a lightness filling my chest. "You think we can get away?"

Trevor's mouth splits into a smile, but then his phone buzzes in his pocket. He looks down and shields the screen from me while he checks his texts. "Let's meet out front in fifteen? That'll be enough time. We can bike over."

"Perfect."

Trevor slips through the crowd, heading toward the beach. When he hits the sand, I watch as he walks over to Erica, Lucy's best friend. She's standing by herself, looking out at the water, and when Trevor stops next to her, she turns to face him and nods in his direction.

I fold my arms over my stomach and realize I'm standing all alone while everyone else seems to be deep in conversation or concentrating on their food or offering the Godwins their condolences. Without Trevor as my anchor, I'm unmoored, and I don't dare look around for fear of making eye contact with someone who's trying to sneak a peek at the girl who let Billy drown. Even though I know it's not my fault. Even though Mrs. Godwin just offered me absolution. I *know* I couldn't have helped him. I try to stay calm by breathing in and out, focusing on how nice the warmth of the sun feels on my cheeks.

But my try-to-Zen-out moment is interrupted by the crashing of metal pizza trays to my left, and I glance up to see Frankie leaning forward, helping a caterer pick up the mess. I push my way through the crowd toward her.

"Sorry!" Frankie says, grabbing a few of the trays. "I'm clumsy as hell these days." She stretches out her arms and shakes her hands. "My mom says it's because I'm so gangly that I don't know what to do with my limbs."

The caterer glares and gathers the rest of the trays. "Don't worry about it." But their tone suggests otherwise.

"Whoops," Frankie mutters.

"You good?" I ask. Frankie smooths her black skirt down over her thighs and stands up straight. But as she does, she slips something behind her back.

"Totally fine," she says. "Like I said, just making a mess wherever I go."

"What are you holding?" I ask, motioning to her arm, just out of view.

"What are you talking about?"

"Why are you being so weird?"

Frankie pushes her hair back from her forehead. "Enough with the questions! I'm going to get a seltzer."

"Whatever you're doing, don't let Mom see you!" I call, but Frankie's already waving me off, heading inside the house. For the best. Whatever she's up to, I'm not interested in getting involved.

My phone buzzes with a text from Trevor. I'll be out front in five. I reply with a thumbs-up and make my way inside to use the bathroom before we go.

The crowd is still packed inside the house, and when I reach the powder room, I find a line snaking all the way around the hallway into the foyer.

"There's an en suite off the maid's room over on the far side of the house." A waiter smiles at me, holding out a tray full of pigs in blankets. "That's where we're all going." She winks at me and keeps moving through the crowd.

I follow her advice. There are fewer people on this side of the house, and I poke my head into an open doorway, which must be the maid's room. It's sparsely decorated compared to the rest of the home, which is covered in wool wall coverings, modern art, and sleek light fixtures. This room is plain, painted a pale baby blue, and has nothing on the walls. No art, no photographs, not even a mirror.

I step inside and close the door behind me, already feeling calmer now that I'm away from everyone else, now that I can hear myself think, the thumping of my own heart, the reminder that I am here. I am still alive.

I head for the door on the opposite side of the room, which must be the bathroom, and press my hand to the doorknob, but as I start to turn it, I hear a noise from the other side.

"Hello?" I ask, leaning forward to press my ear on the door. "Is someone in there?"

No one answers, so I turn the knob and push the door open slowly, only to find Ethan sitting on the floor with his knees pulled up under his chin, rocking back and forth. His cheeks are red and puffy, and his dark suit is crumpled, his tie hanging sloppily around his neck. He looks up at me with a flash of recognition—relief—and I shut the door behind us.

"Ethan." His name rushes from my lips.

My phone buzzes in my pocket, but I ignore it and drop down to the floor beside him.

"I had a panic attack," he says, pressing the heel of his hand into his forehead. "I held it together for a while, but as soon as we got here, as soon as everyone kept coming up to me . . . talking to me . . ." He lets out a *whoosh* of air. "I've been in here for basically the whole time."

I rest my hand on top of his and hold his fingers in mine, warmth spreading through me. "Do you want me to get Lucy?"

Ethan shakes his head. "No," he says. "She's . . ." But then he stops and looks up at me. "Can you stay with me for a while? Talk about literally anything besides Billy?"

A sharp pang stabs my stomach, like I'm being pierced all the way through.

"I need a distraction. Please."

"Okay," I say, tucking my feet under me so I can sit up on my shins. "Well . . ." I rack my brain for something—anything—to bring up. "*Little Women* is my favorite book," I say.

Ethan nods, his hair flopping down over one eye. "I know that. We all know that."

"They're releasing a new edition this summer. Illustrated sprayed edges. A new foreword about Amy March and her surprising place in feminist history."

"Okay," Ethan says. His fingers flex, then span out on the tiled floor, starting to relax.

"The cover is printed right on the book, a beautiful embossed kind of thing. No jacket. It's supposed to mimic the old editions."

"Sounds nice," Ethan says. He's smiling now, the V between his eyebrows easing slightly. Comforting him like this feels natural, and I wonder if it was fate that brought me to him here in the bathroom. I could have waited in line for the powder room or wandered upstairs to find another restroom. But I came here, to Ethan, and right now that feels important. I grip his hand tighter, emboldened.

"I keep meaning to preorder with Dre at the Bonanza. I love when they put out old books like this but make them new. It's like seeing something you've seen your whole life but in a totally new light, you know?"

Ethan's eyes are dark and focused as they flick up to mine. My mouth goes dry, even when I try to swallow.

"I know that feeling," Ethan says.

"Yeah?" I ask, but as Ethan nods, the door pushes open, and he drops my hand, his head tilting up to the wall of light pouring in from the bedroom.

"There you are," Lucy says, reaching in to pull Ethan to stand. "I've been looking *everywhere* for you. Mrs. Godwin wants to talk to you for a minute. Can you do that?"

Ethan stands slowly, resting his hands on the counter for support. "Yeah," he says. "I can do that."

"Great," Lucy says, leading him out.

As she pushes him ahead, she looks back at me over her shoulder, pressing one hand to her neck. *Thank you.* Then she disappears back into the party, leaving me alone in the bathroom, the tips of my fingers tingling with an exhilarating secret: Ethan Silver finally sees *me.*

LUCY

"You nailed those constituent calls earlier. Sounded like a pro." I look up from my desk to see my supervisor, Anjali, leaning over the cubicle holding a clipboard.

I stand up and brush my skirt down, hoping she doesn't notice that my desk is piled high with stacks of paper and files I pulled from the archives to study. I've only been here for ninety minutes, but it already looks like I've been one of Mayor Cho's interns for weeks, even though today's my first day. Which, in my opinion, is a good thing.

"Thanks so much," I say. "Sorry, that round took longer than expected."

"Figured. Especially now." Anjali shrugs. "Helluva day to start, huh?"

She's right. Even though my first task of the internship was to call all of the business owners on Main Street and ask them to show up to Mayor Cho's next town hall session, where she would hold a meet and greet with the Small Business Association, most everyone only wanted to talk about safety concerns, the high-traffic complaints now that reporters have started to circle the town, and the investigation into Billy's death. Especially once they realized it was me, Lucy Gold, calling.

Donny Glick, who owns Sunday Best, the high-end luncheonette known for their sugar-dusted lemon ricotta pancakes, spent ten minutes complaining about how the news crew vans took over his entire parking lot before he lowered his voice and said in his posh British accent, "Hope you and Ethan are taking care of each other, dear."

"We are," I said, which was only sort of true since Ethan spent half of yesterday's shiva hiding in the bathroom with Millie. I've been waiting to ask him about the party and what happened at the police station. But there never seems to be a good time. Last night, when we got home, he admitted he had a panic attack, and we spent the rest of the evening at his house watching reruns of *The Office*. Seeing him like that, so exhausted and on edge, was made even more painful by the fact that I still haven't told him about Penn. I hate to admit it, but my dad was right. I have to wait a little bit longer, once we have some more answers about what happened to Billy.

"It's a good thing when folks want to talk," Anjali says. "It means they trust you."

I tilt my chin up and press the heels of my palms together in front of my stomach. "I was actually wondering if you have a few minutes. I'd love to chat with you about the mayor's environmental response to the—" But before I can finish, the front door to the office chimes open, and Anjali cranes her neck to see who's there.

"Ah, she's here."

I glance around the cubicle, and the first thing I see is the hint of pale pink peeking through the space between the desks.

"Who—" I start to say but promptly shut my mouth because standing at the front door in an A-line dress and matching Mary

Jane shoes is Olivia. A chocolate-brown ribbon holds back a wave of honey-blond hair, and she's raising one hand, wiggling her fingers in my direction, a strained smile on her face. There is no plausible reason for her to be at the mayor's office on a Thursday morning, but without thinking, I raise my hand, too.

Anjali turns back to me. "You know her?"

"Old classmates," I say, and manage to wipe the frown off my face by the time Olivia makes her way over to us.

"Sorry I'm late. Took forever for me to get the paperwork done."

Anjali waves a hand in front of her face. "All good. You're going to be set up right here next to Lucy."

"Set up?" A slick of panic rises in my throat, and I look between Anjali and Olivia, though neither one responds.

Anjali pulls out the chair beside my desk and reaches inside the drawer, retrieving a laptop. "Liv's our other intern. We met at a career fair at her high school, and when she told me she was going to be out here all summer, I knew she had to join the team." She knocks her shoulder with Olivia's. "Actually, you two have a lot in common. You both mentioned Mayor Cho's environmental work in your cover letters."

"I thought I was the only intern," I say, not wanting to make eye contact with Olivia.

Anjali's cell buzzes in her hand. "Ah, I have to take this. Lucy, can you walk her through the phones and email? Back in a few."

I'm stuck staring at Anjali's back as Olivia sinks into the seat beside me. She clasps her hands together, her knuckles turning white, and I wonder if she's as caught off guard as I am. "So," she says. "This is . . ."

"Unexpected." I face my computer, trying not to look at her. I've only seen Olivia from afar since we learned Billy died—at the shiva, where she stood with her other aunts and uncles; at the Club, where she walked on the beach alone; across Main Street while she was buying a book at the Bonanza—and I'm not about to use my precious work hours to discuss the way she hugged me that day when she learned the news, not that I've thought about it much at all since then. Not one second.

She's grieving, of course. All I have to do is be nice and kind and not get close enough for her to hurt me. Again.

"I didn't know you'd be working here, too," Olivia says. "I don't want this to be weird."

I keep my eyes focused on my laptop screen, even though the words begin to look fuzzy. "It's not weird. Who said it's weird? It's normal. Totally normal." My palms are warm, and I flex my fingers then rest them on the keyboard like I'm about to start typing a very important email to a very important person.

"That day at Scoop DeVille, I didn't mean . . ." She trails off, and out of the corner of my eye I see her fidgeting with the hem of her skirt. "It was such a shock, and . . . I hope I didn't make you feel uncomfortable."

I pull my shoulders back, and finally I look at her. Her eyes are wide, but her mouth twitches like she wants to say more. "You didn't," I say, keeping my voice even. "I'm sorry, by the way. About Billy. I know you two were close."

"Thanks," Olivia says. Her voice softens, grows quiet. "We weren't that close."

Olivia's complexion takes on a blue tint from the screen. She looks so much like she did when we were younger, except now she's grown into her high cheekbones, her curved jaw. If she was pretty back then, she's beautiful now, elegant and polished, sharp at the edges, too, like getting too close might cut to the bone.

But the last thing I want is for her to think that I've been wondering about her for the past two years—which I haven't, obviously—and so the best thing to do is make sure she knows I don't care at all about our history.

"I want you to know," I say, trying to sound as smooth and confident as I can. "There's no bad blood between us. I don't hold any grudges or anything like that. I barely remember it, really."

Olivia twists her head and looks at me with a curious expression, her lips slightly parted and her head cocked. "Why would you hold a grudge?"

"Well," I say. "I mean, you, like . . . dumped me." My cheeks flame, warmth spreading down my neck. I never say the word *like*. Banished it from my vocabulary when I started doing mock trial. Words like *like* and *um* are telltale signs that you're ill-prepared, which is the last kind of adjective I want associated with me. Especially in front of Olivia.

Olivia shakes her head. "We remember things differently, Lucy."

"I don't think so." Olivia moves back in space but only slightly, and I tuck a stray curl behind my ear. "It doesn't matter, though," I say. "It's all in the past."

"Right," Olivia says slowly. "And you and Ethan are still together, so it was clearly the right call."

I jerk my head up. "What is that supposed to mean?"

"I know you had a crush on him when we were together," Olivia says. "And I know you guys kissed on that vacation. It's okay. Really, it is. Like you said, we were basically kids. It's all ancient history now."

The heat on my neck travels down to my chest, and suddenly I need a drink of water. "Ethan and I didn't start dating until after you moved away."

"Okay," Olivia says.

"It's the truth."

"Hey." Anjali's head pops up over the wall of my cubicle. "Would you two be interested in working on this archiving project? I need you to go through some property records for local businesses. It's not as boring as it sounds, I promise."

"Of course," I say quickly.

Olivia presses her lips into a smile, and we both duck our heads as Anjali's email comes through. But even with this distraction, I can't stop wondering why Olivia thinks Ethan and I kissed. I push my tongue into my teeth, pressure spreading to the roof of my mouth. When she broke up with me, she never gave a concrete reason, only said we were through and that she wanted a clean break. I tried to get her to explain, but she stonewalled me.

Suddenly, a lump forms in my throat as a thought pops into my head: If she thought I kissed Ethan behind her back, maybe that's why she dumped me. But she would have had to hear that information somewhere. Who would have told her the lie that changed everything?

FRANKIE

"Look what I got!" I hold up Erica's purse by its thick strap and let it dangle from my finger in front of Alex. I would have been able to take just the camera if I hadn't knocked over the entire pizza tray tower at Billy's shiva, but when Millie basically bombarded me, I had to slip Erica's purse behind my back and smuggle it out of the house. Thankfully, it's one of those tiny ones, and when I looked inside, I only found the camera and an old lip gloss.

Alex and I are sitting cross-legged in the sunny spots on my bed, the afternoon sun warming my cheeks.

"You didn't!" Alex leans forward to grab it, but I yank it away.

"I *did*." I unzip the bag and pull out the camera, presenting it to Alex in both hands. "You should thank me because I waited to go through the photos with you."

Alex's brow knits in worry, and he shakes his head forcefully. "I don't think we should look at that," he says. "It's not ours."

"Seriously? I thought you wanted to do this." I frown, taken aback.

"*You* wanted to investigate. *I* wanted to go swimming. And I still do. We only have a few hours of sunlight a day when we're not inside the shack. We should be out in the pool or the ocean instead of . . ." He motions to the bag. "Whatever this is."

"You're not the least bit curious?" I cross my arms over my chest.

"Fine. Let me see it." I toss the camera to Alex, and it lands in his hands but then bounces off my comforter and onto the hardwood floor with a *bang*. "Shit, sorry. Do you think it's busted?" Alex asks.

I jump down and retrieve the camera, inspecting it. "Dude, you dented the corner."

"Whoops," Alex says. "Sorry."

I frown and press the power button. "Aha! It still works. Wanna see?"

Alex begrudgingly scoots down to the floor beside me, and we both lean back against the bed.

I start scrolling through her most recent photos, seagulls and clouds and selfies Erica must have taken with her arms outstretched. In one, Lucy kisses her cheek as Erica sticks out her tongue.

"You can see the date," Alex says, pointing at the screen. "These are from before Billy's party."

I detect a hint of relief in his voice, which annoys me. I wish he were as into this as I am.

"Looks like she didn't take any photos that night," Alex says. "Can we get in the pool now? It's like ninety-five degrees outside." He points to the window, where sun is streaming in.

I keep staring at the camera, flipping through old photos, full of party shots from other kickbacks. If Erica documented *those* parties, there's no way she would have left her camera at home for Billy's. "Maybe you were right," I say. "After Billy died, maybe she didn't want anyone to see what happened that night. Maybe she deleted them."

Alex looks like he's about to protest again when there's a knock on my door. Millie pokes her head inside.

"We're all gonna hang at your pool, Alex," she says. "You guys wanna come? Trevor's setting up the waterslide."

Alex stands up and dusts off his shorts. "More than anything."

But I'm not ready to give up on this camera. Not yet. And based on Alex's desperation to get away from me, he won't be any help. "You guys go ahead. I'll be over in a few. I gotta . . . take a dump."

Millie rolls her eyes. "Gross, Franks."

"We all do it!" I call, but they're already gone. Once their footsteps recede, I turn Erica's camera over in my hands. There's a little button on the back, and when I push it, the SIM card pops out.

I reach for my computer and dig deep into my box of wires to pull out the dongle that connects the SIM card to my computer. It only takes a few moments before the folders load, and when I double-tap it open, I see a slew of images, the same ones we saw on her camera, and miraculously, a trash folder.

There's a quickening in my chest as I click the trash icon and dozens of images load. "Bingo," I whisper. My heart beats fast as I scroll down to the date of Billy's party and see there are fifty photos.

I open the first one, and it's immediately clear why she didn't want anyone to see these.

The first photo is of Dylan doing a keg stand, and then the second is of a bunch of girls in their class taking shots from small plastic cups. Then an image of Justin Vreeland with his arms crossed over his chest, scowling at something off-screen the same way he did to me on Main Street the other day. I inhale sharply and remember what I'm looking at: *suspects*.

Quickly, I grab a paper and pen and start making a list of everyone in these photos. I see no one surprising—so many members of the senior class, Billy's cousin Olivia, Ethan.

I keep scrolling, getting a sense of what the party felt like—beer pong and cartwheels in the sand, the thinning of people, a mad dash into the water, excited faces when they come up for air. Nothing to suggest that someone might have been plotting to hurt Billy.

This is a dumb idea. It is foolish to think I could find anything in these images other than a renewed dedication to *not* partying like these people. Instead of making it look fun, they all look like they're acting in a bad movie where someone winds up pregnant or, I realize with a shock, dead.

There's only one image left, and I open it, expecting more of the same. But this one's a photo of the water, the dock extending into it in the distance, no faces in frame.

Except.

I lean closer and turn up the brightness on my screen, which is when I see it. *Him.*

In the corner of the photo is the small silhouette of a boy wearing no shirt, only a pair of jeans rolled up at the ankles, his feet submerged in the ocean. He's turned to the side, so I can only see half his face. I zoom in and bring the screen closer, expecting the image to change in front of me. But it stays exactly the same, an anonymous boy, one of our own.

I scratch my pen against the paper and finish my list. *Shirtless mystery kid.* I snap a photo of the screen with my phone so I can come back to that one later.

The SIM card fits into Erica's camera easily, and I slip the device back into her bag, but when I do, my finger catches on a hard corner poking out of the zippered pocket, a slip of paper coated in something that feels glossy, like a professionally printed photograph. I pinch it between my fingers and pull it out, blinking when I see it in my hand.

It takes me a moment to fully take in what I'm looking at: an abstract image. Black, with grainy white and gray lines. An outline of something that looks like a small turtle. Or maybe a bean. A little alien. The picture looks just like those pages in my health textbook, in the chapter on how babies are made. But that can't be what *this* is. *That* was a sonogram from a pregnant person. *This* was in Erica's bag. *This* . . .

I squint at the slip of paper, study the contours, the border. In the top corner is her name—*Richardson, Erica.*

Holy shit.

This is a sonogram. Because Erica is pregnant.

THE NEXT DAY, I'm a live wire at work, unable to sit still in the welcome hut. I could barely sleep last night, thinking about the sonogram I found in Erica's bag. There were so many moments that I almost told Lucy, that I almost texted Alex. But something about that little image tucked away in her bag made me keep the information to myself.

The wind picks up, blowing up the corners of the towels in the hut, and I pull my hoodie tight around my middle.

"I'm gonna get a lemonade. You'll be okay?" Alex asks.

"Yep," I say. "It's not like someone's going to attack me *here*." I wave my hands around at our little office as Alex nods and rushes off to the clubhouse. But I have to admit that as soon as he leaves, my stomach starts humming. It's quiet today, the only sound coming from the pitter-patter of a drizzle picking up overhead.

Spinning around in my chair, I reach for my book of logic puzzles and steady my breathing. But just as I'm about to crack it open, someone knocks on the welcome hut, and I lean out the window. "Hello?"

"Oh, good. Someone's here. Wasn't sure with the weather." Erica's standing there, shivering in a thin T-shirt and shorts, flip-flops strapped to her feet. Her hair is damp, from the pool or the rain, I'm not sure, and she's got an anxious look on her face. There's a buzzing in my stomach, and I grip my pencil so hard I think it may snap in half. "Mind if I come in?"

But she doesn't wait for my answer, just barrels through the door. "What's up?" I say as nonchalantly as I can.

"I can't find my purse," she says. "Small black thing with a thick strap. I thought it might be in the lost and found. Mind if I check?" She motions to the cardboard box behind me. Everything inside my body tenses. Obviously, the bag isn't in the lost and found. It's in my room, hidden under the bed with a pile of sweatshirts I was supposed to fold last week.

"Actually . . ." I start, the admission hot on my tongue. But when Erica snaps her attention to me, her skin sallow and her eyes wide and frantic, I hesitate.

"What?" she snaps. "Actually *what*? Because this is kind of important, and I don't have time for *actually*."

"Um . . ."

Erica pushes past me and starts digging through the box.

I can picture the sonogram in the bag, the wobbly lines etched onto the paper. I could tell her I took her bag by accident. I wouldn't even have to say I saw what was inside. But the way she's tossing things around like they did something to hurt her makes me nervous. I haven't thought this through. I haven't even considered what she might do when she finds out I know.

"Fuck," she says, her voice sharp, all edges. "It's not here."

"Why don't you fill out this form, and if we see it, we can let you know?" I reach inside my desk for the paper and hand it to her, trying to keep my fingers from shaking.

She snatches it and scrawls across the page before thrusting it back into my chest. "Useless," she says, and storms out of the hut.

"What was that about?" Alex ducks back into the shack holding a grease-stained paper bag. "Rishi threw in some French fries so we could at least wait out the storm with full tums." He points to the sky out the window, a full downpour only moments away.

"Nothing. She wanted ponchos for the pool in case it rained." The lie comes out quick, but I know if I tell Alex what she was after, he'll ask me why I didn't just fork it over. I should just tell Alex about the sonogram, too, but something in my gut says to keep it a secret for a little longer. Alex didn't want to do any of this anyway. Maybe I'm doing him a favor by keeping him in the dark. After all, I haven't told him about that photo of the shirtless kid on the beach. The one I've been staring at, trying to figure out *who* it was. *Who* else might have been at the party. I make a mental note to keep studying it. Who knows, maybe I'll find a hidden clue.

"Cool," he says at the same time that his cell phone rings. Ethan's name scrolls across the screen, and Alex picks it up quickly. "Yo, what's up?" He stops chewing, and his eyes go wide, making direct contact with mine.

"What?" I ask, and lean in close to the phone so I can hear Ethan's voice, too.

"—and they searched the *Sea Witch*," Ethan says.

"Is that Billy's boat?" I ask.

Ethan's quiet for a moment, then speaks. "Frankie?"

"Yeah, we're at work."

Ethan sighs. "Fine, put me on speaker, then."

Alex taps the screen and Ethan's voice fills the hut. "You'll find out anyway. Might as well hear it from me," Ethan says, almost dejected. "Detective Hampton told the Godwins that they searched their family boat, the one moored in the Sound, the *Sea Witch*."

"Did they find anything?" I ask, pressing my palms together.

"Billy's fingerprints are all over everything. The boat was deep-cleaned that day, so they know he was there sometime after that, in the early hours of the morning."

"Okay," I say, glancing at Alex, who's chewing on a cuticle.

"And they also found DNA samples. Blood. Spit. From a few different people."

"Blood?!" I can't help but scream the word.

"What does that mean?" Alex asks, nervous.

"It means," Ethan says, his voice trembling, "that Billy wasn't there alone. Mrs. Godwin thinks whoever was with him may have . . ."

Ethan doesn't need to finish the sentence. Alex and I are stunned into silence, and though I have no idea what he's thinking, the only thing running through my head is this: *If Erica's pregnant, then Billy has to be the father, and if she told him that night, maybe he was furious. Furious enough to start a fight.*

A shock of cold rushes through me when I realize what that means. That DNA may be Erica's.

MILLIE

Even though there were rumors that the Club's annual summer solstice party would be canceled this year, our boss, Jordan, sent out an email this morning saying the party was, in fact, on and that none of the members who were also staffers had to work. Instead, we were instructed to take the night off and enjoy the celebration.

But it's hard to relax. The perimeter of the Club is lined with newly hired security guards, wearing all black and bulky vests that appear bulletproof. They checked everyone's IDs as we entered the Club, which seemed silly to me. It's not as if anyone's Pelican Island Academy badge would have also said I KILLED BILLY on it.

I look around the beach for Trevor but can't find him. I've barely seen him since the shiva. Well, since I left him outside Billy's shiva for thirty minutes while I helped Ethan calm down.

At first, Trevor seemed to understand, but based on his reluctance to return my text messages, I'm not so sure.

I wrap my arms around my middle. If things were normal, we'd spend the whole evening curled up in the Adirondack chairs overlooking the eastern lawn so we could get primo spots for sunset. Take turns getting plates of watermelon salad and shrimp cocktail and, when we finally got sick of debating the merits of horror versus romance, settle into our usual rhythm of reading side by side.

There's a dull ache in my chest. Not the kind I get when I'm around Ethan, where it's all I can focus on. This one is a drumbeat, providing background rhythm, a reminder that things have already started to change, that I *miss* how life was a week ago, before Billy died.

Part of me even wanted to stay home from the solstice party, but when I told Mom I had a headache, she said there was no way in hell she was leaving me on my own. "You will go and you will act normal," she said while putting on her earrings. "We all will."

So here I am, standing on the cornhole lawn by myself, trying to make it seem like I'm definitely paying attention to the middle schoolers who are negging each other as they try to sink beanbags.

"Fascinating, isn't it?" I look to my right, and Trevor approaches wearing khaki shorts and a rumpled short-sleeved button-down.

"Riveting." The ache subsides just a little, and I wonder if this is his peace offering. If we're okay. I nod to the two twelve-year-old boys as they shove each other back and forth. "I think that one's gonna win."

"Which one?"

"No idea."

Trevor laughs once, then presses his lips together. "Are we okay, Mill?"

My chest unlocks a tiny bit, like it's making space for whatever kind of apology he's offering. "You tell me," I say.

"Yeah," he says. "I guess I've been a little . . ."

"Distant?"

He nods, sheepish. "I was pissed at you for ditching me at the shiva."

"I figured." I clasp my hands together and squeeze. "I should have texted, but I saw Ethan like that and . . ."

"I get it. It was good of you. You shouldn't have left him alone."

I know that, but part of me wonders why Trevor's allowed to be mad when he's barely made time to hang out with me and I haven't made a stink at all.

"Anyway," he says. "My bad. I just wanna be cool again. Can we call a truce?"

"Yeah," I say, conceding. "Of course."

"Great. I was waiting for you to hit the buffet."

Together we head inside the clubhouse, where long tables are covered in white tablecloths, set with sterling silver cutlery and heavy china plates bearing the insignia of the Beach Club. Security guards surround the exits, and everyone seems to ignore them, but their presence makes me uneasy, a constant reminder that something terrible has happened here and we don't know why.

All the windows and doors are open, and there's a sudden gust of wind blowing through my hair, lifting up the edges of linen napkins. A few people yelp in surprise, jittery and jumpy, as if everyone in town is as on edge as I am.

"Come on," Trevor says, leading us to the buffet. This party is usually raucous, signaling the real beginning of summer, but tonight the din is quiet as we load up our plates with grilled zucchini and smoked ribs, dilly potato salad and marinated tomatoes. The only sounds I hear are urgent whispers and the scraping of knives against porcelain, the wind lapping at the clubhouse, rattling the windows.

Trevor uses a free hand to rub his shoulder. "You okay?" I ask.

"Yeah," he says. "Forgot to do my physical therapy stretches this morning."

I wince. "Want me to carry your plate?"

Trevor shakes his head. "I'm good, but let's get out of here."

Once we're outside with our piled-high plates, I can breathe again, inhaling the salty cool air. Everything smells of seaweed and damp rocks, melted butter from the lobster bar, and the sweetness of summer, as vivid as the peonies blooming by the tennis courts. As we walk to our usual area on the eastern lawn, I can pretend, for a moment, that things are just as they were last year. Easy.

Once we sit down, the party receding behind us, Trevor asks, "Are you okay going back to work? Especially after . . . you know."

My throat is sandy, and for a moment I find it hard to speak. When I exhale, I turn my face up to the sun. I haven't had my first shift back yet, haven't climbed the ladder and settled into the chair. In fact, I've been putting off thinking about it, not wanting to wonder what it will be like to sit up there and look out at the same ocean where Billy floated face down, waiting to be found.

"I don't know," I say. "I guess we'll find out."

Trevor wrinkles his nose. "I think Ethan's terrified."

"Really?"

"Yeah. At least you guys have each other, huh?"

"Yeah." A warmth spreads over me because it's true. When I get back up there, I won't be alone. I'll be with Ethan. I tear at a piece of garlic bread, oil greasing my fingers.

"Do you like working with Ethan?"

I glance sideways at Trevor, trying to read him. We never talk about his brothers, at least not as they relate to *me*. But he's looking straight down at his plate, spearing a piece of asparagus with his fork.

"Yeah," I say. Trevor furrows his brow and nods once. "But it'll be great when you're back up there. Finally, someone to talk about books with."

Trevor smiles weakly. "For sure," he says.

"How's the pool?"

"It's okay," he says. "Not that exciting. But maybe that's a good thing."

"Erica's a lifeguard for the big-kid pool, right?"

"Uh-huh."

"That must be nice."

"Sure," Trevor says. "She's cool."

"Maybe she can help you with the stretches?" I ask. Erica volunteered at the outpatient rehab place Trevor frequented after his surgery and was probably the only reason he came home from those sessions with a smile on his face since she would crack jokes and bring him snacks. At least, that's how he described it.

"Yeah," he says. "Maybe."

I look down at his arm, and the only sign that it's different from its counterpart is the fading scar slicing across his skin, the slight atrophying along his muscles.

Out of the corner of my eye, I see Frankie speed-walking toward me, her arms pumping by her side as the setting sun creates a gold glowing effect behind her.

"Is there a last call on cherry pie or something?" Trevor asks.

"Who cares?" Frankie says. "You know I'm a blueberry girl."

"Freak," Trevor says, flicking a piece of corn at her.

Frankie rolls her eyes, then crouches down beside me. I can practically feel her high energy, that intensity she gets when she's working on one of those puzzles. She looks around, bug-eyed, and I flick the space between her eyebrows. "What's wrong with you?"

"Nothing." She grips the back of my chair and leans in, her eyes moving to Trevor. "You know," she says, "they *were* running low, actually. On cherry pie."

Trevor springs up. "Oh crap. Mill, you want some?"

"Sure," I say, and Trevor jogs back toward the clubhouse.

Frankie grips my arm. "Did he say anything?"

"Anything *what*?"

"I don't know, about the DNA found on Billy's boat?"

I've been trying to avoid anything related to the murder investigation. It's almost like pretending it didn't happen might make the whole thing go away.

"Maybe he knows something." Frankie's got the kind of nerves that make me think she's about to rob a bank.

"You're being *weird*, Frankie. Go do a puzzle or something."

Frankie checks over her shoulder like she's trying to make sure no one's watching us, and then she reaches into her pocket and pulls out her cell phone, shoving the screen under my nose. "Look at this." I look down and see a photo of the beach, some waves, clearly taken at night, since it's all blown out with the flash.

"Good thing you quit yearbook. This photo is bad."

"I didn't take it." She zooms in on one corner of the photo. "Erica did."

"What? How'd you get this?"

Frankie shakes her head. "It doesn't matter. This photo was

taken the night of Billy's party," she says, her words rushing together. "I wanted to find out who was there."

Suddenly, I'm annoyed. "You're not a *cop*. Stop meddling."

"Millie, look," she says, and hands me back the screen so I can see the zoomed-in corner. "I'm trying to figure out who this is. At first, I didn't recognize him, but I've been looking at this picture like every minute since the shiva, and the more I study it, the more I think it might be . . ." She trails off, her voice urgent, and I take it from her and hold it close to my face.

It's only a second before I understand what she wants me to see. My stomach tenses when I zoom in on the face. The curved jaw and the dark hair. The sloped shoulder, the tiniest shadow of a scar. It could be Ethan, but of course I know it's not.

"Is it . . . ?" Frankie asks, forcing me to finish her sentence.

When I speak, it comes out chalky, like I can't believe I have to say his name out loud. "Trevor."

LUCY

The drive to the town hall is only seven minutes long, and on the way, I pass every important landmark on the island. I cruise by my high school and its expansive grounds, the recently renovated triplex, and the entrance to the golf course before careening toward the Tennis and Beach Club.

As I pass over the train tracks, I notice there are nearly twice as many cars as usual in the parking lot, nearly a dozen people gathering, huddled up near news trucks. An unsettling feeling takes hold of my stomach as I get to the end of the block and pull into the municipal lot behind town hall, which is bursting with reporters.

When I get out of the car, I grip my tote bag close to my chest and flick my eyes to the entrance, now flanked by policemen. "They're everywhere." Olivia steps out of a black sedan next to me, pushing her sunglasses up onto the crown of her head.

"The police or rubberneckers?" I ask.

"Both." She grimaces. "It's all because of that one story in the *Times*' Metro section. People hear 'rich white boy murdered in a beach town' and come running."

"Ick." I scrunch up my face and hold the straps of my bag tighter.

"Did you see news crews trying to get B-roll of the Beach Club on your way in? It's nuts." Olivia shudders. "It's like we're living in a documentary." She holds up a loyalty card to Sweet Pete's, the café on the corner. "I am most certainly not caffeinated enough for that. Want a coffee?"

We still have another fifteen minutes before our workday starts, and the answer is obvious. "Yes."

Together we walk into the café, and I get a whiff of her perfume, sweet and floral as it lodges in my brain. Inside, the shop is packed full of people wearing ill-fitting button-downs working on their laptops. "Do *any* of these people even live here?" Olivia asks.

"Definitely not," I say, and Olivia snorts as we get behind a family of four fighting over which pastries are the best.

"Luce?" I look up and see Ethan turning around with a cold brew in his hand. He's wearing lifeguarding trunks and a thin white T-shirt, his sunglasses perched on top of his head. "What're you doing?"

"Oh!" I say, my cheeks flushing. "Coffee." *Duh.*

His eyes drift to Olivia by my side. The corners of his mouth tug into a smile, but it's a fake one, not the kind that lights up his whole face. "Hey, Olivia."

"Hi," she says.

The tension's palpable, thick and heavy between us, and I fight for something to say. "Weird weather, huh?"

Ethan cocks his head at me and laughs softly. "This is bizarre. Right? Sorry. I don't mean for it to be."

Instantly I relax, grateful that Ethan's got the social graces of a born networker, and I can feel Olivia ease up, too.

"Very much so." Olivia shrugs. "But, hey. Just about everything else this summer is bizarre, so . . ."

"Very good point." Ethan sips his cold brew. "Anyway, I gotta get to my shift." For a second, I think he's going to brush past me, maybe lightly touch my hand as a goodbye, but instead he steps forward and wraps his hand around the back of my neck. His lips meet mine, and he kisses me hard, his tongue pushing forward, grazing my teeth.

Ethan's never been big on PDA, and I'm so shocked that it takes me a moment before I step away, out of his grasp.

"Bye, Luce," he says, leaving before I can say anything.

Heat rushes to my cheeks, and a prickle of shame fills my chest. Olivia doesn't say a thing as we move up in line, which almost makes it worse.

"Separate or together?" the barista asks.

"Separate," I say at the same time Olivia says, "Together."

She turns to me. "Don't worry, I got it." I start to protest, but Olivia's already focused on her order. "Iced mocha for me," she says. "With oat milk."

"I'll have a small latte. Regular milk."

The barista taps a few buttons on the screen, then looks up. "That'll be twelve fifty."

I fight all of the urges telling me to reach for my wallet. I've always been allergic to anyone spotting me. When Ethan and I go out, I insist we split, even down to the nickel. He once asked me what the deal was, why he couldn't grab sandwiches for us or why I insisted on paying him back. I'd never thought too deeply about it, but once he asked, the answer was obvious: I never wanted to feel like I owed someone something, even if it was only Ethan, who did nice things for me all the time.

Even now, six months later, I still think about what he said next.

"It makes *me* feel good to take you out," he said. "Sometimes I feel like you don't need me for anything. Like if I disappeared for a few days, you'd be fine." At the time, I didn't respond with what I really wanted to say, which was *Of course I would be fine. I don't need you. I want you, and isn't that better?* But I said none of those things and instead let him cover our tab at the diner.

I fiddle with the strap on my tote bag to stop myself from making this whole thing weirder when Olivia sucks in a breath of air.

"Shoot," she says, rummaging around in her tote. "I must have forgotten my wallet. Oh my god, I'm mortified."

I reach into my bag. "Don't worry." I slip out a twenty and slide it across the counter. "You can get next time."

"Sure." Red splotches form on Olivia's neck, and her jaw tenses.

When we collect our coffees and walk outside, she says, "I'm really sorry. I've been so absent-minded since Billy died."

I wave my hand in front of me. "It's coffee. Don't worry." Besides, I'm just grateful to talk about anything that's not Ethan so clearly claiming me as his in the coffee shop. Olivia looks like she wants to melt onto the concrete. I rest my hand on her forearm and stop walking. "Seriously. Forget about it."

She stops, too, and her eyes search mine like she wants to say something else, but instead she nods once, and says, "Okay." Her mouth forms a smile. "You know, I always thought that people change so much from year to year, but you're the same. Very 'no bullshit.' It's what I always liked about you."

The skin on the back of my neck tingles but I ignore the sensation. "We can't really change who we are," I say. "At least you put in a nice way. Ethan says I need to let other people do things for me sometimes. Make other people feel needed." As soon as I say the words, I want to take them back. There's no reason in the world I should let her in on that aspect of our relationship.

Olivia laughs, leaning her head back and exposing the soft, long part of her neck to the sun. "I don't think that's a very good reason to let people do things for you."

"What's a good one, then?"

"Because you trust them."

A spring pulls apart inside my chest, and I take a sip of my latte to keep my teeth from grinding together.

Olivia tilts her head. "Do you think I've changed much since you last saw me?"

"I don't know. We've barely spoken." Which is by design. It's not like I've spent my out-of-work hours trying to track her down to hang out. In fact, it's probably best if we spend as little time together as possible.

"Fair," she says. "I have, though. Changed."

"Oh yeah?"

"I'm not interested in playing pretend anymore," she says. I want to ask her what she means, but Olivia skips ahead, pulling the door open to Mayor Cho's office. "Come on," she says. "Let's go inside."

The first half of the workday goes by in a blur of press releases and meetings with Anjali, who dumped a dozen files on our desks for our property records project. As I pore over document after document, I barely have time to think about what Olivia said. Well, that's not true. I'm *choosing* not to think about it, not to let the words sink deep, deep into my brain.

Because you trust them.

I'm only interrupted by incoming texts from Erica, who has been sending the strangest messages, checking in constantly.

Have you heard anything new? What do you know? Are your sisters saying anything?

They're cryptic and desperate, as if knowing what people are saying might change what's happened. I keep telling her the same thing: I haven't heard anything, but I'll let you know if I do.

I turn back to the folder on my desk and get ready to file it quickly, just like the others. But then I realize it's not just a simple property record but a whole stack of papers clipped together. The front page says *VREELAND V. GODWIN.*

A lawsuit.

I duck down and flip through the sheets of paper as quickly as I can. It doesn't take me long to find out the Vreeland family sued the Godwin family a few years ago over a property line dispute when the Godwins began cutting down the Vreelands' trees.

I'm about to ask Olivia if she knew about this, but as I turn the page, I see a deposition taken from Billy, then a freshman in high school.

Justin had a tree house in the big elm we cut down, and after it was demolished he threatened to kill me. That's why I punched him after school.

I read the sentence twice and try to remember ever hearing about Justin and Billy getting into a fight. It's not like they hung out together, but I never noticed bad blood, only a mutual understanding that their circles would only overlap in certain instances.

I want to keep reading, but Anjali pops her head above our side-by-side cubicles and assigns us a project. "Can you two head over to the police station?" she asks. "Detective Hampton has some paperwork she wants hand-delivered to the mayor."

Olivia raises her eyebrows at me with a conspiratorial look, and within a few minutes, we're on the street, rushing over to the station. The air outside is thick and humid, and the sky is gray, clouds rolling through fast.

Once inside, I lead us to the reception area, where we're directed to take a seat in the waiting room until they can get all the files together for us. The station is busy, with officers rushing back to their offices and the sound of urgent chatter floating through the room.

"You'd think they were trying to solve a murder or something," Olivia whispers, and I reel my head back in surprise and try to stifle a laugh. "It's okay," she says. "If I can joke, so can you."

I relent and crack a smile. "Morbid."

Olivia's gaze moves above my head, and a shadow from the window darkens half her face, which seems to tense.

"What?" I ask, and spin around. But when I see what she's looking at, what's framed on the wall, I clench my jaw. "Oh," I say. "I had no idea that was here."

We're both staring at a photo of the two of us when we were fifteen, our arms intertwined, as we hold up a trophy from that year's annual Club Tennis Tournament, which the PIPD sponsors. We'd won girls' doubles in our age group, and our smiles take up most of our faces, our hair slicked with sweat. I peer closer at the photo, remembering how comfortable it felt as her arm snaked around my shoulders. We look so young, still growing into our features, our bodies. There's an awkwardness about us, the way we lean into each other, but an ease, too, like if we were made to pose for a photo by some professional photographer, we were glad we could do it together.

"Your serve was monster," I say.

Olivia shrugs. "Still wasn't good enough."

"What do you mean?"

Olivia's quiet for a moment, and when she speaks, her voice is low. "I thought I'd get a scholarship to play."

"Is that why you're taking a gap year?" I ask.

"Yep," Olivia says. "I got into some schools but without tennis, so I'm not exactly sure where I want to go. I was so single-minded that I didn't really think about the *schools* themselves. Just the teams."

"What are you gonna do instead?"

"I *was* going to stay here," she says, letting out a huff of air.

"But not anymore?"

"What about you?" she asks, changing the subject. "You're going to Cornell, right?"

"Mm-hmm." I clench my hands in front of my stomach. "Where are those files? We should probably be getting back."

"You don't sound too excited."

"I *like* work, actually."

"I mean about Cornell." Olivia narrows her eyes. She knows I'm avoiding the question. "Your parents went there, right?"

"Yeah. Ethan's, too. That's where they all met."

"So was it a choice? Or did you feel like you had to go there?"

Heat creeps into my chest, spreading to my collarbones, and I push myself to stand. "You really think I'm the type of person who would pick a college just because everyone wants me to go there?"

"Maybe I don't know what kind of person you are." She crosses one leg over the other and starts tapping her toe, impatient, as if I'm not going to say anything interesting or useful at all. Something in the way she turns away from me makes me want to tell her the truth, to prove to her that I'm not actually following some boy to school, that I've made up my own mind about my future. But telling her before telling Ethan would be the ultimate betrayal. He has to know first. I have to tell him soon. I—

"Actually, I'm going to Penn." As soon as the words leave my mouth, I want to wrap my arms around them and yank them back, like they never existed at all. "It's a secret." My earlobes are on fire, a wild sensation but one that makes sense when I realize it's not just my earlobes but my whole face. "Only my parents know. And Erica." I turn away from her, making a tally mark on the legal pad. "I don't know why I told you that. Please don't say anything."

Olivia stops tapping her foot. Her whole body stills, and when she speaks, her voice is hushed. "Ethan doesn't know."

"I haven't told him yet."

"How come?"

Don't say anything, I will myself. *You don't trust her. You barely know her anymore.* She's looking at me with such intensity I feel like my heart is going to stop beating. But then, as if a trance has been lifted, Olivia blinks, like she's surprised with herself. "Sorry. You don't have to answer that." Her cheeks redden. "My mom says I try to make people feel bad when I'm on the defense."

There's a weight on my chest as heavy as an elephant's foot. "You don't have to be defensive with me."

Olivia opens her mouth like she's about to say something, but just then, there's a loud banging coming from the back of the police station, the sounds of doors slamming, and shouting.

I spring to my feet, craning my neck to see, and three officers appear, rushing back to where the commotion's coming from.

"What's going on?" I ask the guard behind the desk.

He glances at us, then back toward the hallway, where the sounds of metal scraping against the floor and officers' yelling get louder and louder.

"You can't keep me here!" someone calls. "You have no proof. You have *nothing*!"

A calm female voice rises above the rest, and when she speaks, it sounds like she's getting closer. "We need to take a DNA sample. It's standard procedure. It's—ouch! Jesus Christ! He bit me! Arrest him for assaulting a police officer!"

A moment later, Detective Hampton rushes forward clutching her hand, her eyes wide and her hair out of place. She doesn't register us as she dips her head down to the reception. "Don't let him leave," she says. "Not until I'm back."

"Where are you going?" the guard asks.

"To process this." She holds up her hand. "At least he left DNA on *me*." I gasp, and that's when she turns and sees Olivia and me. "You shouldn't be here," she says, and dashes off into the street before we can explain why were sent to the station in the first place.

But none of that matters, because as I tiptoe to the hallway, I see that deep in the bowels of the police department, there are three officers escorting Justin Vreeland into a conference room. And it sure doesn't look like he's leaving anytime soon.

THE PARTY

1:30 A.M.

Billy stood near the half-empty bottles of booze with Ethan and Dylan, trying to remember the words to some Billy Joel song his dad used to sing to him when he was young.

"Einstein, James Dean, Brooklyn's got a winning team," Billy sang, his voice off-key. "What's next, dude?" He elbowed Ethan in the stomach.

"How should I know? I'm a Bruce guy."

"Long Island traitor!" Dylan wrapped an arm around Ethan's neck, and Billy threw his head back, laughing.

But when he opened his eyes, he realized the crowd on the back patio had thinned, his classmates slipping away into the night. He still couldn't find Erica, who this whole party was for. "Yo, did Erica leave?" he asked.

Dylan looked around and pointed to a small black purse. "I think that's her bag. She's probably around here somewhere."

Billy wanted to look for her, but Ethan clapped him on the back. "Didn't you want to find Justin?"

He did, Billy remembered, and as luck would have it, Justin was sitting in an Adirondack chair, vaping with one of his buddies from the football team.

"That, my dude, is an excellent call." Billy wiggled out of Ethan's

grasp and leapt across the lawn until he was standing directly in front of Justin. He could do with a little blow. Maybe a bump of ketamine. He wanted something that would keep him up, that would keep this party going and make him a little more confident when he finally talked to Erica.

"What do you have tonight?" Billy asked.

Justin shook his head. "I'm not your vending machine."

"I'll pay. Obviously."

"Not tonight, man."

Annoyance prickled the back of Billy's neck. He pulled out a few crisp bills from his back pocket and held them up over Justin's head, then released them so they fluttered in the air, landing on his face.

"C'mon," Ethan said behind him in that worried tone of his. "Be nice about it." But Billy smirked, waiting for Justin to do something. If this kid—this trust-fund baby who was just as well-off as the rest of them—wanted to act hard all year, like he was a real-life Scarface, then Billy wanted to see him do something other than hand over a bunch of pills he swiped from his mom's medicine cabinet. Billy could do that, too, based on his own mother's stash.

Justin stood up, the money floating to the ground. "I'm not selling you shit." The kid turned his back on Billy and started to walk away. But that wasn't going to work. Not for Billy.

"Hey!" Billy called, reeling his elbow back in space, and when Justin turned around, Billy leaned forward and made sure to land his fist right on Justin's jaw, hard enough to hear a cracking sound split through the air.

FRANKIE

Accompanying Millie to the Book Bonanza is like running a marathon. You have to prepare by making sure you have water, a snack, money for an iced tea, probably another snack, and so much patience. Something I definitely lack.

We're here because Millie's refused to talk about that photo of Trevor since I showed it to her at the solstice party a few days ago, and insisted that if we were going to do it, we'd have to go far away from home. And yet, we've been at the shop forever, browsing books.

"C'mon, Millie," I say, tapping my foot against the wooden floorboards. "Can't we sit over there for a sec?" I point to the cozy reading corner where two overstuffed purple armchairs face each other against the window.

"Chill out," she says, pulling another hardcover from the romance section, where she'd been methodically moving down the aisle for the past twenty minutes. "I still haven't gotten to the new releases."

I smack my palm against my forehead. "Why are we hanging out with the books you already know?"

A small smile spreads on her lips. "Because," she says, "it's fun."

"Fun for you. We have *things* to discuss."

Millie turns back to the stacks like she doesn't hear me. I cross my arms over my chest and give her the most powerful glare I can muster, but she doesn't look back at me.

"Millie," I say, growling her name.

"I don't want to go around accusing him of something, okay? Maybe that photo was from another night or something. He and Erica are friends. It's not that weird."

My chest tightens with anxiety. Yesterday, I slipped Erica's bag into the welcome hut's lost and found, but I haven't had the guts to call her yet and tell her that it's waiting for her. Maybe it's because I know that once she gets it back, she'll start to wonder where it went—who took it. Who knows about that photo of Trevor and the baby.

Millie shakes her head. "Go wait over there, okay? Or outside on the benches," she says. "And text Mom that we're still alive. She's been blowing us up for the past ten minutes."

I stomp my way out of the shop and plop down on the bench in front of the store. I pull out my phone and see Mom's messages.

> Are you girls still at the Bonanza?
> Let me know asap.
>
> I see your locations but I want to HEAR FROM YOU.
>
> HELLO?
>
> If you don't respond in two minutes, I'm going to have to come down there myself.

I let out a puff of air and type fast.

Still at the Bonanza, don't freak out!!! Millie just has to read the whole store before we leave.

Mom responds immediately. Ha. Ha. Home by four.

I drop onto the wooden bench and a bead of sweat forms on my forehead, the heavy heat of summer burning my scalp. I should have brought a hat. I stretch my achy legs out and catch a big whiff of wet sand and deep-fried food from Hot Diggity. Yep. It's definitely summer.

The street is lined with the same type of security guards we've seen at the Club, plus Pelican Island police officers. From my perch, it looks like they're all scrolling on their phones, trading pieces of gum back and forth. Not sure how they're going to keep us safe, but *sure*.

Up on the announcement board staked into the grass is a piece of paper with Billy's face on it. Above the image, the words JUSTICE FOR BILLY are typed in bold. But someone's scrawled red devil horns above his head, which seems like a little much. He may have been a douche, but he's dead. Yeesh.

I pull out the puzzle book I bought when we first got here and crack open the spine, but I don't get through more than a few lines before I hear bike tires crunch over gravel. *Shit.* It's Erica pulling up on her bicycle. She's got big sunglasses hiding her face, and even through that shield, her distress is obvious: Her dark hair is tangled, and her skin is red and splotchy. A lump forms in my throat and nerves flutter in my stomach.

"Oh," she says when she sees me, pushing her hair away from her face. "Hi."

"Hi," I say tentatively, clutching my book.

Erica whacks the kickstand of her bike with her heel and lifts her face.

"Your bag," I say, the words coming quickly. "It's in the lost and found."

Erica's eyes go wide. "Really?"

Shit. What if she suspects I put it there? "I think so. At least, there's *a* bag in there that matches the description you gave us."

Erica's shoulders relax. "Thank god," she say. "I'll get it today."

"Cool." My heart rate begins to slow as Erica turns around so she's facing the poster of Billy, the one that's been vandalized.

"Messed up," I say. "Whoever did that's sick."

Erica spins around, and she's got a strange look on her face, her skin bright red.

"I mean, he's dead. It's like, *be nice*." I should really shut up, but the words come out of my mouth like vomit.

"You don't know *anything*, Frankie," Erica says, her voice a mixture of venom and rage. Then she gets back on her bike and hurries away.

I watch her go, speechless for a moment. Is that how someone would act if they found a defaced poster of their dead ex-boyfriend, their potential *baby daddy*? I have no idea, but it sure as hell seemed weird. Wouldn't she have agreed with me? Or at least torn it down?

But Erica did neither of those things. Her tone almost made it seem like she was *justifying* the poster, like maybe Billy deserved to have those devil horns drawn on him, even in death. If she believed that, then maybe . . .

Maybe she's not pregnant with Billy's baby after all. Maybe she's pregnant with someone else's.

"Frankie?" Millie calls from the front door of the Bonanza.

I head over to her and gulp, not wanting to say anything and have my voice betray me. She's got a book tucked under her arm—*A Young Person's Guide to Grieving.* I take a deep breath and finally feel like when I speak, I'll sound normal.

"Is that for Lucy?" I ask, though it doesn't really seem like Lucy needs any form of self-help. She's been cool as a cucumber since everything happened, barely showing any emotion as she heads off to work at Mayor Cho's office. When I asked her how she was doing, she said she was mostly worried about Ethan and Erica, not herself. Hearing her talk about Erica and *not* saying anything felt like a total betrayal.

"Oh," Millie says, covering the title with her palm. "No, it's for Ethan."

"That's nice of you," I say.

Mille slips it into her tote bag and grasps the straps tight. "Come on. Let's go home."

But just as we're about to get on our bikes, our phones ping with a text from Lucy to our family group chat. Millie gets to her phone before I do, and her hand flies to her mouth, her fingers pressed to her lips.

"What?" I ask.

She looks up, her eyes wide in shock. "Justin Vreeland was just arrested."

WE'VE NEVER BIKED faster in our entire lives. All I can focus on is that the investigation is over. Justin killed Billy. "What's his deal, anyway?" I ask Millie, my breathing shallow as we pedal uphill.

She glances over her shoulder. "Lucy says he deals drugs."

"Drugs?" I'm not naive enough to think that no one on Pelican Island dabbles in the dark arts of substance abuse, but to hear Millie say it so plainly is jarring. "Like what kind?"

"I don't know," she says, slowing down so we're side by side on the shoulder of the road. "It's not like he's offering them to *me*."

"Right." I pause. "So, you think Billy was into drugs?"

Millie sighs. "Frankie, how many times do I have to tell you? I don't know. Come on, we're almost there."

We turn onto Pelican Island Road, but as we bike toward our house, Mom rushes out the front door and starts waving her hands. "Girls!" she calls. "There you are!"

"We're fine, Mom." I brake to stop and let my bike drop onto the lawn as Mom reaches for both of us, wrapping us in her arms. "We're *fine*," I repeat.

Behind me, Lucy's car pulls into the driveway and she steps out, shielding her eyes from the setting sun. "Let's go next door," she says, her voice clipped. "The boys are all there."

"*Now* everyone's interested in the investigation!" I say, throwing my hands up. "But when *I* was trying to figure out what happened, no one cared."

Mom snaps her attention to me. "You were trying to *what*?"

Lucy makes big eyes at me and runs her pointer finger across her neck, telling me to cut it out. "Nothing," I say.

Mom hurries us across the driveway and as we walk, it's like she's trying to keep her hands on all three of us at once, like letting any of her daughters go might cause one of us to spontaneously combust. My first instinct is to elbow her away, but I can't deny that it's nice to have her attention, even though I'm sharing it with Millie and Lucy.

We head around to the side door, and Mom knocks on the glass so Paula can let us in, the alarm beeping behind her as we file inside.

"Oh good, you're all together," she says, kissing each one of us on the forehead. "We ordered Chinese for everyone."

"Thanks, Paula," Lucy says, pressing her lips together. "Can I help with anything?"

Paula's face softens, and she shakes her head. "No, dear. I can't believe you heard first."

Lucy winces. "Perks of working at the Mayor's office, I guess. I thought it was weird when I saw him in the station yesterday, but never did I think . . ." She shudders and Paula pats her shoulder gently.

"Why don't you keep Ethan company, okay?" Lucy nods and trots off, but Paula looks at Mom and drops her head. "Have you talked to Deirdre?"

"No," Mom says, her voice a hiss. "What would I even say to her? *Did your son really murder Sally's boy?*" Mom shivers. "No doubt they've brought in that criminal attorney friend of theirs from the city."

Mom and Paula keep talking, but I push through to the couches, where everyone is sprawled out. I once calculated that I have spent at least four months of my life sitting on the Silver family living room couch, sunk into the corner of its L shape, feet tucked under Alex's butt to keep warm. So much of my life has existed in this room—so much of my sisters' lives. I know which throw pillows are frayed at the corners and which blankets still smell like their old cockapoo, Oona, who passed away last year. I know that while sitting on the couch, I can throw my hand up over my shoulder without looking and reach directly into a bowl that holds chocolate Kisses, the wrapper colors changing with the seasons. Today's are red, white, and blue, in honor of the upcoming Fourth of July parade.

Ethan's hands are steepled in front of his face, so I can only see his eyes. Trevor clutches a pillow in front of his stomach, leaning so far forward his back is hunched. Only Alex gets up to greet us.

"You guys want anything to drink?"

We all shake our heads no and I watch Lucy plop down on the couch next to Ethan, his arm snaking around her shoulder.

"I can't believe it," Ethan says. "Justin's supposed to go to Trinity in the fall."

"Not if he killed Billy." I reach behind me and grab a handful of Kisses.

"Have some *tact*, Frankie." Lucy flicks my shoulder. "Besides. He wasn't arrested for murder."

"What was it, drugs?"

All around me, I can feel eyes boring into me like I said something wrong, like I shouldn't have mentioned anything about that. Mom and Paula's conversation stills.

"Drugs?" Mom asks. "What about *drugs*? Deirdre's son deals *drugs*?"

Thankfully, Ethan pipes up. "We don't know anything yet. Just stay calm."

Lucy nudges me with her foot. "I'm pretty sure they arrested him for assaulting an officer," she says. "Yesterday, he *bit* Hampton at the station. That's all they have."

"For now," I say, which earns me a glare from her.

Behind me, Paula and Mom duck their heads together and

whisper to each other, their words barely audible. Leaning back, I strain to catch Mom asking, "Did you hear about Reid?"

"What?" Paula says.

"He's been at the station nearly every day talking to those detectives," Mom says. "Maybe he knew something about Justin."

I stand up slowly and act like I'm walking to the bathroom behind Mom, hoping to butt in a little. "What did you say about Billy's dad?" I ask.

Mom shakes her head. "Nothing, Frankie. You must have misheard."

"But you said . . ."

"Frankie." Mom says my name like it's full of sharp edges. Then she sighs, and says, "Sweetie, you have chocolate on your face. Why don't you take care of that?"

I wipe my arm across my mouth, my heart sinking, and flop back on the couch, folding into myself.

"Oh!" Mom calls, and we all spin our heads around.

"What?" Millie asks.

"It's Deirdre. She texted our group chat."

"You have a group chat?" I ask.

"Yes, Frankie. I'm not a hundred."

Alex bumps my shoulder, trying to conceal a laugh, and we both break into giggles.

"What did she say?" Lucy leans over the back of the couch toward Mom.

"She says . . ." Mom starts. "'I know there are a lot of rumors floating around, but I want to clear something up.' Wow. Bold!"

"Keep reading!" I say a little too enthusiastically.

"'I want to clear something up,'" Mom continues. "'My son, Justin, *was* arrested this evening. But it was for a misunderstanding to do with a police office. He is still being questioned, and I can assure you he had NOTHING to do with Billy's death.' All caps, yeesh. Then she wrote, 'Thank you for your support during this difficult time.'"

"Difficult time?!" Paula says. "Support?! I'm not supporting her or her drug-dealing, police-biting son right now."

Mom and Paula lower their voices and continue gossiping, so I turn back to the couches.

"You were right, Luce." She looks a little too chipper at that, but I ask, "What happens now?"

Ethan stands, wiping his hands on his shorts. "They're probably gathering evidence. Trying to match his DNA with whatever was on the boat. Seeing if they'll bring any other charges."

I cross my arms over my chest. Alex turns to me and raises his eyebrows. "Crazy, huh?"

"You kids still can't go anywhere alone, okay?" Paula says as she unloads cartons of Chinese food from paper bags, setting them out on the dining table behind us. "There's too much chaos going on, and we want you safe." She pauses. "And well fed. Come on. Eat."

Everyone darts into the dining room and starts helping themselves to plates of food. Mom and Paula settle in at the kitchen island, their backs to us. Millie and Lucy take two seats at the far end of the table, twirling lo mein noodles around their chopsticks. All three boys hover over the cartons, their banter light and similar as they edge one another out to get to the egg rolls first.

From where I stand, Ethan and Trevor look identical. Heads bobbing with the same shape of nose and shoulders, same height and swoops of hair. Alex nudges his way in, grabbing a dumpling off Ethan's plate, and for a moment, the three of them seem to meld into one silhouette, one Silver boy. A moment later, they divide back into three.

For my entire life, I've wondered what the three of them do when they're alone. If they talk about us like we talk about them, if they tell each other the secrets they've scavenged from us—if Alex reveals what I've told him about my crushes, my wishes, my embarrassments.

But then I focus on Trevor, who's barely said a word during this whole ordeal, who's now sitting at the far end of the table, hunched over his plate. Millie and I never did get to talk about if it was him in the photo—about what it might mean. But looking at him now, the curve of his jaw, the profile so exacting, I know without a doubt that it's him. I just don't know why he doesn't want anyone to know that he was there, too.

MILLIE

The Club grounds are quiet since it's so early in the morning, before the gates open to guests, and a low mist rolls in from the sea. I used to love this time of day, but now it feels like a pair of hands may reach out from the haze and grab my ankles.

I'm standing in front of the service entrance holding a box full of freshly pressed tablecloths that Jordan asked me to bring to the clubhouse, my lifeguarding backpack strapped to my shoulders. I really should have planned this better. But I said yes before realizing that by "box," she meant an enormous, trapezoidal package that weighs fifty pounds and is nearly impossible for me to carry on my own. Now I struggle to balance the monstrosity while taking even one step forward, not that I really want to anyway. Walking the grounds alone right now feels like tempting fate.

The box teeters in my grasp, and I stop it from falling by balancing the corner on my hip. But the puttering of a golf cart careening around the circular driveway makes me lose focus enough to nearly drop the whole box.

"Oh shit, I'll help you." Ethan stops the golf cart directly in front of me.

"Thanks," I say as Ethan grabs the box, placing it in the flatbed behind the driver's seat.

"Clubhouse?" he asks. "Want a ride?"

"Desperately."

I hop in beside him, and Ethan takes off, winding over the gravel walkway. The air smells of salt and sand, not yet tainted by fryer oil and sunscreen. I sneak a glance at him. I haven't seen him alone since Billy's funeral, and based on the bags under his eyes, it looks like he's barely slept since then. My heart pounds in my chest as I grip the straps on my tote bag. Inside is the book I bought him at the Bonanza yesterday, *A Young Person's Guide to Grieving.* I thought about giving it to him last night at his house, but I couldn't bring myself to do it with everyone else around. I was worried it might be too intimate, too much. But Ethan looks so distraught, so unlike himself, and I all I want to do is help.

I reach inside the bag and grip the book. "I got you something," I say gingerly.

Ethan glances at me out of the corner of his eye. "Really? What?"

"Here," I say, handing it to him face up.

Ethan's cheeks flush, and the golf cart comes to a stop. He takes it from me, holding it with both hands, but he doesn't say anything, just examines the cover, which pictures a teenager looking up at the moon. There's a quickening in my heart. *Crap.* I made a mistake, assumed Ethan would want something like this. It's too personal, too forward. I shouldn't have done anything, should never have been so presumptuous. I open my mouth to apologize, but at the same time, Ethan turns to me, his eyes glassy, and his mouth splits into a smile.

"Millie," he says. "Thank you."

"Really?" I press my finger pads together in my lap. "It's not too . . . ?"

"I can't believe he's gone. I know he could be an idiot sometimes, but he was my best friend. All anyone can talk about is what happened and if Justin did it. It's almost like it's become a game or a puzzle."

"Freaking Frankie."

Ethan shrugs. "She's not the only one. I wish everyone could remember he was a person, too."

I rest my fingertips on his biceps. An act of comfort. A reflex. His skin is hot, sparking under my touch, and I pull away like I burned myself.

Ethan's never been shy when talking about his feelings. His fearlessness over his emotions is as much a part of him as his dark eyebrows or the small gold hoop dangling from his ear. But he's never spoken to me like this. Not like I'm a confidant.

Ethan forces a small smile. "It's weird. It's been hard to talk to Lucy. She's so busy with work." He shakes his head. "This is nice. That's all."

A lump forms in my throat. Those are the words I've been desperate to hear for years. That he *wants* to spend time with me. But it's so strange to hear him talk about Lucy like that, like she's not perfect, and there's a funny sensation in my stomach, like my gut is trying to tell me something. But I'm not quite sure what that is yet. I'm not sure I want to know.

"Anyway. I shouldn't have dumped that on you." Ethan brushes his hair out of his face. "Would you mind keeping this between us? I know how close you guys are, but . . ." He trails off for a minute like he's catching his breath.

"I won't say anything," I promise, and force myself to look forward, not directly at him.

"I don't know what I'd do without you this summer."

I press my mouth closed, unable to find the words to respond as Ethan sets his foot to the gas, and we take off toward the clubhouse, where he helps me deposit the tablecloths inside the lobby with one of the chefs. There's an ease with which we move around each other, our steps in sync, and a cavern opens in my chest. I'm going to miss him so much when he goes to college.

Once we're back outside, the sun has started to peek out from behind the clouds, the mist dissolving into the warming air, and everything in my body starts to relax. I stretch my arms above my head, turning my face to the sun. I close my eyes for a moment and when I blink them open, Ethan's standing in front of me, a small smile on his face and his arms crossed over his broad chest. His black sunglasses are perched on top of his head, which makes his dark hair stick up at odd angles.

"What?" I ask, embarrassed for a moment.

Ethan shrugs. "Wanna grab iced coffees from the Snack Shack?"

I don't have the heart to tell him that I only drink iced tea, because right now he's looking at me with that bold smile, holding the book I gave him to his chest like it's a gift that means something. Instead, I focus on the fluttering in my stomach, the sparkle in Ethan's eyes, visible only to me. The answer is obvious. "Yes."

LUCY

When I get to work, the office is frantic, like someone dialed the volume up a few notches since the last time I was here. As soon as I step through the door, Anjali rushes up to me and motions for me to follow her to my desk.

"What's going on?" I ask, dropping my bag to the floor and taking the seat across from her.

Anjali glances around like she's trying to see if someone is coming. "Don't move. Either of you." She points to Olivia and then rushes over to Mayor Cho's office, slipping in through the door.

"Do you have any idea what's up?" I ask.

Olivia leans forward and ducks her head down like she doesn't want anyone to hear. "Detective Hampton's here," Olivia whispers. "Apparently the Vreelands are throwing a *fit* because they kept Justin in there overnight."

"Whoa." I lean in.

"Yup. His parents got him out first thing this morning." Olivia cups her hand over her mouth. "Not even twenty-four hours in custody. But they confiscated his passport. At least, that's what Aunt Sally said."

"They think he's gonna flee or something?"

"I guess so."

"They must be waiting to see if his DNA matches whatever they found on the boat."

Olivia wrinkles her nose. "Uncle Reid is a *wreck*. It's obvious what happened."

"It is?"

"I mean, yeah. Multiple people said they saw Justin and Billy fight at the party, so later that night, he probably went to the boat to go after him again. Billy was being a dick to Justin, but he didn't deserve *this*."

I glance up at the closed door and wonder what they're saying in there. Justin has been as much a part of Pelican Island as the sandpipers or the beach cruiser rental stand at the corner of Shore Road and West Street. He's third-generation, and there's even a Vreeland gymnasium at our school, named after his grandparents, who ponied up millions for the facilities. Not to mention the fact that his family started Hot Diggity, which has been around for forty years.

I never understood why Justin became the de facto dealer. Why he deemed his future worth throwing away. It wasn't about money. Of course not. Power, maybe. A perpetual invite to whatever was happening. But it seemed so foolish. So careless.

"I don't really know him very well. Do you think he is capable of something like this?" Olivia asks. Her voice is quiet but sharp, and she's pressing her teeth into her bottom lip, her fingers curled around the armrest of her chair.

"I have no idea," I say. But then I remember the file I found yesterday. I lean in toward Olivia. "Did you know that Mr. and Mrs. Godwin were cutting down trees on the Vreelands' property?" I quickly fill her in on the tree house drama I found in the files, but Olivia just shakes her head.

"That is the most suburban shit ever," Olivia says. "But I can't imagine that would lead to *this*."

"I don't know. It's hard to imagine *anyone* on Pelican Island would be capable of this." My fingers tense as a rush of fear surges through me. It's not like I've said more than "hello" to Justin in the hallways. He never popped up in mock trial or my AP classes. He was just *someone* who lived here, too. No one I wanted to engage with. Someone who always indicated danger, which has never appealed to me.

Safety, though. That's what draws me in. To me, safety has always meant learning the rules of Pelican Island—knowing the familiar faces in town and which beaches require local permits, avoiding the jagged coastlines at high tide, being aware of the last train home from the city, spending time in the comfortable company of Ethan, of Erica, of my sisters. Danger has not been a part of my life on Pelican Island. The stuff you hear about on the news—violent gangs and armed robberies—are unheard of. So is spending too much time off-island with kids who go to different schools with parents mine don't know.

But now I wonder if my definition of safety is all wrong. If I'm mistaking *safety* for *familiarity* and that perhaps they are not the same. The thought sends a rattling through my body.

I haven't been *safe*. I've been sheltered.

Olivia settles into her seat beside me, and pretty soon she sucks in a breath of air. "She's leaving."

Mayor Cho's office door slides open, and Detective Hampton

appears, hunching her shoulders as she heads toward the door. Anjali walks her out, and Olivia and I stand, craning our necks to see Hampton get into her squad car and drive out of the parking lot.

Anjali darts back inside, making a beeline to us. "Why don't you two take the rest of the day off?" she asks.

"You don't need any help with . . ." I nod in the direction of Hampton's car.

"We'll see you tomorrow." She raps her knuckles on top of my cubicle and hurries away, slipping back into Mayor Cho's office.

"Do you think they're trying to get rid of us?" I ask, but Olivia is already gathering her things.

"One hundred percent," she says, slinging her bag over her shoulder. "Let's do them a favor and get out of here."

Ten minutes later, Olivia and I settle into a corner booth at Little Vincenzo's, the pizza spot in town.

"I cannot believe how much I've missed this," she says.

"They don't have cold cheese slices in the city?" I ask, looking down at the grease-stained paper plate in front of front of me. We both ordered slices of Pelican Island Plain, which is basically a delicacy here. It's a slice of piping-hot plain pizza topped with a handful of cold shredded cheese that slowly melts into the already-melted *other* mozzarella, resulting in the cheesiest, most comforting bite east of Manhattan. To so many outsiders, it seems overindulgent, a bit gross, even, but here, it's heaven.

Olivia bites into her slice and moans with pleasure. She swallows and wipes her mouth with a paper napkin. "I gotta say, there are so many things I missed about Pelican Island, but this is number one."

"Is your dad still at that company?" I ask, folding my slice. "That's why you moved, right?"

Olivia nods and pulls at a piece of cheese. "Yeah, but the *why* didn't really matter to me. I was so glad to be leaving after . . . you know."

I set my pizza down on the table as a boulder settles into the pit of my stomach. Olivia's looking at me, and our eyes lock for a moment. I hold her gaze, afraid to look away. She doesn't flinch, and all I want to do is lean forward and press my fingers to her cheek, to get close enough to see if her skin is as soft as I remember. Her lips part slightly, and I wonder if she's thinking the same thing, if the question on the tip of her tongue is the same as mine: *What could we have been?*

But then she blinks, and her eyes flit upward to the ceiling. "Can I tell you something?"

"Of course."

"You know how I'm taking a gap year?" she asks. "I said it's because I didn't get a tennis scholarship, which is true," she continues. "But the real reason is because my parents can't pay for school."

I tear at my crust to have something to do with my hands.

"The job my dad took in the city . . . The company went bust," she says. "It was a total tech-bubble thing. He put everything into it, including my trust, the one my grandparents set up."

"Oh my god."

"I was supposed to get all this money when I turned eighteen, use it to pay for college, start a life. Now—*poof.* All gone." Olivia raises her eyebrows and picks a speck of cheese off her pizza. "None of my friends in the city know. It's not something that's *done* in our circles, you know? Take out loans for college?" She blushes. "I can't believe I'm embarrassed by this. How much of a snob am I?"

"Look around," I say. "We've both grown up like royalty. If that changed . . ." I want to say something comforting, but the truth is I don't know what it's like. I've never had to worry about paying for school, paying for anything. And neither has Olivia.

"I'm taking the year off to figure out what I really want to do before saddling myself with some huge student loan." Olivia blinks and her eyes are glassy, like she's trying not to cry. "That's why my parents are in Europe this summer. Dad's trying to get some funding for a new project, and Aunt Sally said I could live with them while I figured things out."

"Olivia, I'm so sorry."

"It's ridiculous," she says. "There may be other ways, but . . ." She waves her fingers in the air. "I don't know. It's my own shit to deal with. I hate that it scares me. It wasn't even my money to lose."

"You're not a bad person for worrying about that," I say. "If I was in your position, I'd be losing my mind."

"Really?"

"Yes," I say definitively. "We've all grown up with things we don't deserve, that we didn't do anything to earn."

"Yeah," she says quietly.

"But what we do with that privilege is what matters. That's how we determine if we're good people or not."

"Do you think I'm a good person?" Olivia asks.

Her desire to connect lands deep within my chest. It reminds me of the conversations we'd have when we were together, when we were an *us*. Lying on the sand after school in the fall, wrapped in our tennis hoodies, we'd curl up close to each other and ask questions like this: *What do you think I'll be like in ten years? If you could live anywhere in the world, where would you? What would you change about Pelican Island?* Our answers were aspirational and high-flying, full of promise and purpose and dreams. But, above all, honesty.

That autumn, after joining the mock-trial team, I asked Olivia if she thought I was smart enough to become a Supreme Court Justice one day, and she paused, thinking. Nerves hummed in my stomach until finally she answered.

"I don't think it's just about smarts," she said hesitantly. "It's about how hard you want to work. And you, Lucy Gold, are the hardest worker I know. So the answer is yes, but not without grinding like crazy."

The answer comforted me because I knew she wasn't just *saying* that. She meant it.

Sitting at Little Vincenzo's two years later, I want to do her the same courtesy.

"Do I think you're a good person?" I ask. "I think we have to work at being good people, that we have to make the right choices and consistently decide to do good things. But you seem to do that."

She reaches over the table and rests her fingers on my wrist, her touch so warm I want to melt right into it. "I think you do, too."

LATER THAT NIGHT, when I'm alone in my bedroom, the sounds of the cicadas chirping loud outside my window, I can't seem to fall asleep. A sliver of light from the moon shines through my curtains, and I toss and turn, digging my elbows into my pillow to make it comfortable. But it's no use. I'm fully awake, all live wires, and I can't stop thinking about what Olivia asked me. *Do you think I'm a good person?*

I've never thought to ask someone that question, never wondered that about myself. Took it as a given. I wonder what made Olivia ask that.

I squeeze my eyes closed, then let out a long breath and throw the covers back. Even though Millie's the resident bookworm in this house, reading usually puts me to sleep. My feet hit the fuzzy rug, and I make my way to my desk in the dark, looking for the bag I brought to work. Inside, there's an Emily Henry book Millie said I *had* to read before the summer was over, and though I haven't started it, I've been carrying it around for weeks. Maybe now's the time.

Back in bed, I switch on my lamp and flip open the hardcover. But when I do, a postcard falls out and I hold it by the corner. Millie must have used this as a bookmark and left it here.

The image is of a white-sand beach in Anguilla, footprints in the sand. We took a family vacation there with the Silvers two years ago, but I have no idea why Millie would have kept *this* as a bookmark. How odd. But when I flip it over, I realize it's not Millie's.

There, on the back of the postcard, is Ethan's loopy, messy handwriting, a short greeting on the left side, and on the right, he had addressed it to Billy Godwin.

I squint, making out the faded words.

BILLY! Made a move with Lucy and it WORKED. Best vacation ever. SEE YOU SOON!

I push my tongue against the back of my front teeth, and I read the words again, trying to get them to make sense. That vacation was a standard spring break trip, like so many others our families had taken before. We rented two villas and went boogie boarding and sailing, snorkeling to see the multicolored fish. At night, we ate ice cream and watched movies, the six of us piled onto a big sofa as the ceiling fan spun lazily around in circles.

But at the time, Ethan and I had been *friends*. I was still dating Olivia. There had never been *a move*. There hadn't been *anything* romantic, just the promise of sun and sweat and French fries as salty as the Caribbean Sea.

Part of me wants to pick up the phone and call Ethan right now and ask him what the hell this is, how it found its way into my bag, this book. But as soon as I hold my phone in my hand, I stop. Ethan has been acting strange all summer, hiding pieces of himself. There's no way to know that he'll tell the truth now.

I turn the postcard over, study the handwriting, the address, the soft edges where the cardstock has worn down. Someone kept this for two years, and with a startle, I realize someone slipped this into my bag. Someone *wanted* me to find this. To see Ethan's lie.

A pit opens in my stomach, and I press my head back into the pillows, one word bleating in my brain: *Who?*

FRANKIE

It's been three days since they brought Justin Vreeland in, and all morning at the welcome hut, I've been trying to overhear snippets of conversation, but the general consensus seems to be "we know nothing."

So annoying.

"Don't you think they'd want to put out some public safety announcement telling us what's going on?" I ask Alex, kicking my feet up on the desk.

"Not really," he says, his hands moving quickly over a wooden pocket puzzle.

I blow out a raspberry and cross my arms over my chest. "So unfair."

"Oh my god, lay off." He tosses me the completed puzzle, and when I catch it, I wiggle it around so I can start from scratch. "I thought you were done with this investigation. It's *over*." His tone is sharp and biting.

"Not until they say they actually got him for Billy." I lean in toward him. "What's up with you? You're totally on edge."

"No, I'm not," Alex says, turning away from me. I want to protest, but there's a knock on the front window of our little hut.

"Hello?" someone calls. "Can I get a little help here?"

I swing my legs around and roll my desk chair over to see a tall Black woman peering into the window. "Hi!" I say. "What can I do for you?"

"I'm checking in for a pickleball lesson." Her voice is high and bouncy, like she's had ten cups of coffee before noon. "Ellen Davis."

I glance up and try to place the woman, with her high cheekbones and coiled locs. She looks so familiar, but I can't remember where I've seen her before.

"Sure," I say. "Let me check." I scan the sheet for her name. "Are you a member here?"

"No. I'm a guest. Maybe the reservation's under their name?" She looks around, then lowers her voice as she leans in. "Vreeland?"

That's when it clicks. She was standing with Justin and his mom outside the police station last week. I try to catch Alex's eye to see if he recognizes her, too, but he's tapping something out on the staff computer.

"Vreeland?" I repeat.

The woman nods, checking her phone. "Hold on, I have to take this." She steps away and presses her phone to her ear. "Deirdre? What is it?" She pauses. "No, I'm at the Club. Was going to get a lesson in before . . . They *what*?" She pats her forehead with the heel of her hand. "Well, that's circumstantial." She pauses. "I'll be there in ten minutes."

Alex's eyes flick to mine finally, and I mouth the word *Vreeland* to him, a look of recognition passing over his face.

She hangs up and turns back to us, apologetic. "Never mind. Thanks anyway."

As she rushes off to the parking lot, I spin around and press my palms into my knees. "Dude, that was totally his lawyer."

"Seriously? What was her name?"

"Ellen Davis," I say as Alex starts typing on his phone.

"Ooh, look here. Says here she's worked on dozens of murder trials in Manhattan."

An electrical current zaps through my body. "Do you think we should go down to the station on our lunch break? Do a little stake out and see what's going on?"

"Frankie, no."

"Come on, it'll be fun!"

"That's not fun. That's messed up." Alex turns away from me and starts drumming his fingers against the desk.

"What's up with you?" I ask, an edge sliding into my voice.

"Nothing." He stays turned around, not looking at me.

"So, don't you want to solve the puzzle?" I crack my neck this way and that, suddenly impatient. I want to shake him and drag him over to the station, but Alex curls his knees up under his chest, leaning away from me almost like he's scared.

"It's not a puzzle," he says. "It's a murder."

"A better reason to figure out if Justin did it or if there's some other freak on the loose." I throw my hands up in the air. "Don't you want to *know*?"

"But it's not our *job*," he says. "And besides, Billy sucked anyway." Alex's voice rises to a peak, then cracks when he says Billy's name. I try to catch his eye, but Alex turns away from me, looking at the water.

Alex's chin quivers, and suddenly, a puzzle piece clicks into place inside my brain. Alex's indifference to finding out what happened. I swallow and try to calm my voice, make it as kind as possible. "Alex, what did he do to you?"

"Nothing. Never mind."

"Come on. It's *me*."

"It's too embarrassing," Alex says.

"As embarrassing as the time I farted so loud on the bus to the Met that everyone opened their windows and called me Frankenfarts?" I ask.

"Worse."

"Well then, it sounds like you've been torturing yourself by keeping it a secret."

"Fine," Alex says. His spine curls into a C shape, and he sneaks a look at me before resting his cheek on his knee. "You know how when I came out, I said there wasn't any specific reason why I was doing it then? Only that I was ready?"

"Uh-huh." I had long suspected that Alex was attracted to boys, mostly because in middle school, he kept wanting to watch *The Kissing Booth* movies over and over, pausing on the Jacob Elordi scenes. But I had never asked him point-blank, assuming if he wanted me to know, he would tell me. And he did, in January, when we were sitting side by side with the logic puzzle book splayed out on the coffee table in front of us. We were halfway done with the clues when Alex said, without looking up, "I'm gay, you know."

"That's great," I said, squeezing his hand. "I love you."

He told everybody else in quick succession, and that was that.

"Well," Alex says slowly, "that's not entirely true. All fall, I had been talking to someone that I met in that game theory forum online."

"Okay," I say slowly.

"This guy . . . We talked to each other about real stuff," Alex says. "He was the first person I told I was gay. He said he lived in Kimber Cove, and at one point we talked about meeting up. We had this whole plan, and I was excited. But I wasn't an idiot. I'd heard horror stories about this kind of thing. Seen all the documentaries about creeps trying to hang out with kids or whatever."

I nod, but my stomach ties itself into knots.

"So anyway, I did some sleuthing. Checked out the Kimber Cove yearbook, looked up some databases. It was so obvious this guy didn't exist, and I felt like a freaking fool."

"Billy," I say, my fists tightening by my sides.

Alex blinks, his eyes wet and glassy. "I basically shut off contact with him, deleted my account. Everything. But then at school one day, I opened my locker, and right there were the print-outs of our entire conversations."

"No." I cover my mouth with my hand.

Alex nods. "Billy goddamn Godwin was standing right behind me, smirking like an asshole. He saw me holding the papers and did this dumb little wave. Then he walked right up to me and asked me to solve the same problem we'd been working on in the forum."

"I'd kill him," I say. The words come out like I have no control over them. "If he hadn't . . . already . . . Shit."

Alex shakes his head. "I couldn't figure out why he did that, but then I realized that was his shtick. Being an asshole. He was taunting me for being gay, even though who the fuck cares. So, I said screw it, he's not going to out me before I out myself. That's why I told everyone. After that, he never talked to me again, like I had ruined his prank."

"Did you ever tell Ethan?"

Alex nods. "Yeah," he says, sucking in a big gulp of air. "Ethan said not to take anything Billy did seriously."

"He didn't kick his ass?"

Alex shrugs. "You know Ethan. He just wanted to keep the peace. Trevor told me to ignore Billy, so that's just what I did. I hate to admit it, but in a weird way, I'm kind of grateful that he's gone. He didn't deserve . . . *this*. But you know what, neither did I."

I open and close my mouth, not knowing what to say, only knowing that I prize Alex's safety and well-being above almost anyone's, that whoever hurt him would have been dead to me anyway.

"I don't want anything to do with him. Even now that he's dead." Alex looks up, his usually bright eyes dark, searching for recognition. "Does that make sense?"

I reach for his hand and hold it tightly in mine. "Yes," I say, even though I'm not quite sure it does. "Of course."

Alex swallows and looks up toward the Snack Shack. "Now, can we never talk about this again?"

MILLIE

I stretch my arms above my head until they shake, vibrating in my sockets. It's been over a week since they arrested Justin for assaulting an officer, and even though there's still a shadow hanging over the Club, today was the first time since summer began that it felt like everyone in town descended on the Club, prepared to have an *actual* fun day. Though I couldn't help but notice all the whispers behind cupped hands as people let their eyes wander over the other faces at the Club, wondering, *What do they know?*

Now all I can think about is curling up under my duvet with the new romance novel I picked up at the Bonanza, especially before all of the Fourth of July festivities due to take place tomorrow. I gather my bag from my staff locker and pull on my jean shorts and a T-shirt, then head to the bike rack. I'm unlocking it when a voice lilts behind me.

"Wanna go for a drive?" Ethan asks.

He's standing there with his hair sticking up straight, wet from the shower, his own bag hung over his shoulder. He uses his other hand to toss me his keys.

I catch them with my palm outstretched. I shake my head. "You're gonna trust me with your jeep?"

"Sure, why not?" He flashes me a smile and nods to his car. "Come on. I need a distraction."

That's all it takes. Two little words. *I need.*

A few minutes later, I'm sitting in his car, moving his seat way up so I can reach the pedals. I place my hands at ten and two, gripping the steering wheel so hard my fingers began to hurt. In my periphery, he's got a big goofy grin pasted across his face. It's the first time since Billy died that he looks a little carefree, like maybe everything really is going to be okay.

"Home?" I ask as we turn onto the main road. The cloying sweetness of summer is heavy in the air, but when I pick up speed, the afternoon breeze rushes through the car, sending the ends of my hair swirling around my face.

"Can we make a pit stop first?"

"Anywhere," I say, and immediately regret how desperate it sounds, as if I admitted I would follow him to the ends of the earth.

"Keep going." I drive a little farther down Pelican Island Road. It's a five-mile circle that loops around the whole island, with smaller streets shooting off it like spokes on a wheel. I've biked or walked every inch of this island and know the roads by heart. But being here in the car with only a few feet of space between us and all of Pelican Island out the windshield, the terrain looks new and foreign, like I have to focus on road signs to figure out where I'm going. But it doesn't matter because Ethan has a plan.

"Hang a left here," Ethan says as we approach Great Dune Road.

I do as he says, my stomach buzzing with recognition of where he wants to go. The concrete turns to loose gravel, then to dirt. We bump up and down over the rough terrain, but inside the car is quiet; the only sounds come from seagulls circling overhead, the engine puttering as we drive under the shade of the willow trees.

At the end of the narrow path, we come upon a clearing, a small pond in the distance. We've all been coming here since were little, swimming with the frogs and tiny fish, our feet sinking into the squishy bottom.

Ethan yanks the car door open, and I follow him, neither one of us saying a word as we walk toward the clearing. Ethan pulls off his shirt and drops it onto the pebbles, wading into the pond until he disappears beneath the surface. When he pops up, farther into the water, he turns around and looks right at me, beckoning for me to follow.

My mind whirs, helpless in his presence. I should turn back. Or wait for him on the sand. Is it normal to spend all this time with your sister's boyfriend? But just because we haven't done this before doesn't mean it's wrong, doesn't mean the apprehension in my gut means anything.

Ethan smiles and any hesitation evaporates into the thick humid air. I pull my shirt over my head and tug down my cutoffs, revealing my lifeguarding bathing suit, still damp from my shift. I've made these movements in front of Ethan a hundred times by now, but now that it's just the two of us—no children laughing in the background at the Club, no siblings playing chicken in the pool—I wonder if it feels different to him, if he can sense that the world has tilted off-kilter and the only thing tethering me to the ground is sheer will, preventing me from blowing away.

There's no way to tell because Ethan dunks his head underwater, disappearing.

I cut through the surface and swim to him, holding my breath as long as I can, until I come up for air and find Ethan so close to me that if I extend my legs all the way while treading, they might accidentally intertwine with his. And for the briefest moment, they do, our ankles knocking against each other's. When I feel his bones against mine, it's like a light switch flips inside my chest and I am illuminated from within.

The fresh water is bright and cool against my skin, so different than the Sound. I turn onto my back and flutter my feet, floating away. It's safer like this, with distance. But Ethan comes closer, the water rippling around me.

I right myself and begin treading water, moving my arms in circles, catching bits of grass and blown leaves between my fingers. There's a crease in Ethan's forehead, like he's worrying. "Everything's going to be okay," I say.

Ethan lets out a rush of air. "It's hard to believe that." I watch his Adam's apple bob in his throat, and my chest aches. I want to wrap him in my arms and hug him so tightly that I can feel every rib.

"What will help?" I ask.

Ethan's blue eyes are made even brighter by the crystal-clear water. "Nothing," he says.

My throat is raw, and I shake my head. "You know that's not true."

Ethan's lips part as the space between us becomes smaller and smaller, and my whole body buzzes, like if any other part of his body touches mine, I might never be able to get stand on dry land again.

"Ethan," I say, though I have no plan for what follows that one word. A plea. A refusal. He inches closer to me, and our thighs bump underwater, and for a moment, I wonder if it's possible for time to stop so I can be rooted to this very space and moment for the rest of my life.

But then there is a sound—a noise—the sputtering of a car driving up Great Dune Road and parking next to Ethan's jeep, and he dives underwater, away from me, the cord that hung taut between us severed.

With that absence comes pain, sharp and bitter like teeth sinking into the flesh of my lip, but also relief. A momentary exhale. No line crossed. No betrayal realized.

Only a moment of connection, sweet and simple. Fleeting.

"Come on," Ethan says, swimming to shore. "Let's go back."

I let Ethan wade out of the water first, and when I get to shore, I wrap myself in a towel. "Ready?" I ask. Ethan's bent over his phone, the screen close to his face.

He looks up at me, shock on his face, and there's a quickening in my chest.

"They found Justin's DNA on Billy's shirt."

THE PARTY

1:45 A.M.

Billy had never been hit in the face before, and holy shit, that fucking hurt. His back was pressed into the grass, and Justin was on top of him, wailing on him, a fist colliding with his side, his cheek, his shoulder. He'd talked shit to Justin before, but the kid never threw a punch at him like a goddamn mafioso. Who did he think he was?

As Justin pulled his arm back, Billy seized the moment and wiggled his way out from beneath Justin's weight. Scrambling to his feet, Billy backed away.

"Aha!" Billy said, adrenaline pumping through him so intensely he barely felt drunk anymore. "Sucker!" But Justin was looking at him with eyes full of rage, his mouth forming a snarl, and the smile dropped from Billy's face. "Dude, let's—"

The wind left him swiftly, an elbow thrust into Billy's stomach, and he wailed in pain. But instead of clutching his middle, he reached up to Justin's neck and raked his fingernails against skin, eliciting a high-pitched wail. There was blood now, tiny red spots that trickled onto Billy's white shirt.

"You asshole!" Justin's fists slammed against Billy's head, and Billy's vision grew fuzzy, like someone was changing the channel on him, turning his brain on then off again. Justin spit on the ground, a bloody clot of saliva, then wiped his face with the back of his arm. He was on

his feet again, and then before Billy could get up, he felt a sharp pain in his back and realized it was Justin's foot colliding with his spine.

"Argh!" he called out, spots floating in his eyes as he blinked and looked around the patio to see who was watching his humiliation. Thankfully, the party was basically over. The only people left were Ethan and Dylan . . . but Erica's bag was still here. Where was she?

Another kick came swiftly, causing him to curl in on himself, to cry out again in pain. He blinked open his eyes, and in the distance, he saw pink. That bright pink bikini. Erica.

"Dude, stop!" Ethan tried to hold Justin back, but the kid was too strong, and Billy felt another kick land, this time right in his ribs.

"Erica!" He wanted her more than he could admit. He wanted her to come here and make this all stop. He saw her move along the dunes, a flash of color in the darkness. She was rushing to him. Thank goodness. His heart fluttered, and though his body was on fire, he knew it would all be over soon. She couldn't see him lying on the ground like this and ignore him. She had a heart after all.

"Enough!" Ethan said, and Billy looked over his shoulder to see that both Dylan and Ethan had pulled Justin away from him, that they were now standing between them, and Billy was finally able to push himself to stand. Wobbly, but still standing.

He looked back for Erica, for that spot of pink against the inky sky. She was getting closer, and Billy smiled, though he tasted blood. "Erica," he said again, and started walking toward her. But when he got close, he realized she was not the only figure in the darkness. Before Billy could see who it was, his whole world turned black.

LUCY

"Can you believe the bloody shirt?" Olivia asks. There's an incredulous tone to her voice, like she's trying to contain herself. The timbre reminds me of when we were fifteen and won that doubles tournament, when we cheered and yelped and held the trophy high above our heads.

Today is the Fourth of July, and we're standing side by side on a big blue parade float gliding slowly down Main Street, wearing PELICAN ISLAND STRONG T-shirts that Anjali handed us earlier this morning. Mayor Cho's white vintage convertible inches forward ahead of us and we wave to the crowds.

"My aunt is losing her *mind*," Olivia says. "She's so grateful this is going to be over soon. Hoping he enters a guilty plea and everyone can avoid a trial."

"That's so crazy," I say, shaking my head. Ever since the news broke that Justin's blood was on Billy's shirt, it's as if the entire town has exhaled, knowing that there's an explanation for Billy's death. Most of the extra security has disbanded, and Billy's parents were seen walking around town for the first time in weeks, eating at Sunday Best and getting bagels at Schmear & Co. No one's seen or heard from the Vreelands except for Alex, who swears he saw Justin's dad wiping graffiti off the Hot Diggity window.

All around us, people line the sidewalks as they wave American flags in the air and blast music from enormous speakers. Every so often, a *poof* of confetti rains down, and I have to tamp down the impulse to pluck stray pieces of gold and red and blue foil from Olivia's hair. Plumes of smoke from a nearby portable grill waft into the air, and I catch a whiff of burgers and charred corn on the cob.

The Pelican Island Fourth of July parade has always been one of my favorite days of the year. It's tradition for families to gather along Main Street starting at six in the morning and snag prime watching spots by unfolding chairs and sun umbrellas, coolers full of orange juice and iced coffee, and to wait around, together, singing songs and skipping from one family's setup to another's.

Dad and Gil were always in charge of securing spots for all ten of us, laying out two big blankets on the sidewalk and weighing down the corners with tote bags full of sand toys. By the time we joined them, the Godwins would be close by. The Vreelands, too.

But this year, none of us kids will watch on Main Street, because we are all *in* the parade. Me with Mayor Cho's brigade and the rest of them on various Pelican Island Beach Club floats a few blocks behind us.

"There they all are," Olivia says, pointing toward my parents, huddled up with the Silvers and the Godwins. The group is usually split by sex, the wives hanging out on one blanket and the husbands on another, but today my dad stays close to Mom and the other women while Gil and Mr. Godwin stand side by side. There's a pained look on Dad's face, even as he gives me a wave. It's probably nothing. Just stress. Nothing for me to worry about, even though I can't help myself.

"Anyway. Do you mind if we try to have *fun* today?" Olivia asks. "I need to let loose." A smile rips across her face, and she throws her arm around me, leaning her weight on my shoulder, and waves at the crowd. She hasn't been this close to me since that morning at Scoop DeVille, and the feel of her pressed against me, the smell of her shampoo . . . It's enough to make me dizzy. "Come on," she says. "Give our subjects what they want."

I bring my hand up and wiggle my fingers at the crowd, which makes Olivia laugh, her hair tickling the soft skin on the inside of my elbow. Without thinking, I sling my arm around her back, press my fingers into her ribs. She inches closer to me so we're hip to hip, and I swear I hear her inhale sharply, her laughing hitch.

I drop my arm, suddenly self-conscious, and my insides swim. I drew her too close.

Olivia leans over the railing and calls to the crowd, "Happy Independence Day!" like nothing has happened. She didn't notice anything weird. It's all in my head. But if that should bring me relief, it doesn't. Instead a hint of disappointment bubbles up in my chest.

My phone buzzes in my pocket, and when I pull it out, I see a text from Erica. Did I just see you and Olivia acting chummy AF?? Are you VIBING??

I look over my shoulder and see Erica on the float behind us looking right at me with her eyebrows raised and a devilish smile on her face. I shake my head, but she shrugs, then looks down at her phone.

A moment later, I get another text. I don't hate it!!!!

I send her a rolling-eyes emoji and stuff my phone away, refusing to let her nudging burrow into my brain. The next block goes by in a haze of humidity and languid laughter as the float nears the end of the parade, stopping at the Beach Club, where all the participants are invited to an all-town barbecue. When we round the corner and our float comes to a stop, Olivia climbs down first, then extends her hand up to me to help me off the steel stairs.

"Thanks." I grip her fingers and step down onto the concrete, but someone bumps my shoulder, causing me to fall into Olivia, my other hand bracing against her waist. "Sorry," I say, my hand still attached to her, pressing against the soft cotton of her skirt, the hint of bone beneath the fabric. She's warm beneath my touch, and there's a tightening in my stomach, a strong desire to be completely alone with her right now.

Olivia steps back and smiles as a piece of confetti flutters in the air, settling on the crown of her head. "All good," she says.

I can't help myself. I reach out and pluck the tiny piece of confetti from her hair and let it fall to the ground between us.

"I'm sorry I dumped all that stuff on you about school, by the way," she says suddenly, her voice low. "It's not your problem."

"I'm glad you told me," I say. "It makes me feel close to you." My cheeks blush instantly. I don't know why I said that, and the word *close* lingers between us, an offer.

"Are you reading anything good lately?" she asks, and the change of subject gives me pause.

"What?"

"I saw you carrying the Emily Henry book at work the other day. Is it good?"

I never read a word of that book the other night, was too preoccupied by the postcard I found inside the pages. Olivia's mouth twitches, and everything goes very still, and I study her face.

"Did you leave me that postcard?" I ask, my voice still. "Did you slip that into my bag?"

Olivia's cheeks flush, and her fingers fly up to her hair like they're trying to keep her in place. "I found it when I was going through a box of Billy's stuff. He showed it to me right before we broke up. I thought he threw it out, but there it was when I went in the other day, sitting on top of his Spanish homework." She shrugs. "You said it never happened, but I wanted you to have that postcard. I wanted you to know I wasn't lying."

My throat is suddenly raw, and even though all around us people are cheering and shooting off confetti and barbecuing burgers, the only thing I can focus on is the timidness on her face, the hint of guilt written in the lines on her forehead.

"It never happened," I say. "I have no idea why he would write something like that. Ethan never told me he sent Billy a postcard from that trip or anything."

Her pink mouth parts, her tongue darting out quickly to coat her upper lip. "That's how I knew about you guys. Billy was clearly trying to start shit, but he also had my back. At the time, I was appreciative."

I shake my head, a rush of hot anger washing over my body. Olivia doesn't need to tell me the chronology because I'm wildly aware of it. One week after we returned from vacation, Olivia ended things, saying she didn't have to explain herself, and that I *knew* what had happened. I was baffled at the time, utterly shocked, and cried to Erica about it for weeks.

That only means one thing: Ethan lied when he wrote that postcard. He knew Billy would tell Olivia, that Olivia would break up with me.

My breathing grows ragged as I start to form my next thought.

"Are you okay?" Olivia asks. "It's all in the past. I just wanted you to know."

I barely hear her. As the rest of Mayor Cho's staff unloads her float, I push my way through the crowd, desperate to get away from the Beach Club as fast as possible before Ethan and the others arrive, ready to celebrate.

Everything becomes clear. Ethan made it all up. Our entire relationship—the one that's been the backbone of my high school experience, the one that he talks about extending into the future, into *forever*, the one that I don't even know if I want anymore—was built on a lie.

MILLIE

The weather is picture-perfect today—all blue skies, no clouds, light breeze. An ideal day to stand on a parade float in your sunglasses and wave out to everyone you've ever known, singing random songs at the top of your lungs.

Today I want to forget that anything bad ever happened since we got out of school. I want to shout to everyone, *We are safe! It is summer, and it is fleeting and magical, and if we spend all of it worrying, we're going to miss it!*

But as we pass Hot Diggity, it's hard to ignore what's happened. Even though Justin's dad paid someone to clean the window, I can still make out the graffiti someone spray-painted: MURDERER!

I swallow the lump in my throat and force a smile back on my face as we move forward in the parade. At the end of our route, I hop off the float, and Ethan appears, pushing his curls off his face. He brings me in for a side hug, his fingers pressing into my shoulder, and whispers, "Hey, Mill."

"Hey," I say, daring to look up at him, the sun casting a golden glow on his cheeks.

"Would you mind finding Trevor? I haven't seen him all morning. I gotta go help Jordan set up the barbecue, but can you make sure he gets over there?"

"For sure," I say, and watch Ethan jog away, looping his arm around Alex's neck and bringing him in for a noogie even though Alex is a few inches taller. There's a lightness between them. Good. Maybe that means Ethan is feeling calmer, more at ease.

I crane my neck to search for Trevor, but amid the sea of staffers, he's nowhere to be found. I dial Trevor's number and press the phone to my ear, but after three rings, it goes straight to voicemail. I shake my head and send him a text instead. **Barbecue at West Shore Beach. Ethan wants to make sure you got the memo.**

I pocket my phone and start toward the parking lot, weaving between staffers tossing red, white, and blue confetti in the air. But just as I'm passing the alley between Little Vincenzo's and Schmear & Co., I hear a familiar voice rising over the waves.

Trevor. But I don't see him. Must have been a mistake. My subconscious working overtime since I'm looking for him.

Then there he is again, his voice sharp and hurried. I can't make out the words, but I walk in the direction of the noise, closer to the garbage cans in the alley. I peer around the corner of the building and see him hidden behind the boats. Trevor leans forward with his arm pressed high on the brick wall. His mouth is twisted, and his eyes are wide and dark. He's tapping his back foot against the ground. Impatient.

He says something again, but I'm not close enough to make out the words, can only hear the exasperation. He tilts his head back so his curls bounce, catching the glare of the sun. I try to reposition myself so I can see who he's talking to without coming into full view, but I don't need to. Because suddenly, she steps forward, out from behind the boats, and wraps her arms around Trevor's neck, and when she does, it's all I can do to hold back a gasp.

I clamp my hand over my mouth and watch as Erica angles her face up toward Trevor's, pressing a palm to his cheek. He leans into her touch, as if she's soothing him, as if she's a salve. She presses her lips to his, her whole body to his, like they were born to do this.

Trevor pulls back, brings one hand to her forehead, and pushes back a piece of hair. Erica looks up at him, her eyes focused, smiling, but then she says something I can't hear and his demeanor changes, a storm cloud passing over his face. Trevor throws his shoulder back, shakes his head, and starts running toward the beach, in the opposite direction of me. I expect Erica to follow him, but she leans back against the brick wall and then slides down until she's squatting on her heels, her face buried in her hands, the faint echo of a sob floating through the air.

I could go to her and comfort her or run after Trevor, but it's like my body has a mind of its own, and before I can think, I'm back at my bike, spinning the dial around to enter my combination, hopping onto the seat and pedaling away as fast as I can toward the barbecue.

It takes me six whole blocks to catch my breath, to understand what I saw, and to realize, with confusion, that for some reason, my cheeks are wet and my eyes sting. I blink, wipe my forearm across my face, and shake my head as if that will stop the tears.

I shouldn't be crying. I shouldn't even *care*. Actually, I should be happy that Trevor has found someone to kiss in an alley, someone whose waist seems to fit perfectly in his grasp. But then again, I should also be concerned that whatever was going on between them seems to have an ugly side, something I was never meant to see.

And yet, the only question I want an answer to is this one: How, after seventeen years of friendship, did Trevor and I reach a place where he wouldn't think to tell me about Erica? That he would *lie* to me about where he's been, what he's been doing, who he's been thinking about?

But just as I begin to wonder, just as the fury begins to grow, I realize that's exactly what I've been doing to him.

Lying. And perhaps my lie has bigger and worse consequences. Because there's no way in the world I would ever tell him about my love for Ethan, so how can I expect him to be honest with me?

LUCY

The farther away I get from the Beach Club, the more notifications I receive on my phone. At first, they're only from Ethan.

I thought you got here before us.

The mayor's float is here, but I can't find you.

Where are you?

Hello??!!

Then I see a text from Erica come in.

Are you here? Can you find me??

I stop on the side of the street, which is full of parade detritus—confetti and popped balloons and little bits of foam that fell off the floats as they glided down our main drag—and sit on the sidewalk, dropping my head down. I think about what Olivia told me: Ethan did what he could to break us up.

I squeeze my eyes shut and try to remember what it was like to be sixteen and heartbroken, what Ethan's exact movements were like in the aftermath in those tender weeks. Olivia's proclamation came swiftly and without much time to process, a text asking me to meet her behind the tennis courts after school. When I got there, she looked at me with a hard stare and said the words I never forgot.

"We're moving to the city in June, and it's easier to break up now."

That was it. As swift and shocking as a beheading. It was Ethan who found me an hour later, sitting in the same place, long after Olivia had left.

He didn't ask me questions or force me to talk about it. All he did was take my backpack and walk alongside me in silence, as if he knew that was what I wanted most.

When we got home, he hugged me long and hard, and said, "This is the worst part. I'm sure of it. Tomorrow will be better."

And he was right. Every day did get easier. Mostly because I had Ethan by my side.

Toward the end of that summer, I remember we were sprawled out on the sand, baking in the sun. His eyes were closed, and the sun made the freckles on his nose more pronounced, gave his skin a deep tan. I had always known Ethan was objectively good-looking. Obviously so, with a symmetrical face and straight teeth and eyes that locked in: *I'm listening, I'm here.* But that day, I looked at him and noticed a stirring in my core, a pressure against my sternum.

"One day, you'll tell me what you're thinking," he'd said. "What about today?"

"Maybe." His eyes held mine, and a zippy sensation shot down my spine. Ethan's hand drifted over to my towel, and even though we didn't make contact, I could feel the heat from his skin, wanted to lean toward him so that the tips of his fingers grazed my thighs.

"I'll go first," he said.

I could see our future about to unfold, and I wanted him to say it out loud, an exaltation. I had an acute understanding that whatever we did moving forward—however we chose to define our relationship—would change the course of our lives, create a ripple effect in our families, our friendships. Our worlds were so intertwined that if we chose to redefine whatever *this* was between us, it would have consequences and we had to be ready to face them.

Ethan didn't hesitate. He propped himself up on his side, too, so our eyes were at the same level, so there were only millimeters of air separating us.

"You are my favorite person on the planet, Lucy Gold. And I think that you feel the same way about me."

"Oh?" I asked, a smile forming on my lips.

"Yes," he said with utter confidence. "I like you. So much. And I think there's a chance you like me, too."

"I do," I said, immediately aware that my words sounded like an oath, a promise, and in that moment, I didn't care.

Then there were good-morning texts and breakfast orders, walks through the school halls and side-by-side lunches, study groups and movie nights, bike rides to parties and trying things for the first time together, always together. Fervent roll-arounds in the back of his car, in the pool house, on the beach. First times for everything, for touches and kisses and explosions that, in the beginning, were like tidal waves and then gradually crested into security and comfort. Simple directions like "I like that" and "Over there" and "Yes" and the secret admissions that *we are the lucky ones* and *how horrible to do this with someone you don't know, someone you can't speak openly with* and *I will never love someone like I love you.*

And yet now I know that all of those moments—every single one—happened because Ethan lied. My stomach ties itself in knots, a ball of rage forming in my chest. Ethan didn't have the right to do this. To steal from me. Because that's what he did. He took my autonomy. My freedom. He made something happen *to* me instead of letting me figure things out on my own. And that is unforgivable.

FRANKIE

I jolt awake, my brow sweaty and the covers twisted around my legs. I blink my eyes open, and my chest rises and falls so fast, like I was having a nightmare. But I can't remember anything, only the claustrophobic sensation that the ceiling had been dropping lower and lower until it was directly over my nose, like it was about to smush me down into the bed. Thankfully, the ceiling is where it should be, and I'm relieved to find it was just a dream.

I roll over onto my side, and outside the window, the sky is such a dark blue, it's almost black. I curl my fists under my chin, ball the covers up close to my neck. But I'm wide-awake. It's no use pretending sleep is only a few breaths away.

That's when I see it. Something nudged under my door, a slip of paper. Curiosity grabs me, and I sit up in bed, slide out of the covers, and tiptoe to where it pokes out from beneath a stripe of light. I kneel down on my shins and reach for the paper, folded into quarters. When I open it, I see a drawing of a heart, sliced into three equal pieces.

Millie.

My heart rate picks up, and I stand, resting my hand on the doorknob until I twist it slowly so it won't make too much noise. Millie's room is across the hall, and I don't even knock, just inch open her door until I can fold myself inside her room and shut the door behind me. She forms a lump in her bed, turned the other way so I can't see her face.

"Mill?" I whisper. "Are you awake?"

"Frankie?" She sits up, revealing dark half-moons underneath her eyes, like she hasn't slept at all since we all went to bed hours ago.

"I saw your note," I say. "You could have woken me up." Within a few steps, I'm at her bed, and she scoots over so I can climb in beside her. My room is all striped curtains and mismatching sheets, balls of worn clothes and lone socks without their partners, and Lucy's is hotel white except for the color-coding system she employs for her clothes, which hang in her closet, all facing the same direction. Millie prefers soft and cozy pastel throws, fuzzy everything, like the stuff inside her four walls is made of clouds. Tonight her bed is made with lilac sheets and a matching duvet, embroidered with small flowers at its scalloped edges.

And yet, despite the differences, Millie's room smells like mine, our shampoo and curl cream the same. The Gold-girl scent wafting under doors, embedding itself in everything we own.

"I saw something," she says.

"What?" I lick my lips, inch closer to her.

"Trevor," she says slowly. Millie glances at me sideways but stays lying on her back, won't face me head-on. "I saw him kiss Erica."

I inhale sharply, my heart launching into my throat.

"Behind the kayak stands over on Birch Street. They were *kissing*, and then she said something, and he got furious and ran away from her."

I try to keep my face still, but Millie sees through me immediately. "What? Why do you have that look on your face?"

"Remember how I said Erica took that photo I showed you?"

Millie nods, her eyes growing wider, like she's putting puzzle pieces together.

"I found something else in her bag when I borrowed that camera."

"What?" Millie whispers.

"A sonogram," I say, and then, without stopping myself, I say the words I've been holding in for weeks: "She's pregnant."

"No," Millie whispers, her voice warbling. "Trevor's going to be a father?"

"He never mentioned anything?"

"Never."

I swallow the lump in my throat and press my head against her pillow. I don't know what I would do if I learned Alex kept something like that from me. We tell each other *everything*. Or at least, we used to, because, I have to remind myself, I never told him about this.

"Does Lucy know?" Millie asks.

I shake my head no.

"She's going to lose her mind."

"Are you going to confront Trevor?" I ask, butterflies humming in my stomach.

"No." Millie doesn't elaborate, but in that moment it's like I can read her mind. *He won't tell me the truth anyway.*

MILLIE

"Okay, so the first order of business is we can't get caught." Frankie walks quickly down Main Street, her eyes focused straight ahead, trying not to let Erica out of our sight. We've been following her as casually as we can for the past three days, but we haven't seen her do anything more interesting than meet up with Lucy for ice cream or play Skee-Ball with Dylan at the arcade. No sign of her hanging out with Trevor.

"This is getting ridiculous, Frankie." The humidity makes my T-shirt stick to my skin. Beads of sweat roll down my back. "Honestly, I should just talk to Trevor."

Frankie stops in her tracks and spins around. "Are you serious?"

"Yes. The more I think about it, the more horrible I feel. He must be terrified and isolated. He's going to have a baby, and no one knows." When I say the words out loud, there's a tightening in my chest. Just because I'm mad that Trevor didn't clue me in doesn't mean that I want him to suffer alone. "Maybe he needs someone to talk to, Franks."

Frankie rolls her eyes. "Don't you think he would have actually, I don't know, talked to you if that were true?'

"Maybe he's scared." My voice is small, but I mean it.

"One more day," Frankie says, exasperated. She ducks her head toward mine. "If we don't find anything out, then you can talk to Trevor. Okay?"

"Fine."

Up ahead, Erica tosses a Popsicle stick from Scoop DeVille into the trash and hops on her bike, heading down Main Street.

"Come on," Frankie says, and we take off after her.

"She's probably going home." I expect her to make a hard left onto Pelican Island Road, which would lead up toward her house on Highland Drive, but she doesn't. Instead, she makes a right, which takes her past . . .

"Is she going to *our* house?" Frankie asks. "Or to the Silvers'?" Frankie picks up speed, and I reach one hand out to her.

"Slow down," I hiss. "She's going to see us." There are lots of cars on the road, but a pair of bikes is more obvious. Thankfully, Frankie coasts down the hill, and from our perch above Erica, we watch her keep going, our house already behind her.

Frankie's brows narrow in determination, and then she comes to an abrupt stop.

"What are you doing?" I ask, whipping my head around as I brake, too.

"Look," Frankie says, pointing to the space behind me where Erica is hunched over in the bushes, her bike leaning on the ground beside me. "Gross."

I swat Frankie's arm. "She's *pregnant*. It makes you nauseous."

Frankie grimaces. "Still. Gross."

I watch Erica retch into the bushes, and I suddenly feel so sad for her, going through this all alone. It takes everything in me not to step forward and rub her back in the way that Mom does for me when I get a stomach bug.

"Duck!" Frankie says. She yanks on my shirt, and I fall back into the brush with her, thorns sticking into my side.

"Ouch! What are you doing?" But when I glance back at Erica, I see she's wiping her mouth on the back of her arm and swiveling her head around like she hears something. Like she's *looking* for something. My stomach lurches.

"Did she see us?" I ask, my voice strained.

"I don't think so." Frankie slowly pokes her head out, and her shoulders drop. "She's going." We stand and brush ourselves off, watching Erica pedal away until Frankie motions for me to follow her. "Come on," Frankie says.

We ride in silence for another half a mile, the air still and tense around us. The heat is oppressive, and sweat builds under my arms, dripping from my neck, my hairline, the insides of my thighs. Blisters start to form where my ankles rub against my sneakers, and all I want is to go home and jump in the pool. I'm about to say as much when Erica makes a wobbly right turn on French Moor Drive.

I slow down and call to Frankie. "We have to wait."

"Why?"

"It's a dead end. She'll see us behind her." Frankie knows this. Everyone on Pelican Island knows every square inch of our town, can tell you which cul-de-sacs are waterfront, which beaches are made of rocks and which of sand. French Moor Drive is one of those old roads that used to belong to one single family back in the 1800s before it was parceled off into three eight-acre plots.

The last time I was here was at the shiva with nearly everyone else I know. Because down French Moor Drive is Billy Godwin's house.

Frankie blows a stray curl out of her face, her head cocked in frustration. "Come on. It's been enough time."

"We know where she's going."

"We have to at least *see*," Frankie hisses.

"She's probably visiting Olivia. Or saying hi to Mrs. Godwin."

Frankie takes off before I can stop her, and I have nothing to do but follow her down the street. A canopy of trees darkens the road, and for a moment, I get sweet relief. It's cooler over here in the shade, and I don't have to squint to see against the sun. Goose pimples rise on my skin, and my sweat turns cold. I grip my handlebars tighter and glance at Frankie, who has a determined look on her face, her gaze straight ahead.

We stick to the other side of the road, hugging the shoulder, and when we get to the Godwin house, I duck behind an enormous maple tree, hoping it conceals my bike, but . . . Shoot. I should have remembered.

"We can't see anything." I groan and point to the hedges blocking the entire Godwin home, which sits nearly a quarter mile back from the road behind not only manicured rows of greenery but also an iron gate.

"Dammit," Frankie says. "Ah, well. That was fun, I guess."

"You are delusional." I shake my head. "Come on. Let's go back to town."

Frankie looks longingly at the Godwin estate but follows me, pedaling slowly as she gripes behind me. "We should have stayed!"

"Can it, Frankie." I look back at her and roll my eyes, but as I do, her voice rings out.

"Millie, look out!"

I brake fast, swerving onto the side of the road just in time for a black SUV to come careening past us.

"Oh my god," I say, placing my hand over my heart. "Don't they know there's a speed limit?"

Frankie's right behind me, panting and gripping the handlebars of her bike, but she's still looking at the car turning into the driveway up ahead.

"Isn't that . . ." she says, her voice trailing.

"What?" I ask, checking my body for any cuts or scrapes. My adrenaline is still through the roof, and I smooth down my hair, hoping to catch my breath.

"It totally is. Come on." Frankie hops back on her bike and pedals so fast that I have to rush to keep up.

"You're going to get us killed!" I call after her, but when I catch up to her at the next driveway, I see what she's looking at. A brass nameplate tacked to the brick pillars on either side of the driveway, the name VREELAND stenciled into the metal.

"So it's the Vreelands' house. Big whoop. Let's go. I want to sit in the pool for the next six hours straight."

"Look," she says, pointing toward the house. The black SUV that almost ran me over is parked at the end of the circular driveway, and we watch for a moment as Justin's parents climb out, adjusting their clothing, their sunglasses.

"Again. I do not understand why we're waiting like a bunch of creeps—"

But that's when I see it.

Rather, *him*.

Justin Vreeland stepping out from the back seat of the car, stretching his arms overhead, an enormous smile on his face like he's . . . free.

THE PARTY

2:00 A.M.

"Billy!" Erica's voice cut through the night, and Billy lifted his head to see her run toward him from the dunes. She was barefoot, still in that bikini, but her hair was wet and when she knelt down beside him, he realized her skin was, too. She smelled salty, like the sea. "Are you okay?"

Billy pushed himself to sit and swung his head around to see that Ethan and Dylan were holding Justin back.

"Get off me!" Justin called. "He deserves to get his ass kicked."

Billy tasted blood and he looked down to see red stains on his T-shirt. When he brought his fingers to his cheek, he flinched, touching the scratches etched into his skin.

"Relax," Dylan told Justin, yanking him back. "Let it go, man."

"Fine!" Justin wrenched loose but he stopped swinging.

Billy turned away from Erica so he could spit out a loogie onto the deck.

"Come here," she said, pulling him to sit on one of the lounge chairs. "Let me see." Her fingers were cold when they touched his skin, right above his eye where Justin had landed his fist. Billy winced.

"I'll get a first aid kit," Trevor said. Billy glanced up and saw him standing close to Erica, his fingers light on her shoulders. Trevor's jeans were damp at the bottom, and his hair was slicked wet, too.

He was down there with her on the beach.

He had taken Erica away from the party. Which didn't make sense. None of this made sense.

"Fuck off, Little Silver," Billy said, glowering at the kid.

Ethan appeared next to his brother, grabbing him by the forearm. "Come on, Trev. Let's go."

"I'm gonna make sure Justin gets out of here," Dylan said from behind Billy's back. "You guys okay?"

Billy nodded. "Thanks." But he kept his eyes on Trevor, who was looking at Erica expectantly.

Dylan jogged off after Justin, and the two of them gathered their bikes from the lawn and rode off down French Moor Drive. The only people left were Trevor, Ethan, and Erica, and right now, Ethan was talking close to Trevor, whispering something into his ear. Ethan's jaw was tight. So was his grip on Trevor's arm.

"Hold still," Erica said, dabbing his forehead with a wet towel.

Billy gritted his teeth and strained to listen to what Ethan was saying to Trevor. "You said it'd only be an hour," Ethan hissed. "We gotta go."

Trevor knelt down next to Erica. "Let's go. He's fine."

Ethan put himself between Trevor and Billy like he was guarding them from each other. "Dude, stop."

Erica twisted her head around to Trevor. "You go home, okay? We'll talk later."

"Can someone please tell me what is going on?" Billy asked, though the knot in his stomach told him that he already knew the truth.

"Nothing," Erica mumbled.

"We're together, Billy," Trevor said. "Have been for weeks. She didn't want to tell you yet, but that's the truth."

Billy stood up, yanking his arm out of Erica's light touch. "What?"

"Trevor." Erica was stern as she turned to him, using the same kind of voice she used when she broke up with Billy. "I think you should leave, okay? Let me talk to him."

"He's serious?" Billy turned to Erica, demanding an answer.

Erica didn't say anything, and Billy shoved Ethan, trying to get to Trevor. He couldn't see straight, couldn't hear anything. Just wanted to get his hands on the kid.

Ethan jumped between them again. "Trevor," he said. "You can figure this all out in the morning."

But then Billy realized what Ethan had said only moments earlier. You said it'd only be an hour. *"You knew about this?" Billy said, jabbing a finger at Ethan. "You knew your brother was screwing my girlfriend?"*

"I'm not your girlfriend," Erica said. Her voice was shaky now, like she might burst into tears.

"Is that why you came tonight?" Billy asked. "So you could distract me while they hooked up? So I wouldn't try to destroy your brother?"

"Let's all calm down," Ethan said, pumping his hands. "Billy, we'll talk everything out in the morning."

Billy scowled as Ethan pushed Trevor in the opposite direction, leading him back toward the dunes.

Only Erica remained and when Billy turned to her and saw the desperate, helpless look on her face, it was as if every emotion he had ever experienced exploded from his chest, an eruption he had never felt before. He couldn't help but burst into tears.

FRANKIE

Bursting through the front door of our house, I feel like the Kool-Aid Man. "Hello?" I call, panting.

Mom comes rushing into the foyer, her hair in rollers, her phone glued to her ear. "They're home. Oh, thank god. They're home." She gathers Millie and me in a hug and holds us tightly until I wriggle out of her grasp.

"Who are you talking to?" I ask.

"Sally, I'll call you back," Mom says, then turns away. "They will find who did this. I promise you." Mom faces us, worry etched into her forehead. "That was Sally Godwin. Did you girls get my texts?"

"We haven't looked at our phones, Mom," Millie says. "We were biking past the Vreelands' and saw—"

"The Vreelands'?" Lucy emerges from the kitchen holding a bowl of green grapes, her eyebrows so far up her forehead, they near her hairline. "What were you doing over there?"

Millie glances at me, and I stand up straight. "Just going for a ride. But we saw Justin there, walking around like nothing—"

"They let him out," Mom says, pressing her hand to her chest. "That lawyer of his was able to find footage of him from the cameras around town riding his bike home before three in the morning."

"So?" I ask. "It's not like they know a time of death. Billy was floating in the water! That'll mess with any dead body's—"

"Frankie!" Mom nearly screams. "Have some respect."

"I'm just wondering why they let him out."

Lucy steps forward, closer to me, and chimes in. "She's kind of right, Mom. What else did Mrs. Godwin say?"

I lean into Lucy, a silent thank-you, and she pats my shoulder.

"If you girls would let me finish, I could explain that the Godwins know that Billy was on the family boat early in the morning, after three. So he was *alive* after Justin went home."

"Wow," Millie says next to me, her voice small, at the same time I say, "How?"

"What?" Mom asks.

"*How?* How do they know that?"

"I don't know, Frankie," Mom says, exasperated. "It didn't really feel appropriate to question Sally after everything she's been through. But you girls don't leave the house unless I say so, okay? Whoever hurt Billy is still out there, and we need to keep you all *safe*."

"But—" I start.

Mom holds up her hand. "No buts. Got it?"

"Got it," we say in unison.

Lucy looks down at her phone and pops a grape in her mouth. "Erica's coming over," she says.

"She is?" I ask, elbowing Millie, who's suddenly very interested in the hem of her jean shorts. "Her parents are letting her outside?"

"They're stuck in the city," Lucy says. "But you know how they are."

Negligent is the word I would use, though Lucy would probably say *relaxed* to be kind.

Lucy disappears upstairs, and I grip Millie's hand, but she yanks it away. "I know what you're going to say," Millie says softly. "But I don't want to figure out what Erica was up to over at the Godwins' house. I don't care anymore. I just want some peace and quiet, okay? We can talk about it later."

"But—" I try to protest as Millie rushes up the stairs, leaving me all alone. *Great.*

I let out an enormous sigh, suddenly so annoyed with everyone in this house. How can no one else want to find out what happened, especially now that the only suspect is walking free?

"Ridiculous," I mutter to myself as I step outside, finding the air still hot and heavy, a thick humidity unbroken. There's one person I could try to talk to about all this. He said he wasn't interested, but that was back when Justin was for sure guilty. Maybe . . .

I dash to the back of the yard, where our property lines up with the Silvers', and slip through the archway separating our homes. Alex is just where I thought he might be, sitting on a pool float in the middle of the deep end with a Rubik's Cube in his hands.

"Al!" I take off running and cannonball right into the water, everything disappearing for a moment as I'm under the surface.

When I break through the surface, Alex has a panicked look on his face. "You scared me half to death, you freak!" he calls, and splashes water my way.

I swim over to him and rest my elbows on the float, treading water below the surface.

"Justin's *innocent*," I say.

"I know."

"So . . ." I say slowly. "Do you want to . . ."

Alex leans back against the float and looks up at the sun. "I told you, Frankie. I'm not interested in solving any crimes or whatever."

"But—"

"Frankie!" His voice is loud and sharp, a sound I've never heard come out of his mouth, and I back away from the float like he's pushed me. "Sorry," he says. "But I *told* you. Billy was a jerk, and this is all too much. Can you just drop it?"

I want to say no, but the pained look on his face is a warning. "Fine," I say, and swim to the ladder on the side of the pool. "Have it your way."

"It's not my way," Alex calls after me. "It's the *normal* way."

"Whatever." I climb out of the pool and grab a towel from one of the lounge chairs, wrapping it around myself.

"You can't be mad at me!"

"Watch me," I mumble, stalking across the grass. I half expect Alex to follow me, but he doesn't, and it's not until I'm back on our property that I can fully realize how furious I am, how much is buzzing around in my brain. It's crazy-making that no one else in my life seems to care about what's actually going on around here. Of course, there's Billy, but then there's also *Erica* and Trevor.

I thought sharing the secret with Millie would make me feel less alone, would make us aligned. But now it seems like I'm further away from *everyone*. I hold the towel close around my body, my bare feet rooted in the prickly grass. *Breathe*, I remind myself. *Breathe*.

The sound of the sliding door makes me open my eyes, and I peer at our house to see Erica walking inside. I freeze but she doesn't notice me, only greets Lucy with a hug. I watch them beyond the glass and try to detect whether Lucy knows, whether anything is out of sorts. But they look as they always do—in sync, relaxed, like friends.

Lucy starts up the stairs and Erica follows, but just as she's about to disappear from view, she turns around, and I startle as her eyes meet mine, direct and unflinching. Inhaling a sip of air, I stay rooted in place until Erica spins around and hurries up the stairs.

All the air leaves my lungs, and I have to take a seat on the lounger to steady myself. She has no idea I know. It's not possible. But that look was so unnerving, so strange. I lean back against the chair and hold the towel tight around my chest. The tips of my hair are still wet from the pool, and they tickle my neck as I close my eyes. Maybe all I need is rest. Maybe that will help me figure out what to do next.

Overhead, leaves rustle and birds caw, as if the sounds of summer are lulling me to sleep, and the next thing I know, I wake with a start, unaware of how much time has passed. It takes me a few seconds to realize I'm still outside, the corners of the towel still clenched in my fists. My hair is mostly dry now, and the sun has begun to set. Stretching my arms up above me, I swing myself up to sit and swing my feet to the ground, feel the stone warm against my bare feet.

Well. One of them. The other foot lands on a piece of paper, thin against my skin. I reach down and find a plain white envelope, the letter *F* written on the front in small block lettering.

I pick it up and flip it over, see no obvious marks, no address, no stamp. Glancing around, I realize I'm still alone. But someone else must have come here and left this for me while I was sleeping. The idea makes my stomach flip. A tingling sensation starts in my toes.

I slide my pointer finger under the flap of the envelope and open it carefully, finding a folded-up piece of paper inside. It's white, the kind you'd find in any type of printer, and when I open it up, there's only one sentence etched in pen.

Stop looking, Frankie, or someone will get hurt.

The edges of the note crinkle as I clutch it, read it a dozen times. I don't recognize the handwriting, so neat it's as if the letters had been traced, but I glance back to our house, look for movement in Lucy's room. The curtains at her window flutter, the only sign of life, and the only thing I can think about is that Erica must have left this for me somehow. She must know.

And she had no choice but to leave me this: a threat.

LUCY

"You good to get home on your own?" I ask Erica at the front door as she gets onto her bike. "I can give you a ride."

"I'm okay," she says. "Promise."

I glance up at the sky. The sunset behind her is a mix of pinks and blues, all cotton-candy colors that meld together to create something totally new and spectacular. On any other day, I'd suggest we go down to the Club and watch it to completion with ice cream cones in hand. But today is not a normal today. Today is the day Pelican Island has been thrown into chaos.

"Text me when you get there." I lean against the doorframe as Erica nods and puts on her helmet. "Are you sure you're okay?" I ask. "You know you can tell me anything."

Erica lets out a low and shaky breath. Her skin is sallow and the hollows beneath her eyes are dark. We've been together for hours, but she's barely said a word, ducking out to use the bathroom more than usual, not really watching the *Gossip Girl* episodes I put on, even though it's her favorite.

"I know," she says. "It's all so overwhelming."

"I love you, Er," I say, pulling her in for a hug. She's limp under my touch, and part of me wants her to stay. There's clearly so much going on beneath the surface. But part of being in a family of girls is knowing when to stop pushing, when to let someone come to you, so I let her go and watch her ride off on her bike.

"Text me!" I call after her, and she puts up one hand without turning back.

Inside the house is quiet, save for Mom yammering on the phone. She's been toggling back and forth between calls with Sally Godwin and Paula Silver, and even had a call with Deirdre Vreeland.

"We *never* thought Justin did it," she whispered, giving me a death stare when I rolled my eyes at her.

All I want to do is flop down on the living room couch, get Millie on one side, Frankie on the other, and press play on the next episode of *Gossip Girl*, but there's a bubbling in my stomach, anticipation building, because even before we heard the news about Justin, I knew what I had to do today, and I'm afraid if I don't do it, I'm going to chicken out.

It's only been three days since the Fourth of July parade when I learned Ethan lied to Billy about when he and I first kissed. Three days of avoiding Ethan, telling him I had the stomach bug, sneaking off to work early so he wouldn't see my car leave the driveway. Three days of fending off offers for him to bring me Popsicles or lemonade or just sit with me and rub my back.

But enough time has passed that I finally know what I want to do. What I want to say. Up in my room, I look at myself in the mirror and apply my usual mascara, dab blush on my cheeks. My curls have gotten wild over the past few weeks, and I can't remember the last time I did a deep conditioning treatment, which I used to perform every other wash like clockwork. The corners of my mouth dip into a frown, and for a moment it feels like a fissure has appeared in my chest with the intent of splitting it in two.

I hold my breath and send a text to Ethan. Bonfire? The beach is about as far as my parents will let us go right now.

Yes, he writes. See you in two.

I step into the hallway at the same time Millie does, and when she sees me, it looks like she's hit with a wave of relief.

"You okay?" I ask.

"Can we hang for a while?" she asks, her voice small. I know that tone, the one that says, *Don't leave me. We don't have much time.* But if I don't do this now, I don't know when I'll get my nerve back.

"Later, okay? I'm just meeting Ethan for a bit."

Millie grips the stair railing like she's trying not to fall over.

"Okay?" I say again.

"Okay."

I give her a quick hug and peck her on the cheek. "I'll be back soon."

Skipping down the stairs, I feel her eyes on me, but I don't turn around for fear of staying put. Outside, the temperature has dipped, and I'm hit with a waft of seaweed and ocean so salty, it almost makes me stop. A wet towel is draped over one of the pool loungers, likely from Frankie forgetting to put her stuff away. But I don't have time to clean up her mess now. I rush forward, to the grass, the blades damp, tickling my ankles, and by the time I reach the sand, a wave of nerves has begun to swell in my stomach.

"There you are!" Ethan says. I'm ambushed in a hug so tight, I'm nearly knocked off my feet. The usual comfort I feel with him is gone, replaced by nerves, and that's when I realize that nothing about this night is normal. "You haven't returned any of my calls or texts or anything. I was starting to freak out."

"Sorry," I say. "Been a little crazed."

"Seriously." Ethan shakes his head, and I can smell his soap, the scent of fresh laundry, of his home, so familiar to me it's almost like my own. "Here." He leads me over to the fire pit where he's already lit the kindling and set up a few blankets.

"Great." My voice is raw, and I hope he doesn't notice the tension in my jaw, the fear in my eyes. As we settle down onto the sand, he rests one hand on my hip and smiles, leaning forward, closing his eyes. His lips are pursed, wanting. But I don't meet them, and he stops midair, confused.

"Everything all right?"

I try to remember my words, the monologue I practiced. But when I look at him, my mind goes blank, and all I say is this: "I know about Olivia."

"What about her?" Ethan cocks his head, his face wide open.

"The reason why she broke up with me sophomore year."

"Because she was moving, right?"

"No." I try to keep my voice even. "Because she thought you and I hooked up in Anguilla."

"Why would she think that?"

"You tell me."

Ethan purses his lips but doesn't say anything, which only infuriates me more.

"I saw the postcard," I say. "The one you wrote to Billy. She found it in his room."

He nods slowly like he's considering the information. "And?"

"Excuse me?" I cross my arms over my chest, plumes of rage rising in my stomach.

He drops his hands by his sides, and his shoulders inch up toward his ears. "I should have told you," he says, "but it was such a long time ago."

The shock is so sudden, so abrupt that it takes me a moment to realize he's not denying any of it, not a word. He lied in order to get what he wanted. To get me.

"How could you *do* this? You knew how upset I was, and you *made* that happen. You caused it."

"I'm sorry, Lucy." He reaches for my waist again, and I pull back, away from him. He doesn't sound sorry. In fact, he sounds like he doesn't care at all, like he'd prefer it if we wrapped up this whole conversation fast so we could hook up or search for shooting stars.

"I don't understand how you're being so *whatever* about this," I say, scrambling to stand. "Our whole relationship was founded on a *lie*."

Ethan lets out a laugh, then runs both hands through his hair, his face turned up to the sky.

"What is so funny?"

"You," he says, getting to his feet. "You're being so hypocritical."

"Me?" I ask, shoving my thumb into my chest. "How am *I* a hypocrite?"

Ethan raises his eyebrows at me like he's waiting for me to say something, and all of a sudden, the bottom of my stomach drops to my feet, my sense of gravity shaking. *He knows.*

"Yeah, Lucy," he says. "I found out about Penn."

A force slams into my chest, and I try to find something to say.

"I know you got in and you've been lying to me." He takes a deep breath, pushing air out through his teeth.

"Did Olivia tell you?"

"Olivia?" Ethan bowls over and presses his palm to his forehead. "Jesus Christ, you told *Olivia* and not me? No wonder you're so mad about something that happened two years ago. You're not over her. You were *never* over her."

"That's not the point."

"You're not even denying it!"

"Of course I'm over her," I say, ignoring the pulsing in my gut. "But right now, I'm mad at *you*. This is about *us*."

"Yeah, well, I'm mad at you, too, Lucy. You didn't tell me about one of the biggest decisions of your life. You made it without me." He pauses like he's catching his breath.

"How did you find out?" My voice is small, but I try to keep it steady even though panic is creeping into my throat.

"I called the housing office to try to see if we could get on the same floor," he says, his voice lower. "I thought I was doing something nice. Something that would make you happy. But when I gave them your name, they said they didn't have a record of Lucy Gold in their database."

I squeeze my eyes shut. It's a gesture that in another life I would have thought of as sweet but now feels like one that comes with a collar and a leash.

"Then what?" I ask. "Did you go through my email or something?"

"It took me two minutes to find your acceptance letter," he says.

"What's wrong with you?" I'm yelling now, but I don't care who hears, who knows what Ethan did. "Ever since we got together, you've done everything to keep me *yours*. God, you couldn't even let me live in another dorm."

"Well, it doesn't matter anyway because you won't be there."

"Ethan, you lied to me."

"And *you* lied to me. For weeks. Every single day. I gave you so many opportunities to tell me the truth."

"So many opportunities?" I ask. "When did you do all this sleuthing?" He shakes his head once and I say it again. "How long have you known?"

"Right before Billy died."

More than two weeks.

I should be sorry. But the only emotion bubbling up is disgust—disgust that he lied for so long, and disgust that he didn't have the courage to confront me about college. Yes, I should have told him. We are both in the wrong. We both messed up.

But Ethan's a coward, and I'm the one who doesn't want to move forward, so I'm going to have to be the one to break us. I drop my shoulders and steady my breathing as the words crystallize in my mind.

"Ethan." He looks up at me expectantly, like he's waiting for a reason, an answer, an apology. But I have none of those things. I wait for the rage and fear to hit me, for all of those base and raw emotions to take over. But the only thing coursing through my veins is relief. "I should have told you earlier," I say.

"So you're going."

"Of course I'm going."

"But we planned this out. We planned our lives out. Our futures."

"*You* did, Ethan," I say. "You had it all set in stone even while I was still with Olivia. You manipulated everything. I'm not going to forgive that."

"But it was worth it, right? We got together."

"You *hurt* me, Ethan." My mouth twitches, and a look of recognition comes over Ethan's face.

"You hurt me, too," he says, throwing up his hands. "You know what? This is fine. I can get over this. I can move past it. It's only a four-hour drive. Besides, we'll both be here for breaks. It's doesn't matter. Like when we're married with a million kids, we'll be like, *That was so hard*, but who will care by then?"

"Ethan . . ."

"I'm serious. I've *been* serious about you since the day we got together."

"The day you *lied* to get us together."

Ethan shakes his head. "All I've ever wanted was you."

"Yeah, and you'd do anything to keep me just as I am in your mind—like a doll in a box."

"I've supported you through *everything*. What made you think that I wouldn't support you going to Penn? I *would*. I want to be together while you do it."

A jolt of heat spreads through my body, and everything in me recoils like I'm rejecting his words, the very concepts they suggest. Even though I could picture my future so clearly at Penn, and even though it didn't feature Ethan, I never imagined having this conversation. Never once, and all of a sudden, it feels like the ground has shifted beneath me.

"What do you want, Lucy?" His words are like little pins pricking my skin, hitting every tiny nerve. "Say it, Lucy." His voice wavers, and I know that if I look at him, I'll see the boy with the bright eyes and the dark hair and the smile that's always been comforting and constant, signaling bliss as soon as he sees me. With only a few words, I'll change all that. He'll no longer be the first person I search for across a room. He won't place his hand on my waist to steady me when I'm wobbly on my bike, won't high-five me after an excellent serve on the tennis court. With only one sentence—one declaration—I'll sever the cord that connects us, has held us together our entire lives.

But on the other side of this moment, there is something else. Something new. A fresh start with new possibilities and new people, new adventures. If I'm lucky, that world will include some form of Ethan—maybe not now, maybe not in ten years, but maybe at some point. And I'd hate myself if I didn't at least venture to see what existed in a world where I'm not defined by Ethan Silver, the boy next door, my *boyfriend*, my mixed-doubles partner, my intended future.

The wind whips my hair all around my face, and I look up at the sky, the first star of the night blinking back at me.

"Ethan," I say, his name now foreign on my lips. I straighten my shoulders and look him square in the eye, see his chest puff in and out, his lips parted and his nostrils flaring, and he says nothing. He's going to make me be the bad guy. But I can handle that. I can be the bad guy if it means moving forward. "I want to break up."

Ethan blinks once, then again, and shuts his mouth. His whole body goes very still, almost like he's stopped breathing.

The night air slows, the wind ceasing, as if it's waiting for him to move, as if the entire universe is on pause, waiting to see what Ethan will do.

He could hug me and tell me we will always be friends, that we will *always* be in each other's lives. Or he could scream and yell and turn to tell everyone that Lucy Gold is a *fucking bitch*. Or he could run.

He takes off so quickly, sprinting on the beach so fast that sand flies into my eyes, and when I wipe it away, I can't tell which direction he went or where he headed.

"Ethan!" I yell, calling into the darkness.

But it's no use. My voice is nearly drowned out by the sound of the waves crashing, and for a split second, I stand still, wondering if he's about to come back.

"Lucy?"

I spin around and see Millie climbing down from the walkway.

"You shouldn't be out here." I brush the hair away from my face, blink against the stinging in my eyes.

"What's going on?" she asks, rushing to me. She's close now, her hands on my elbows, and it only takes a moment before she knows something's wrong, her eyebrows drawing close to each other, her grip tightening on my skin.

"We broke up," I say, and watch Millie's eyes turn into saucers. "Just now. He took off and . . ."

Millie's eyes flick to the water, the darkness, the never-ending expanse of beach, then back to me. "Are you okay?"

"I don't know," I say.

"Oh, Luce." She wraps me in a hug, pressing her cheek to mine, and I let her hold me, feel the weight of her comfort for a moment when I realize I don't really want to be around anyone, not even Millie. All I want is to be alone.

"I need some space," I say.

I walk up the steps to the pathway that leads to our house before she can protest. The sea breeze is light on my skin, the air damp and thick.

All my life, I've craved freedom without knowing I didn't have it. All my life I've craved something *different*, and tonight I gave myself that gift. I wish I didn't have to hurt Ethan in the process. Tomorrow I'll try my best to mend what I broke. But tonight, as I climb up the stairs to my bedroom and shut the door, I allow myself to grasp the greatest feeling of all: release.

MILLIE

"Ethan!" I call his name, but my voice drifts away in the night sky, drowned out by the crashing waves. Footsteps are etched in the beach in front of me, and I know he ran toward the dunes. The wind picks up, pushing me forward, sand flying up against my legs.

I don't have to take off after him, but Lucy doesn't want comfort, and after all that Ethan's been through this summer, the idea of him alone out here at night frightens me, like one wrong step could send him into the sea—or worse, toward someone who might want him to meet the same fate that took Billy. We can't lose him. *I* can't lose him.

"Ethan!" I shout again, though no one responds. I stumble ahead, away from our homes. Finally, a few hundred yards down the sand, I see him, walking away from me, hunched as he trudges toward a dune.

I pick up my pace, calling his name, until he turns around and his eyes widen with surprise as he registers me. The way he looks at me—with relief and gratitude, like he can't believe I would come after him—sends an electric shock through me, but it doesn't slow me down, doesn't stop me from running right at him so fast that in an instant, we're both on the ground, his limbs tangled in mine.

"Sorry," I say, pushing myself to sit. "I didn't mean to tackle you."

"It's all right," he says, shaking out his hair.

"I saw Lucy and heard what happened. I wanted to make sure . . . I was worried about you." I try to compose myself and tuck my hair behind my ears, but the wind whips it right back up again.

"God, what a nightmare," Ethan says. His voice is hoarse, and he makes no motion to stand, instead hugs his shins to his chest and rocks back and forth.

"I'm sorry," I say.

He lifts his head up, and I get a good look at him. His cheeks are pink, and his hair is disheveled, grains of sand sticking to his curls that fall away from his face.

"Did you know?" he asks.

"About what?"

"About Penn?"

I blink and pull my head back. "Penn?"

"She got in. She's going."

"Are you serious?" I ask, heat spreading to my face.

"Yep."

"She didn't tell us." I glance up at the stars. They appeared so quickly, thousands of them up there in a matter of moments, and now they're so bright they nearly blind me. I'm surprised to find tears filling my eyes. *She doesn't trust me.*

"It's weird, but that makes me feel better."

"That's so fucked up," I say, the words biting as they come out of my mouth.

Ethan's eyebrows raise. "Damn, Millie."

I press the heels of my hands into my knees. "Sorry," I say. "I'm just . . . I'm pissed. She should have told me. She should have told *you*." Ethan nods and lets out a puff of air. Together we're aligned in a way I never thought we would be. Against Lucy. "Is that why you broke up?"

Ethan shakes his head. "No," he says. "There were a million reasons."

I know how to comfort him. I can put my hand on his back and offer him soft words of encouragement, but there's a tickling in my stomach, a bubbling warning that indicates whatever he's saying—and *not* saying—is for a reason.

"How did she seem?" Ethan asks.

"She wanted some space, but she's okay."

Ethan's face falls for a moment.

"Should I say she was sobbing and heartbroken?"

He laughs, a small one but still a laugh. "Yeah. Yeah, you should." He shakes his head. "Pathetic, huh? That I want her to be upset? I guess it would prove she actually cared about me."

"Of course she did. Still does."

Ethan toes the sand. "Doesn't feel that way. Doesn't feel like *anyone* cares about me."

"Hey," I say. "Don't say that. So many people do." My heart thrums, a stampede in my chest gaining steam. I reach for his hand, and when he doesn't pull away, I hold it between both of mine, enveloping his fingers that flex beneath my grasp. "I care, Ethan. I care about you. A lot."

A burst of adrenaline rushes through me, but what quickly follows is the realization that I've said too much. As I drop his hand, I watch his face take shape in the moonlight, his eyes stopping at my shoulders, my collarbones, my chin. They move up to my face—stopping at my lips, my nose, and finally, my own eyes, where his gaze holds me.

"I know," he says softly.

It occurs to me in this moment that I would let this boy do just about anything to me. I would wreck my whole life to feel the palm of his hand sturdy against my neck, his fingers winding through my hair. To experience the graze of his lips on mine, his thumb running over of the curve of my jaw.

Now's the time to stop. To get up and walk away and laugh this whole thing off and say, *Maybe you should talk to Trevor or Alex or literally anyone in the world besides me about this.*

But I can't bear to turn away from him, to do anything else except wait. Wait for the pounding in my heart to slow, wait for him to blink and realize that we're sitting too close together on the sand, that our thighs shouldn't be pressed together. Neither of those things happen, and instead Ethan ducks his head toward mine.

"Millie," he says, my name sounding like a spell cast from his lips. "Do you want me to kiss you?" Ethan asks, his voice a whisper.

Everything in my body aches. Everything I have ever wanted right here in front of me, in this boy who is looking at me like I'm made of stars, of fire, of magic. The answer is obvious. It has been so my whole life.

"Yes," I say, and as soon as I breathe the word into the air, his mouth is on mine, a shock, a wave of pressure, like being shot out of a cannon or thrown from a horse. One of his hands is on my shoulder, and the other rests in the bend of my neck, and I blink my eyes open to know for certain that this is really *him*, that this is really happening, and I have to force myself not to think about anything except the fact that *Ethan Silver is kissing me*.

I kiss him back, press my lips against his, and as his tongue slips into my mouth, my stomach lurches, and—wait.

Wait.

This is all wrong.

It takes all my strength for me to nudge him away, to stand and take a few steps back and catch my breath and wipe my mouth and shake my head. "Ethan, we can't."

Ethan blinks like he's in a daze, still on the ground, shaking his head. "I thought you wanted this."

"I do," I say. "I did. I mean, I desperately do. I've been thinking about this forever." I squeeze my eyes shut, barely able to comprehend that I've said the words out loud. "But not like this. Not when you're five seconds out of a breakup with Lucy and not . . ." My throat is suddenly raw, like I've swallowed half the sand on the beach. "Not when I'm the consolation prize."

Ethan sucks on the inside of his cheek, his head turned down to the sand. "Not what you thought it would be, I guess?"

"That's not what I mean," I say, panic rising in my throat. I messed this up—all of it—and yet I can't seem to find a way out.

"Both you and Lucy, you project this idea of who I am onto me."

"What are you—"

"I knew you had a crush on me."

His words knock the wind out of me, and I want him to stop talking. I want to turn back time.

"It's sweet, Millie. But you don't know me. You don't *like* me. You think you do based on some image you have of me in your mind. But what if that's not the real me?" Ethan drops his head into his hands, and his words morph into sobs.

"I *do* know you."

"No, you don't." He looks up at me through tears, his eyes rimmed with red, his jaw tense in a way that makes me step back, move aside.

"That's not fair," I say.

"Yeah," Ethan says. "Nothing that's happened this summer is fair. *Life* isn't fair." He pushes himself to stand and drops his head back, looking up at the sky. An enormous dark cloud sails by, obscuring the moon and in a moment, we're plunged into darkness, the stark shadows of the waves dancing behind him. "You'll learn that when you grow up, Millie," he says, his words piercing, and for a moment, I wonder if they're a threat.

And then Ethan walks back to our homes, away from me and what we've done.

FRANKIE

I have to tell Lucy about Erica. About this note.

The threat looms over me.

Stop looking, Frankie, or someone will get hurt.

The piece of paper burns a hole in my pocket as I sit at the kitchen table with the rest of the family for breakfast. We're all sitting in our usual spots, and the table is full of our favorites: a platter of bagels and smoked salmon; a small tub of scallion cream cheese; an enormous bowl of sliced strawberries; a glass pitcher of freshly squeezed orange juice; and a plate piled high with sliced onions, cucumbers, and tomatoes. Everything is exactly as it always is. Everything is normal.

Except for the fact that Millie and Lucy haven't said a word.

Instead, they're moving pieces of food around on their plates, looking down or out the window and certainly not engaging with anyone else at the table.

"What's going on?" I ask, hoping *someone* will answer.

Dad perks up. "What do you mean, hon?"

"Everyone is obviously on edge, Frankie." Mom sips her cup of coffee. "I was on the phone with Sally for hours last night. I'm surprised she hasn't called this morning. They're talking about bringing in a private detective. The utter incompetence of that Hampton woman." She clucks her tongue.

"I mean you two," I say, stabbing my fork in the air at Millie, then Lucy. "What's going on with you two?"

"Nothing," they say in unison, and then the room goes quiet. Usually, these brunches are loud, each of us trying to talk over one another as we compete for the last spoonful of whitefish, the last half of an everything bagel. But today . . . nothing.

"Okay, well, I don't believe you," I say, and fold my arms over my chest.

Lucy sighs, her shoulders dropping down in the most dramatic way possible, and then she sets both palms down on the table. "Fine," she says. "I have news."

Millie glances up at her, and both of my parents set down their forks.

"Ethan and I broke up," she says.

The only noise comes from my mother's inhalation, a suction so loud it hurts my ears.

"Mom," I say. "Relax."

But she doesn't listen and instead stands and pushes her seat so far back it falls over behind her. "Lucy, what are you *talking* about?"

"Mom," Lucy says, annoyance tinging her voice. "It's okay. It's for the best. Really."

"Is this about Penn?" Dad says.

"What about Penn?" I ask.

"Dad!" Lucy shouts.

"Oh my god, did you get in?" I ask. Lucy breaks into a tiny smile, and she nods once, an almost imperceptible movement, but that's all it takes for me to push *my* chair back and lunge toward her, throwing my arms around her in a hug. "This is amazing! This is the best news ever!"

Lucy had been talking about that school all of last year and was heartbroken when she didn't get in this spring. It was a shock to us all, considering we thought she could do *anything*, but I should have known she would get off the waitlist, that she would make it there somehow.

"Thanks, Frankie," Lucy whispers into my ear, and when I finally release her, I realize everyone else at the table is still in shock over the *other* news.

"Lucy, *is* it about Penn?" Mom asks, her voice stern, like she's about to dole out a punishment. "Because the schools aren't that far, and I know you two can work it out and—"

"It's none of your business why Ethan and I broke up," Lucy says. "You can talk to Gil and Paula all you want about it and try to figure it out, but I'm entitled to privacy in the same way you are."

Lucy throws her napkin down on the table and crosses her arms over her chest, but that's when Millie stands up for the first time, pressing her palm to her chest. There's a pause in the room, like everything has stood still, and I know in an instant that this is one of their secret salutations, part of their language I'm not part of. I sit back down in my chair and reach for a bagel, tearing it in half and shoving a piece into my mouth.

Lucy stops and smiles, winking with her left eye, then settles back into her seat and resumes eating. "Now, if you'll let me finish my breakfast before another interrogation, that would be amazing."

No one says anything for the rest of the meal, and after, Millie races off to her room, probably to read or something, while Lucy and I hang back to clear up. When it's just the two of us in the kitchen, moving around each other in an easy dance, I remember how nice it feels to have her to myself, her steady presence, her calm demeanor. Even if she was acting weird earlier, she is totally herself now. Calm and collected, a protector.

Which is why now's the time to tell her about Erica.

"Lucy, I need to—" But as I do, her phone vibrates, and she picks it up, holding it to her ear.

"Hey, girl," she says. But then her eyes get wide, and her mouth drops open. "Calm down. What? Erica, I can't understand you."

I set my dishrag down on the counter and peer at her, trying to make out what's going on.

"Okay," Lucy says. "Stay put. I'll be there in five."

She hangs up and I lean forward. "What's going on?"

"Erica," she says, flustered as she pulls her hair into a ponytail. "She's freaking out."

"About what?" My heart pounds in my chest. *Tell her. Tell her.*

"Something's going on with Billy's parents? She could barely get the words out. I have to go over there. She's losing her mind."

"You can't go." I say it forcefully, hoping she'll stop. But Lucy shakes her head.

"Cover for me. Just once, okay? I'll be back in an hour."

"Lucy!" I call after her, fear thumping in my chest, but she's already gone, slipping out the door.

LUCY

"Lucy!" Frankie's voice is soft, but I can still hear it, and I turn around on my bike to see her pedaling fast behind me.

"What are you doing? Get back home."

"I can't let you go over there alone," she says, her voice breathless.

"What are you talking about?" I shake my head but keep pedaling.

"Erica's pregnant," Frankie says, the words clipped and foreign coming from her. "She's been hooking up with Trevor for weeks. It's his."

My brakes screech to a halt. "What?" The sound comes out of me like a puff of air. "No, she's not. What are you talking about?"

"I found a sonogram in her purse."

"It could be nothing. A printout. Her cousin's. . . ." My voice is weak, and Frankie's looking at me like I just said the dumbest thing on the planet because even though Frankie's only fifteen, we both know there's only one reason to carry around a sonogram: because it's yours.

Frankie shakes her head. "She left me this note yesterday when she was at the house." Frankie pulls a piece of paper out of her pocket and hands it to me.

I unfold it slowly, but when I do, the words are a shock: *Stop looking, Frankie, or someone will get hurt.*

The letters are all wrong, though, blocky like stencils, not at all like Erica's slanted handwriting. "I don't know what this is, but she didn't write it," I say.

"But—"

"It's probably nothing. A joke," I say, gripping my handlebars tight. Yet even as I say the words, I don't know if they're true. After all, she's my best friend, and according to Frankie, she just spent the past few weeks lying to me about the biggest thing in her world.

Frankie swallows. "What if this isn't even about Trevor, though? What if this means she hurt Billy and she wants me to stop investigating?"

A nervous hum fills my stomach. "Then you need to turn around and let me figure out what's going on."

"No," Frankie says. "I'm coming with you, and you can't change my mind. Let's go before Mom and Dad find out."

There's no use in arguing with Frankie, not now, and so we ride the rest of the way in silence until we arrive at Erica's house, a beautiful gray-shingled estate set back from the road up a quarter-mile-long driveway. I've been here hundreds of times, maybe thousands. Know every peony bush and hydrangea, can pinpoint the cherry tree that blossoms every April for three weeks exactly, and the familiarity of it always sets me at ease, especially because her parents are rarely home. Coming here usually means uninterrupted TV time and junk food and sleepovers in her enormous feather bed.

But now my stomach has twisted itself into a knot, and I have no idea what I'll find today, *who* I'll find. Thankfully, I don't have to wait long. Erica's sitting on a bench swing hanging from the ceiling of her wraparound porch. Her knees are tucked up under her chin, and her arms are wrapped around her legs. When she hears us drop our bikes, she looks up, her face stained with tears, registering Frankie beside me.

"I told you to come alone," she says, warbling.

"Is it true?" I ask, trying to keep my voice even. "Are you pregnant? Are you okay?"

Erica folds her bottom lip into her mouth and glances up like she's trying to hold back tears. Her shoulders shake, and my stomach drops to the floor. It's true. And she's not okay.

I take the steps up to the porch two at a time and sit beside her, wrapping my arms around her. As soon as her head hits my shoulder, she begins to sob, and I glare at Frankie, standing on the grass. Who cares about a stupid anonymous note? How could this girl, my best friend, ever harm a single person? Can't Frankie see she is in pain, not dangerous?

"I'm here for you," I whisper. "Whatever you need."

"Don't say that," Erica says, her words wet, punctuated by hiccups.

"Tell me what's going on," I plead. "Tell me."

Erica lifts her face and searches mine, her gaze desperate. She opens her mouth, and just when I expect her to say *something*, to offer an explanation as to why I needed to rush over here, we're interrupted by the wailing of sirens, of tires spitting up gravel, and I look up to see two cop cars flying down her driveway headed right to us.

Erica's eyes go wide, and her mouth drops open.

"What's going on?" Frankie asks, fear rising in her voice. "What's happening?"

"Erica?" I ask, leaning away from her.

She grips my arms, her face frantic.

"Did you hurt Billy?" I ask, panic in my throat.

She's breathing hard, her chest rising and falling, and then she looks at me, and says, "I didn't mean to."

"Erica Richardson? We're taking you in. Now." Detective Hampton trots toward us, handcuffs dangling from two fingers.

Erica stands, tears falling down her face. "I'm sorry," she says to me. "I'm so sorry."

Frankie looks at me with wide eyes, and I have no idea what to say, no idea what's going on, can only watch as Hampton peels Erica's fingers off the porch railing one by one, not sure who my best friend is anymore.

THE PARTY

2:30 A.M.

"Shh, Billy. It's okay. It's okay." Erica looped an arm around Billy's shoulder, and he couldn't help but lean into her. She smelled so good, like beer and driftwood, and underneath all that, she smelled like home.

"Erica," he said, her name soft on his lips. He liked the way it sounded. So classic and elegant, just like her. He lifted his face to hers and leaned forward, pursing his lips, waiting to feel her soft mouth. But there was nothing there, just air, the absence of her, and Billy opened his eyes, searching. Erica's head hung down and she was sniffling, like she was about to start crying, too. "Hey," he said. "Is this because of Trevor? Because come on. That kid's a joke."

Erica shook her head, her mouth trembling. "I'm pregnant, Billy."

Billy had never truly been shocked before. He had been surprised or delighted, but this form of shock—the kind that makes the whole world stop spinning, the air in front of you freeze, the hairs on the backs of your arms stand on end—was new to him.

"It's his?" Billy asked. The despair in his voice was new, too. The absolute and utter despair. This was all wrong. So wrong.

But then, miraculously, Erica shook her head and looked up at him, her brown eyes wet. "It's yours."

It wasn't despair he felt. No. It was elation. Joy. He couldn't contain himself. He pressed his hands to Erica's cheeks and kissed her hard. Her mouth wilted against his, but he didn't care. He and Erica would be linked forever by this thing they created, this magic. He knew it was ridiculous to be this happy, but he couldn't help it.

"This is . . . amazing," he said. His mind was moving quickly, a plan forming. "We won't be the teenage parents you hear about on the news. I can transfer to school in New York. Maybe even Columbia. And my parents can get us an apartment in the city and a nanny and all the things we need, whatever they are. We'll be fine. We'll be more than fine! And we'll be together. We can still do all the things we want—like go to parties and concerts and tailgates and . . ."

"But that's not what I want," Erica said. Her voice was small but forceful.

"A wedding? That's fine. We can do that. We can get married. I'll get you a big fat diamond."

"But I don't love you, Billy."

Billy stood up. "What . . . But . . . it's us."

"I'm telling you as a courtesy," she said. "I'm still deciding what I want to do."

"What you want to do? Are you crazy? You keep it. You keep our baby."

Erica's face crumpled and she shook her head. "It's not your body. It's not your life." She turned on her heel and started toward the street.

"It is my life!" Billy called after her. How could she not see that? He grabbed at her arm, even as she tried to wrestle away from him.

"Get off me," she said, her voice firm. "Now."

She looked at him with wild eyes, and he kept his grip firm. If he let her go, she might never come back. She might—

The slap of her hand was a crack in the air, one that changed everything.

FRANKIE

News of Erica's trip to the police station spreads like wildfire, but unfortunately, so does our little venture out of the house, which makes Mom and Dad extremely pissed even though, as I told them, I was only trying to make sure Lucy didn't get hurt. No one thinks the youngest can protect anyone. Ridiculous.

"You are not to leave this property until I say so," Mom says. "Is that clear?"

"What about to go next door?" I say, pressing my back into the couch in the living room. It's mostly to piss her off. I don't have any interest in seeing Alex since he sniped at me yesterday.

Mom shakes her head, standing in front of the TV. "Unbelievable. Alex can come here."

"But we practically live there, too," I say.

"Just listen to your mother," Dad says, resigned, and I decide it's not worth it to fight. Lucy's basically in a coma, silent next to me with her arms crossed over her chest.

"Are you okay?" I ask her when Mom and Dad leave the room.

"No." She stands and walks out the side door into the backyard. I'm about to follow her when I hear Millie's footsteps behind me, so much softer than Lucy's, like she's trying to tiptoe around the house without being heard.

"Trevor texted me that he and Alex want to come over," she says.

I sit up and bang my knee on the coffee table, a fissure of pain radiating down my leg. "Gah," I say, then turn to her. "Really?"

Her eyes move to the space behind me, and she inhales sharply. "There they are."

They're both peering through the glass door that leads to the deck, looking rather sheepish, and as Millie lets them in, I realize it's the first time I've been so close to Trevor since finding out all this information about him. Heat rises in my chest, and suddenly, I'm embarrassed, like I don't know what to say, like I know too much about him. Usually, I'd rush over to Alex, but I'm still miffed at him for the way he spoke to me in the pool, so I look away and hope Millie can do all the talking.

"Let's go to my room," she says.

The four of us file upstairs, and when she shuts the door behind us, we're all awkward and quiet for a moment as we find our places far away from one another. Millie settles into her armchair while Trevor falls into her desk chair. Alex sits crisscross on the floor, so I take the bed, burrowing in Millie's pillows.

"This is weird," Trevor says.

"Clearly," I mumble.

"I'm sorry." Alex blurts out the words like he's been holding them in for a week. "Frankie, I'm sorry I blew you off. I hate fighting with you."

Something softens inside my chest. I hate fighting with him, too. Everything is so much better when we're on the same page.

"It's okay," I say. "Especially now. There's too much other shit going on. You know, like Erica being hauled into the police station."

Trevor's face falls, and I realize that was probably not the right thing to say.

"Sorry, Trevor. But, uh, now that we broke the ice . . ." I pull at a thread on Millie's quilt. "We know about you two, about everything."

Millie grips a pillow, her eyes wide, and I can tell she's worried about him. "Why didn't you tell me?" she asks. "I would have been there for you."

"We wanted to keep it secret," Trevor says, tapping his foot on the ground. "She thought Billy would lose his mind, and we didn't know what we *were* yet. But now . . ."

"What are you going to do?" Millie asks.

"Me?" he asks.

"Don't tell me you're going to make her do this all on her own," I say. "If you're the father—"

"He's not," Alex says, his voice more confident than usual. "Trevor's not the father."

"You knew about this?" I ask, incredulous, and Alex shrugs. It dawns on me then how foolish I was not to assume that the boys told each other things they would never tell us, kept each other's secrets.

Trevor runs his hand through his hair. "We only got together a few weeks ago. The timing doesn't line up." He takes a slow exhale. "It's Billy's, but his parents wanted her to take a paternity test. She refused, so they court-ordered one. She texted me this morning saying she thought she was going to be forced or something. Mr. Godwin's behind it all, I know it. He's such an asshole. Honestly, makes me think *he*'s hiding something."

I press my fingers to my forehead and close my eyes, trying to understand. "Wait, so that's why they brought her into the police station? To take a court-ordered paternity test?"

"I think so," Trevor says. "She's already been through so much." He bites his bottom lip and Alex lets out a weary sigh.

I reach inside my pocket, the corner of Erica's note pricking my finger. I could show it to them, but Lucy already told me it was stupid. There's no way they would listen to me either. So I leave the note hidden, and instead ask, "You don't think she killed Billy?"

In the quickest moment, Alex and Trevor exchange a worried look, almost a blink. A suggestion of a glance.

"No," Trevor says. "No way."

But that look, I fear, tells a different story.

LUCY

Even though I can't leave our property, I walk as far as I can get to the very edge of the cliff on our backyard, where Dad and Gil installed a bench for what they call "alone together time." I think it's where they secretly come to vape. I slump down, close my eyes, and listen to the waves lapping against the rocks. Here, I can forget about everything—about Erica, about Penn, about Ethan. I can exist in a body and feel the breeze on my skin, smell the brackish mussels in the sand, press my feet into the warm pebbles, remember that I am here. I am whole.

I flick my eyes open and look up at the seagulls flapping their wings against the bright blue sky. *Remember this*, I tell myself. *Remember how beautiful this place is.*

"I didn't realize you'd be here."

I lift my head to see Ethan approaching, wearing running shorts, his chest bare, and a white tank top tucked into his waistband. He's drenched in sweat, his curls damp against his forehead.

"Looks like someone was allowed to go on a run."

"Nah, only on the treadmill," he says. "But I saw you out here and . . ."

I slide over, making room. It's not up to me if he takes the olive branch, but the least I can do is offer it. The bench creaks with his weight. We've sat in this exact place so many times before, talking about nothing, holding hands and letting the silence get comfortable. For a brief, terrible moment, I wonder if I'll ever feel that cozy quiet with anyone ever again.

"I heard about Erica," he says. "Are you okay?"

"I don't know what's real anymore." The space behind my eyes stings and I blink, wetness coating my lashes.

"I'm sorry, Lucy," Ethan says, his voice soft.

"About Erica or about last night?"

He makes a coughing noise. "Both? I was a dick."

My chest unlocks, and I take a deep breath. "I wasn't my best self either."

Ethan clasps his hands behind his neck, his elbows pointing up to the sky, and I catch a look at him out of my periphery. He's always his most handsome after he exercises, when there's pink in his cheeks and a sheen of perspiration on his skin. I take in his profile, consider the crooked scar on his nose I've always found endearing, the curve of his jaw, the tiny gold hoop he never takes out of his ear. I didn't expect all that love and affection I've tended to for years to evaporate when I said the words *break up*. But it feels like a betrayal that those emotions are still brewing, right beneath my skin, and yet, nothing in me wants to take back what was said.

"I'm sorry I didn't tell you about Penn," I say. "I was scared."

"I know." He smirks, toeing the dirt with his sneaker. "To be fair, I would have supported you. But I know that wasn't the issue."

"No. It wasn't."

"And I'm sorry about writing that postcard to Billy. It was stupid." Ethan leans forward, rests his elbows on his knees. "I didn't think I could compete with Olivia."

"You shouldn't have done that," I say.

"No. I shouldn't have. Even if we were babies."

I turn to face him, resting one knee on the bench. "Do you think we still are? In the grand scheme of things?"

"Yes," he says.

"I don't know if I'm ready to be a full-blown adult. Not yet."

Ethan shakes his head. "No way."

There it is. That comfortable silence.

What a relief to know that after severing the tie between us, there is still *this*. The luxury of being known.

"I hope we always know each other," I say, the words feeling trite but necessary.

Ethan rests his palm on the bench, facing upward toward the sky. An invitation. I accept it and rest my hand on top of his.

"We will," he says. "In some capacity."

"Are we really going to try to be friends?" I ask.

Ethan shrugs. "Maybe. Let's take it one day at a time."

"Okay," I say.

We sit together for another moment of quiet, listening to the water, the birds, the humming of cars puttering down the street. I wonder if Ethan is also dreading going back inside, back to reality. If he wants to extend this moment for as long as possible to delay the inevitable gossip that will surround us like a cloud of gnats. The horrible details that are about to come out about Erica. Ethan takes his hand away, and immediately I feel its absence, my skin resting on the wood of the bench.

"I'm just glad you're not mad about Millie," he says. "A weird mistake, you know?" He runs his fingers through his hair. "I wasn't thinking."

"Millie." I repeat my sister's name, heat spreading on the back of my neck. "A mistake?"

Ethan stands and rests his hands on his hips. "I immediately felt bad about the kiss. I wasn't very nice about it either. God, I have to go on an apology tour with the Gold sisters, huh? I hope she gets over it. Won't do her any good to keep pining after me."

"The kiss." I blink, my vision blurring the water in front of me until it's a mess of blue.

"She told you, right? You guys tell each other everything."

My throat is sandpaper, and I clench my jaw, force my neck to bob my head up and down. "Of course."

"Anyway," he says. "We're gonna be okay, Lucy. We are."

He reaches for me and squeezes my shoulder, and like a fool, I let him.

"Keep me posted on Erica, okay? It's hard to believe she . . ." He shakes his head. "I can't believe it. I really can't."

"Mm-hmm," I say as he trots off toward home. But I can't get up. I can't stand or move or cry because all I can see is a picture in my mind of my sister's face attached to Ethan's.

The boy whose entire existence I can sketch on a map, whose heart lay on top of mine, overlapping like shadows.

Ethan, who Millie had gone after last night, trekking off into the darkness in order to find. To *kiss*.

Ethan, who Millie had been . . . What did he say? *Pining* after him?

It's not possible. None of it is.

And yet . . .

I spin around and watch as Ethan walks back over the boardwalk between our houses, the massive structures flanking him, our whole lives set on these four acres. I grip the bench, and the wood slats dig into my hands so hard a splinter splits my skin. A sharp pain travels up my arm, and I'm hit with a question so unnerving it knocks the breath out of me: What has Millie been hiding?

MILLIE

I hear her before I see her. Lucy opening the front door, slamming it behind her. The dampening of her footsteps as they hit the wool runner in the hallway, charging up the stairs. A pause at the landing, then a left turn toward our rooms.

I tense as the weight of the air shifts around me. Trevor is long gone, Alex and Frankie are holed up in her room working on a new logic puzzle, and I'm all alone, attuned to Lucy's movements because I've been waiting for this moment all day. Fearing it.

She's standing right outside my door. I can hear her breathing, can imagine her raising her hand to the doorknob, knowing I don't deserve the courtesy of a knock. Not today.

How strange, to know someone by the way their feet hit the floor, the rhythm of their steps. I've lived my whole life inside this house, listening to Lucy shut dresser drawers, draw back the curtains, flip on light switches, pull plates down from the kitchen cabinets. I can tell she's stressed based on the way she pushes the pantry door open with her hip, that she's sleepy if she plops down onto her vanity seat with force so it creaks on that one floorboard in her bedroom. Her movements around this house, even though I can't see her, paint a picture. Just as I'm sure mine do.

Because we *know* each other.

Which is why I can tell that on the other side of the door that separates us, Lucy is standing in the hall, debating how she's going to confront me.

I straighten my spine and press my back deep into my armchair as if by some miracle I might disappear into the cushions. But there's no way to prepare, nowhere to hide, and the only thing I can do is wait for the door to swing open.

LUCY

My lungs are on fire as I rip open Millie's door. She's right where I thought she'd be, curled up on that stupid chair she's always in, doing what she always does. *Nothing.*

We stare at each other, and it takes me a second to realize she's wearing my sweater, the well-loved gray cotton pullover that's so soft at the elbows it's almost threadbare, and for a moment it looks as though I'm sitting in the chair.

"Take it off," I say. "Take off my sweater. Now."

Millie looks down like she doesn't remember what she put on when Mom turned the air conditioner on high, and when she registers the item, she calmly lifts it up over her shoulders and starts to fold it into quarters.

I'm in front of her in two steps and yank the fabric out of her hands. "You think you can take whatever's mine, don't you?"

"Lucy—" she starts, but I slice my hand through the air.

"You don't get to speak. Not yet." A hitch catches in my voice, and I swallow the lump in my throat. I will not let *her* lead this conversation.

Millie shuts her mouth, but her shoulders begin to shake as she grips the arms of her chair. There's fear in her eyes, like she's terrified of me, and I'm horrified that my first instinct is to grab Millie and hug her tight. To make calming noises and tell her that everything will be okay. Because that's what I've done my whole life. Protect my sisters.

Not this time.

I can't protect her from her own bad decisions.

"You kissed Ethan," I say, my words a hiss. "What the hell were you *thinking*?" I'm amazed to hear my voice is brittle like it's already broken. "Actually, I know the answer. You were thinking that we broke up and he might notice you for once. Is that right? That after all these years of being jealous of me, you could finally go after him? You're pathetic." A strange sound escapes my lips. Not quite a laugh but not a sob either.

"That's not—" Millie says. Her cheeks are red and splotchy, and tears threaten to spill from her eyes. But I don't care. Not anymore. "I'm sorry, Lucy. I'm so sorry. It just happened, and he . . ."

"It just happened? Millie, that's not how kissing works."

Millie hiccups, but the sound she makes is more like a wail, and I'm struck by the absence of a denial, how obvious the truth is.

Every moment Ethan had been in our house, in my room, at our dinner table, Millie had been swooning, yearning, devastated by the knowledge that he was with me, not her.

If I were a stronger person, I would feel empathy for my sister. If I were *good*, I would be able to wrap Millie in my arms and whisper into her ear that everything was going to be all right. We were going to be fine. That I could forgive her for such a betrayal.

But I don't feel *good*. I feel mean and rotten, like I want to hurt Millie. Because even though I have no claim to Ethan's heart or his body or his mind, he is still part of me. The person who awakened in me a sense of desire and pleasure, and made me realize that there is beauty in being connected to another human being in the way our parents seem to be, singing and dancing in the kitchen when they think no one else is home.

"I didn't want to hurt you," Millie says, tears running down her face. "I don't even . . . Not anymore . . . It was such a mistake."

"Well, you did hurt me," I say. My eyes sting and my throat is raw like I had screamed for a thousand years. "You really fucking did."

I can't look at Millie anymore. I force myself to turn away from her and walk across the hall to my room, where I shut the door and lock it. I don't open it again. Not when Millie pounds her fists against the wood, not when Mom yells up the stairs for us to quiet down. Eventually, Millie relents, and I hear her open and close her own door, can hear the sag of her armchair, her weight on top of the cushions. The house grows quiet, and then, finally, in total privacy, I let the tears come, hard and heavy, as I crawl into bed and cry.

Going to work the next morning is a relief so great, my whole body seems to relax as I drive away from the house. I haven't heard from Erica since yesterday, and as I sit down at my desk at the mayor's office, all I want to do is forget about everything that's happened over the past few days and focus on my job.

"Got you something." Olivia plunks an iced coffee down on my desk. "Whole milk, right?"

Warmth spreads through my chest. I take a sip, and it's heaven. "Thank you. I needed this."

"I owed you," she said, sliding into her seat. "Besides, figured any sort of pick-me-up would be a good idea today." She pauses, and for a moment I think she's going to bring up Ethan. "After everything going on with Erica . . ."

My spine prickles, and I sit up straight, relieved. "Honestly, I'd rather talk about anything else." I grab a manila envelope full of the property records.

"First one to find an instance of tree-house-induced violence gets a cookie?" Olivia asks. "Too soon?"

I burst out laughing, and for the next hour, we work together in tandem, passing pieces of paper back and forth, as we sort the files in terms of immediacy. It's tedious work, but it's the easiest, most relaxing part of my week. At one point, Olivia reads some of the complaints aloud in a British accent, looking up at me every few sentences in hopes that I laugh, which I do, so hard I snort out a little bit of coffee onto my keyboard.

"Oh my god," I say, wiping it up with a napkin. "Thank you for that."

"At your service." Olivia takes a deep bow in her seat, then cracks up, covering her hand with her mouth.

"I'm surprised you're so chill," I say. "I know I said I didn't want to talk about it, but I haven't heard from Erica yet, and I'm starting to think . . ."

"Think what?" Olivia cocks her head.

"That she killed Billy." The words come out choked, like I can barely get them out.

Olivia frowns. "She didn't kill him."

"How do you know?"

"They let her go early this morning," Olivia says, tucking her hair behind her ear. "Made her get a paternity test, which I told Aunt Sally was a dumb idea anyway. So rude. If she says it's his, it's his. But I don't think they ever suspected her of *murder*."

"Oh, thank god," I say, resting my hand over my heart, the relief immediate and all-consuming.

Olivia's face sours for a moment as she turns back to the computer.

"What?" I ask.

"Obviously, I'm happy it wasn't Erica," she says slowly. "But with every false lead it just means we still don't have an answer." She turns back to her computer, typing quickly, and I realize she's right.

Billy's death is still a question mark.

THE PARTY

3:00 A.M.

Erica's slap stung his skin, and Billy released her wrist, raising his hand to his cheek.

"We can talk about this in the morning," she said, her voice high and urgent. "But I'm leaving. Now."

Billy let her go. He had to. She walked away and grabbed her bike, and then, as if she was never there at all, she was gone. He watched the spot where she had been, wishing that she would come back, willing her to return. He must have stood like that for five, ten minutes. Or maybe it was only thirty seconds. Billy couldn't keep track of time.

He looked up at his house, all of its windows dark, and wondered if his parents were sleeping in the same room tonight, if Olivia was tucked safely in the pool house. He wondered if anyone had puked on the lawn, if Glenda, the housekeeper, would talk shit about him to the gardeners in the morning.

He could climb into bed and sleep for twelve hours. More, probably. But he couldn't let the night end like this. Not when Erica's voice was bleating in his head. Not when he had just learned the most important information of his life.

He turned back around and faced the water. Jutting out from the rocky beach was the family's small dock where they kept a tender, the little boat they used to get back and forth to Sea Witch, *their sailing yacht, moored in the Sound, closer to the marina.*

Billy's feet moved before he could formulate a plan, and pretty soon, he was on the tender gliding over the surface of the water. He would go to the boat and sleep there tonight. Or at least watch the sun come up. It was there that he always felt calm, that he could always find answers. It was there that Billy would find a way forward.

MILLIE

The very last place in the world I want to be right now is on a lifeguarding shift with Ethan, but here I am, trying my hardest not to look at him. It helps that he's positioned down on the sand, holding the flotation device over his stomach, and I'm up on the tower, trying to focus on the single swimmer bobbing up and down in the water. The forecast threatened rain, and the sky is a dark, menacing gray that makes me shiver under my oversize hoodie. The beach is empty, but Ethan and I can't leave our post for another few hours.

We've barely said a word to each other since we got here, but all I want to do is melt into the chair. And yet there's a pulsing in my chest, daring my heart to burst out of me, and finally, after a few more moments of silence, I can't take it anymore.

"I can't believe you told her," I blurt.

Ethan looks up at me, surprised. "*I* told her? I assumed you did."

"Why would I ever tell her something like that?"

"Because you guys tell each other *everything*."

"Clearly not."

"That's the only reason I said something. I thought she knew."

"Well, now she hates me. She probably won't ever speak to me again." My eyes sting and I tuck my hands inside the sleeves of my sweatshirt.

Ethan turns back toward the water. "Are you really in love with me?"

My shoulders tense up by my ears. "I thought so. Maybe. At some point."

"And now? Still?"

"Now I just want my sister back." I look out at the horizon and let my vision go blurry. "Did you mean what you said? That we don't know you?"

"No one really knows each other," he says, his voice soft around the edges. "We pretend to. But there are some things we keep hidden. Sometimes I feel like everyone treats me like the person they want me to be rather than the person I am. I think that's what you did."

I lean back and cross my ankles tight so the bones press together. I want to push back, but maybe he's *right*. My whole life, I've looked at him as a perfect Prince Charming, one of the guys in my romance novels. I'd read a chapter of an epic love story, then look across the backyard and think to myself, *There he is. If only . . .*

But maybe there's a reason why I ascribed those labels to Ethan instead of someone who *was* attainable. Someone I could actually have. Because knowing I could never cross the line with Ethan without losing Lucy made it so that I *wouldn't* ever have to submit myself to rejection or real, actual pain. I could continue living in a fantasy of ignorance, a boxed-in version of what I thought love might be. I could never get hurt because I could never *try*.

And yet . . .

Not only did I get hurt, but I hurt others in the process.

"Yeah," I say softly. "I think I understand."

Ethan lets out a noise that sounds somewhat like a laugh and even though it's not *really* one, the bubble of tension around us seems to pop. "Next time you want to live out a fairy tale, choose someone else to chase after."

"I was not *chasing after* you."

"You *literally* chased me." Ethan smirks, and I kick his shoulder with my toes, causing him to stumble forward and laugh.

"I'm glad this is funny to you." But, surprising myself, I laugh, too, because objectively this whole situation is ridiculous. Incredibly, stupidly funny. "God, I've messed everything up."

Ethan bowls over, clutching his stomach as his laughter gets louder and louder. "You definitely have." He wipes his eyes with his pointer finger and stands up straight, trying to catch his breath. "It's not all your fault. I kissed you, too." He flicks his eyes up to me, and the usual hum in my stomach grows softer, almost imperceptible.

We're both quiet, and I lean back against the tower, watching the waves crest against the shore, getting more violent by the moment, the far-out sea darkening beneath the gray sky.

"Hey," he says. "Can I ask you something?"

"Not like I can say no *now*."

"You saw Trevor yesterday, right?" Ethan asks.

"Yeah."

"How did he seem to you?"

"What do you mean?" I ask.

"I'm worried about him. With all this Erica stuff. I think he got in over his head."

"He's got you," I say.

"And you, hopefully." Ethan drums his nails on the inflatable around his middle. "I'm his brother, but I think he could use a friend."

I press my hand to my stomach as a drop of rain lands on my forehead, rolling into my eye. "Okay," I say. "I can do that."

"Thanks," he says.

A moment later, the rain picks up, the water falling in sheets, the smell of a summer storm suddenly all-consuming. I don't try to fight it, let myself get drenched. My hoodie sticks to my skin, and I turn my face to the sky, the rain pummeling me. When I speak my voice is nearly drowned out by the downpour. "Do you think Lucy will ever forgive me?" I shout.

"She will," Ethan says, loud over the rain. "Give her time."

"How do you know?" I ask, water rolling down my back, over my skin, washing me clean.

"Because I forgive my brothers for all sorts of things. And they forgive me."

Ethan smiles at me, rain pouring down his face, his hair matted to his scalp, and in that moment, I choose to believe him.

LUCY

Erica's sprawled out on a lounge chair next to her pool, exactly where I thought she'd be, and when I open the gate to her backyard, she sits up and pushes her sunglasses on top of her head. "What are you doing here?" The skin around her eyes is red and puffy, and my heart leaps into my throat as soon as I see her.

I drop onto the chair next to her and wrap her in my arms. "Taking care of you, duh."

She lets out a sob, her cheek wet against my shoulder. "Everyone knows, don't they?"

"Yeah," I whisper. "How are you holding up?"

"Well, I'm nine weeks along, so I feel like shit. My parents are furious, and Billy's family won't speak to me until the paternity test comes back."

"And I thought *I* had problems."

"Ha! That's the first thing that's made me laugh in weeks."

"Do you know what you're going to do yet?" I ask. She presses her palms to the sides of her head and folds her bottom lip under her teeth. When she doesn't answer immediately, fear grips me hard, and I reach for her knee. "Erica?"

"I haven't decided," she says.

"You're thinking of keeping it?" I stare at her, incredulous. "But you're only eighteen. You're going to NYU in two months. You're . . . Erica, you're a *kid*."

Erica pouts and leans back against the lounge chair. "I knew you'd react this way."

"Well, *yeah*. Have you thought this through?"

"Of course not," she says, her voice getting louder. "I haven't had much time to process, and honestly I could really use a friend right now instead of another person telling me what to do with my body."

Her words hit me square in the chest. She's right. I can't control her, just like I can't control Millie or Frankie or even Ethan. All I can do is be there for her.

Erica closes her eyes, and her features tremble, a tiny earthquake rippling over her face. After what feels like an eternity, she looks at me. "If Billy were alive, the decision would be easier."

She lets the words hang between us, her mouth trembling, her cheeks growing red. She presses a hand to her stomach, still flat, and when she looks at me, I understand why Erica would consider having this baby.

It may be the last remaining piece of Billy Godwin.

I STAY IN Erica's backyard for a long, long time. Long enough for darkness to fall, for Erica to pull the towel around her shoulders for warmth, and for me to suggest that maybe we go inside and raid her pantry.

In the frigid air-conditioning of her home, over bowls of boxed macaroni and cheese, Erica begins to tell me what's happened.

"I wasn't totally honest with you about why Billy and I broke up," she says. "When I said I liked myself more when I wasn't with him, what I meant was that I liked myself more when I was with Trevor." I scoop up a spoonful of noodles and listen intently.

"He made me comfortable. I don't know how to explain it." Erica sets her bowl on the table. "With Billy, I always felt like I had to perform. But Trevor was so . . . easy. A week before I officially broke things off with Billy, I asked Trevor if he wanted to go for a drive. He suggested we go over the bridge into Kimber Cove to see the sunset from a different vantage point." She shrugs and throws up her hands. "I kissed him that night. That was that."

"Trevor." I shake my head. "I can't believe it."

"I know. Honestly, he seemed surprised, too. I always thought he had a crush on Millie, but after that . . . we just clicked."

I stick my spoon back in my bowl. "Why didn't you tell me?"

"I was mortified. I mean, I cheated on Billy. I wasn't exactly proud of that. And if it got back to Billy . . . It was just easier to keep it a secret." A small smile starts to form on her face. "This is bad, but it was *fun* to have a secret. A summer fling before college. Something sweet and easy."

"But then you found out you were pregnant."

She nods, her eyes downcast.

"And then Billy died."

"I found out the morning of the party." Erica swallows and rests her palm on her forehead. "And I told him that night."

My mind is moving so fast, trying to parse the words, figure out how they translate to what I know about Billy's death. "How did he react?"

Erica smiles, soft. "He thought we were going to get married and live in an apartment in the city that his parents paid for."

I bite my tongue and try not to point out how delusional this line of thinking is.

"The next morning, his dad called me and basically demanded that I keep quiet. I guess Billy told him before he died."

"What was Mr. Godwin's reaction?"

Erica leans in, clasping her hands together. "Maybe I'm losing it, but I really thought they would want me to have it. That they would want some part of Billy alive. But they were furious. Said I was probably lying, and even if I wasn't that they wouldn't support it at all." Erica bites her lip.

"Why didn't you want to take the DNA test? Why did you refuse?"

"On principle," she says. "They're only doing it because they don't want me to have any of their money." She scrunches up her nose. "I don't even want it. I went over there a few days ago before all this craziness," Erica says, "and his dad was such an asshole, screaming at Mrs. Godwin about how Billy would still be here if she had just let him sleep at home that night." She shakes her head. "He was drunk, I think, but it was so creepy, and Mrs. Godwin threw a plate at him."

My jaw tenses, and Erica narrows her eyes.

"What?" she asks. "You have that look on your face that you get before a math test."

"Were his parents home the night of the party?"

"His mom was, but she always takes a bunch of benzos and passes out. I never saw Billy's dad. He's in and out a lot."

"Do you think he could have been on the boat?"

Erica's eyes flash recognition. "When we were together, Billy would say that his dad disappeared all the time and would sometimes sleep on the boat if he got into a fight with Mrs. Godwin."

My mind whirs, the possibilities crystallizing like developing photographs. "What if Mr. Godwin was on the boat? What if he and Billy got into a fight that night over *this*?"

Erica's mouth drops open, and neither of us say anything. We don't have to.

FRANKIE

Rocking back and forth in the hammock in our backyard, a soft breeze cool against my skin, I should be relaxed. But all my limbs are tense, and I'm restless, flopping around, trying to get comfortable, wanting to *do* something.

I cross my arms over my chest and look up at the dark sky, where the stars are so bright they seem to illuminate the whole yard. I try to think of the things I can do that might actually get me closer to figuring out what happened.

I can go to Detective Hampton and show her the note, tell her that I'm positive Erica left it for me—and that they need to keep looking at her. But I can already picture the way Hampton would blow me off, think of me as a dumb kid, just like Lucy did.

I can confront Trevor and Alex and demand they tell me more of what they know, but based on the truce we reached today, I'm not sure I want to rock the boat. Especially with Alex, who hung around for hours doing puzzles with me in order to take our mind off things. It almost felt like we were back to being *us*.

Trevor mentioned that he wouldn't be surprised if Mr. Godwin was hiding something based on how much of a dick he was being to Erica, so that's an idea. I can try to do some sneaky stalking of

Mr. Godwin and see if he's up to anything creepy. But there's no way I'd be able to go to the Godwin house without being detected.

I swing my legs over the side of the hammock and look out to the sea. It's useless. There's nothing I can do that would give me any answers. But at least there's this view. There is *always* this view. The Sound stretches out before me, dark and still, the perfect place to learn to swim, to kayak, to paddleboard, to water-ski. This body of water has been the backdrop to our entire lives, and I can't imagine ever living far from a beach. Not that I would want to.

When Alex and I were five, our families installed a shared dock between our beaches so we could jump out into the water without having to wade in through the rocky shore. I stand up and walk toward it, suddenly desperate to dip my feet, to see how cold it is.

A gust of wind blows through my hair, and I shiver, the salt spray stinging my eyes, landing like mist on my skin. Up above, the stars blink back at me, glitter thrown across the night. Magic.

Sitting at the edge of the dock, I let my legs dangle over, but they don't hit water. Instead, my feet drop into the hard plastic bottom of one of our kayaks. The four-seater inflatable one Ethan got for his sixteenth birthday.

I keep the kayak in place with my feet, when suddenly the answer is obvious. The Godwin boat is moored not too far from here. I could get there quickly. Under twenty minutes. Chances are there's nothing there the cops haven't already seen, but maybe if I could just *get* there, I'd have a better idea of what to do next.

I pause, holding my breath for a moment before I let the air out. Screw it.

Soon I'm in the middle of the Sound, my biceps twitching as I paddle against the current. I can see the *Sea Witch*, dark and swaying, and adrenaline pushes me forward. There's no need for a flashlight, not when I'm illuminated by the moon, and I follow my sight lines to the sailing yacht, the mast a North Star in the night.

As I get closer, the boat becomes bigger, a looming tower, and my stomach flips. I don't actually have a plan. I paddle around the back of the boat and am shocked by its size, by the fact that it's *here* in the water, bobbing about, massive and dark, like no one is on board. On one side, a ladder drops into the water, and I grab onto it, using a rope from Ethan's kayak to tie a knot from the metal so the kayak doesn't float away.

Staring up at the boat, I have a choice to make. I could step onto the ladder and climb on up, searching for . . . something. Or I could turn back. I could give up.

There's no choice at all. My legs move as if unattached to my body, and I hook one foot over the ladder, then the other. Within seconds, I'm aboard, surveying the deck. The place is immaculate, with pristine white couches lining the sides, a sturdy dining table set up at the bow. There are no taped-off areas, no signs of violence, not even a cushion out of place.

Carefully, I walk the perimeter, my eyes searching for something—anything—that might say *Here is your answer.* But all I see are spotless wineglasses stowed away, a single open bottle on the bar cart. The only sound comes from the birds circling overhead, the waves gently cresting below the boat, rocking the ship in the night.

I try to steady my breathing as the adrenaline kicks in. *This is fine. This is all fine.*

In the middle of the deck is a staircase, and I grip the railing, tiptoeing downstairs to the cabins, where I find three doors. My heart pounds in my chest as I push one open with my pointer finger. It creaks, the noise sending a shock wave down my spine, but I hold steady, stay calm, stay put. Inside, there's a queen bed and a floor-length mirror, the space almost as big as my room at home. Not a terrible place to be stuck at sea. I step farther inside and spin around, gaining confidence. No one is here. Nothing looks out of place. Nothing looks strange. In the mirror, I catch my reflection, dark half-moons under my eyes, my curls frizzy from the ocean air. The girl looking back at me is wild, like she's chasing after something, and she emboldens me.

I move to the second door and nudge that one open with my shoulder. But as soon as I do, it's obvious something is off. Light from a small lamp on the bedside table cuts across the room and the enormous bed is unmade, half a dozen throw pillows spread out on the floor. A pair of khakis is slung over the armchair in the corner.

Terror rips through me, and everything in my body is telling me to run. *Get out. Get out.* But I can't move. I can barely think.

That's when I hear it. Above the placid waves, there's another sound. A stream of water running in the bathroom on the other side of the room. And then, suddenly, quiet. A showerhead turned off.

That's when I bolt.

Up the stairs and onto the deck, where I crash right into the bar cart, wineglasses crashing as they knock together in the wind.

"Hello?" a man's frantic voice calls from below. "Who's here?"

Run. Run. Run.

I push myself to make it to the ladder and fling my limbs over the edge of the boat as fast as I can, my knees knocking into the side with a sudden *thud*, my right hand scraping against rope and metal, a screw catching on my palm. The pain is instant, and I bite my lip to keep from crying out as I fumble my way into the kayak. I hear the man above, his feet sliding across the deck. Blood from my hand drips down my arm as I try to untie the rope. My fingers are clumsy and slow, and I'm about to be caught.

Even if I can untie this knot, even if I free myself and paddle as fast as I can, he'll still be able to see me. I have to do *something*.

"Olivia?" the man calls. "I told you to stay *home*."

The voice is closer, so close it's like he's right over me, and I have no choice. I dive off the kayak, into the water, and duck beneath the surface. Immediately, I'm plunged into darkness, the cold rushing through me like I've been pumped full of ice. The cut on my hand stings so much, it's like a jellyfish has found its way into my tendons. I only have a few moments of breath and pray this man sees the kayak and thinks that it's a water toy belonging to the boat, that he forgot about it, that he doesn't notice the girl underwater beneath it.

I'm running out of air. I'm lightheaded, and my brain is demanding more from me. *Breathe. Breathe. Breathe.*

My vision is spotty. My lungs are on fire, threatening to burst out of my chest. I have no choice. I need oxygen.

Bobbing to the surface, I gasp for air and claw at the kayak. I brace for someone to grip me by the shoulders and throw me down onto the boat, or worse—push me back underwater.

And yet, no one comes. No one is there. I force myself to look back up to the *Sea Witch*. The man has his back to me, but he's wearing pajamas, navy blue with white piping along the collar. He's got dark hair and a tall, slim build, and when he turns so I can see his profile, it's obvious the man is Billy's father, a phone pressed to his ear.

"I swore I heard someone on the boat," he mutters. "No. No. I'm not going *crazy*. You never listen to me. I've said it once and I'll say it again, Sally. If you'd let me sleep at home that night, he'd still be *alive*."

The last word has venom in it. Mr. Godwin shakes his head and pockets his phone before descending into the cabin, and it's only then that I can finally heave myself onto the kayak. Water pools around my seat, but with shaking hands, I loosen the knot and slowly start to paddle away.

It takes me nearly three times as long to get home, and when I do, I rest my head on my knees and breathe heavily, my teeth chattering from the cold. But it's only when I retie the kayak back to our dock that I realize the gift Mr. Godwin just gave me: the answer to my puzzle.

THE PARTY

3:30 A.M.

As Billy maneuvered the tender to the side of the boat where a ladder dangled into the water, his heart skipped in his chest. The Sea Witch *was a thirty-eight-foot Bali Catsmart, which made it one of the most luxurious and comfortable sailboats in the world, and Billy knew it was stocked with more booze and a better sound system than every bar on Pelican Island.*

Nothing was better than waking up on that boat, when the sun rose over the water, and the whole sky looked like one of those paintings he saw in Musée d'Orsay when his family went to Paris last winter.

Some of his fondest memories took place aboard the ship, like when they sailed to Bermuda last June or when they took it up to Martha's Vineyard and stayed at his grandparents' estate for the entire month of August. His dad always talked about taking a trip, just the two of them, up to Canada to go oyster farming. Maybe next summer, they'd finally do it.

Billy tied up the tender and swung his leg up onto the ladder, climbing aboard with ease. He made his way to the bar cart, splashed whatever was in the crystal decanter into a glass, and chugged half of it in one swig. The liquor burned, but Billy didn't care. He already felt better.

Soon he would cross the flybridge, go downstairs to one of the cabins and pass out face-first on the bed, only waking when the sun peeked through the porthole. But for now, Billy sprawled out on one of the couches, the cushions damp with sea spray.

He was so peaceful here. So utterly—

"What the hell are you doing here?"

Billy sat up but he did so too quickly and thought he was looking at the person in front of him through a kaleidoscope, four versions of them moving in sync with one another. It was only when he blinked that he realized he was looking right at only one person. His father.

LUCY

Olivia picks up on the first ring. "Hello?"

"Hi," I say, breathless as I bike away from Erica's house. Her voice is sweet, almost melodic in my earbuds. "Are you at home?"

Olivia pauses and for a moment, but then says, "Yeah. What's up?"

There's so much I could say: *I think your uncle might be dangerous. Where was he the night of Billy's death?* But there's only one question I can ask that will allow me to get to all of the other ones.

"Can I come over for a bit?"

"Really?"

"Yeah," I say, turning down French Moor Drive. "I'm around the corner."

"Okay," she says slowly. Olivia rattles off the code to get through their gate, and pretty soon, I'm on the Godwin property, the enormous brick house rising up from the earth with views of the water flanking either side.

I hop off my bike and walk it the rest of the way, but the path from the driveway to the pool house is longer than I remember, and I count my steps, focusing on putting one foot in front of the other to get there. I don't dare look back at the main house, where Mr. Godwin may be inside. When I reach the door, I raise my hand to knock, but it swings open before my fist makes contact.

"Hey!" Olivia says brightly. Instead of welcoming me inside, she steps out into the night and looks up. "I forgot how amazing the sky is here," she says tilting her head back. "I've barely looked up since I've been here. A tragedy, really."

"It is," I say, but I keep my focus on what I'm here for. Answers. Information. Nothing else. Except it's hard to focus. Olivia looks more relaxed than she has all summer, wearing a sleeveless top and jean shorts, and her long hair is wavy, falling down her shoulders. No makeup, no hair accessories, just a thin gold chain around her neck, and up close like this, I can see she's got a handful of freckles sprinkled on her shoulders.

"Wanna go to the beach?" she asks. "See if we can find a shooting star or something equally cringe?" Olivia grabs a blanket from an Adirondack chair.

"Perfect."

The night breeze makes my curls swirl around my face as we walk in silence down the narrow pathway. I kick off my sandals, my toes sinking into the sand. The Godwins' stretch of waterfront is wider than ours, with a dock jutting out from the land, a tender tied to one of the posts in the water.

Olivia lays out the blanket, and together we secure its corners with rocks and pieces of driftwood. It's a small square of fabric, and she drops down first, patting the space beside her even though it's tiny. My stomach leaps into my throat, but I stretch my body out next to hers, so close that our flanks touch, our bare thighs, the outsides of our knees all connected in one line.

I'm thinking about how to phrase what's in my head, how to say *Did your uncle kill his son?* But that's when she speaks.

"You can say what's on your mind, you know."

I glance sideways at her but decide to keep looking up at the sky. It's easier this way. "Do you have any idea who killed Billy?"

Olivia flutters her lips. "No," she says. "No clue."

"You don't have any theories? You were at that party. It sounded like things got intense."

She rolls to one side and tucks her elbow up under her arm. "I left before any of the fighting started. Didn't even see Justin wail on him. Didn't even know about Erica."

"You slept through all of that?" I ask.

She shakes her head. "Tossed and turned for a while, but basically."

"Huh," I say. "Can I ask you something that might sound terrible?"

"Now I'm interested."

"Do you think your uncle could have hurt Billy?"

"Uncle Reid?"

"Erica said he spends a lot of nights on that boat. Maybe he was there. Maybe something happened."

She wrinkles her nose. "I don't know," she says. "He was home that night. I couldn't sleep much after the party and saw him taking a walk around the property in the middle of the night. Guess he was wide-awake, too."

"He still could have been out there on the boat," I say. The police were never able to pin down an exact time of death because Billy's body had been so damaged by the water.

"Maybe, but he was in pajamas. He definitely didn't look like he had been on a boat." She shrugs. "Besides, he waved at me through the window. Smiled. Not something you'd do if you killed your kid."

"True," I say, hesitant. "I didn't realize you two were close."

"We're not. But my parents are dipshits right now. Gotta hang on to the family that's there for you."

I nod like I can relate, but there's no way in hell I would ever call my parents dipshits even when I'm at my most furious.

"You know, I'm thinking about going to Wesleyan in the fall," she says.

"Really?" I glance sideways at her. "You were able to figure out the tuition?"

"Yep," she says, sitting up with her knees tucked under her chin. The wind picks up a few strands of her hair that tickle my shoulder.

"What changed?"

She shakes her head so her hair falls in her face, obscuring her eyes. "It's messed up."

"What is?"

"Remember how I told you my grandparents set up trusts for Billy and me?" she says. "And how my parents drained mine?"

"Of course."

She pauses, sipping air through her barely parted lips. "There was a clause that said if something happened to one of us, the other would get their shares when they turned eighteen."

"Holy shit," I say, realizing what she's saying. "So you get Billy's? Because he's gone?"

Olivia winces. "It's fucked up, right? That I get to go to school because he's not here."

I don't know what to do with that information, because on the one hand, yes, it is messed up. He dies, and she gets what she wants. But it's not like that was Olivia's fault.

"Lots of things about this are fucked up, but you being able to get an education isn't one of them."

She tilts her head up to the sky, the corners of her mouth turning upward. "You think?"

"Yeah," I say. "I do. It's not like you set up the parameters of some random trust fund a million years ago."

She laughs. "That's true."

I turn so I can see Olivia's face in profile, the ski slope of her nose, the sharp bones of her shoulders, her cartoonish eyelashes lengthening up to the sky.

"What?" Olivia asks, a smile tugging at the corners of her mouth. "I can feel you looking at me."

"Sorry." I look down at my feet, bury my toes in the sand as heat spreads in my cheeks. "Ethan and I broke up."

"I know."

"You do?"

"I think everyone does."

"It happened like two days ago."

Olivia bursts out laughing, the skin around her eyes crinkling as she rests a hand on her chest. "No one keeps secrets here. You should know that."

"Nuh-uh. I didn't know about that stupid postcard for years."

I sneak a glance at her to see her head tilting straight up, but then she licks her lips and says, "Is that why? Because of the postcard?"

"No," I say. "Well. Yes . . . and no. It's complicated."

"Everything is."

We're both quiet, and for a moment I worry I've said too much, but then she speaks. "You can say it, you know. For real. We can stop tiptoeing around it."

My mouth is dry, and I force myself not to look at her, because if

I do, I might give in to the magnetic pull toward her. There's a force pushing through the surface of my chest, like it wants to elbow its way through my ribs. I wonder if this is an admission that she feels it, too. I could play dumb, but I don't want to do things like that anymore. I want to be honest and open and accept whatever feelings are tangled in my stomach—and then *act* on them. I'm sick of doing what I'm supposed to do, worrying about everyone else's feelings.

I only want to worry about mine.

But before I can speak, she lies back down and rolls over to one side so she's resting her head in her hand, propped up on her elbow. Her eyes are on me, traveling my body, but I force myself to stay still, to not make eye contact for fear of doing *something* without warning, for fear of my body—my want—taking over. Though maybe that's not a bad thing.

"I think I still have feelings for you." There's a hitch in her voice, a softening.

Slowly, I roll over to face her, and my breath catches when I see her front teeth resting on her bottom lip, a desperation in her eye as she looks right at me. Our noses are only a few centimeters apart, and I force myself not to move, to try to remember this moment and how my chest aches so acutely it might break open right here on this beach.

All the questions about Billy and Mr. Godwin slip out of my head like they were never there at all. The moment is weighty, heavy, and there's heat between my thighs I can't ignore.

"I think I do, too." The words come out fast and slippery, but once I see her eyes blink wide, I can't stop them. I don't want to. I want to tell her *everything*, lay myself bare, because for the first time all summer, I feel like I can trust her, like whatever I say in front of her will be the *right* thing.

"I never stopped wondering what happened to us." I press my lips together, the words hanging between us. "I loved Ethan. I did. I do . . . but you were a question mark." I shake my head. "I'm not saying it right. I don't even know *what* I'm saying."

Olivia's chest rises and falls, each breath bringing us closer, and her fingers reach for mine, hold them tightly. My limbs are made of live wires, like every touch is a spark, an explosion.

"Here we are," Olivia says. "Back on Pelican Island, back on the beach."

"Here we are," I say, repeating her words.

Olivia's eyes drop to my lips, and a thrill rumbles through my core. Heat blooms in my chest, at my very center. I want to taste her, to slide my fingers through her hair and feel how soft it is.

Together, we're quiet for a moment, taking each other in. I focus on the apples of her cheeks, the smooth expanse of her neck, the bare pink skin along her shoulders. Blood pulses in my stomach, my wrists, my need growing with every thump.

"I want to kiss you," I whisper, the words slipping out into the night.

Olivia raises her hand and places it on my cheek. Her fingers are cold, but I don't flinch. I want them to travel over me, and like she reads my mind, Olivia palms my neck, the top of my chest, where goose pimples rise under her touch. And still, I want more. I want her fingers to roam, to find the very center of me and press. I inch closer to her, moving my face toward hers, and finally, Olivia hovers her mouth above mine, and then we meet—a kiss, a flower, a rolling wave of seawater, salty and delicious and wholly new yet just as I remember. Kissing her is like finding my favorite T-shirt, hidden in my closet, like eating a warm bagel from the *good* place on Main, like diving into the ocean headfirst at the beginning of the summer. A familiar revelation. A wakened memory.

I rest my hand on Olivia's thigh, my fingers slipping under the fold of her shorts, grazing her skin, all of it so *much*, so unbelievable, so charged, that in that moment, I forget I've ever kissed anyone else before, that there are mouths that belong to other people, other bodies. All the desire that had come before was nothing compared to what I'm experiencing in this exact moment, and based on the way Olivia kisses me back—the hunger, the need, the tender little noises slipping between my lips—Olivia feels the same.

"Whoa," Olivia says, blinking open her eyes. There is nothing else to say. Only another kiss, another flame, another rolling wave that has nowhere to go but back to shore.

MILLIE

When I wake up in the morning, my back stiff from drifting off in the armchair, any ounce of confidence I had yesterday after my conversation with Ethan has evaporated and is replaced with a sense of dread.

I unfurl my limbs and stretch as I stand, cracking joints and shaking out my feet. Below me, I hear Lucy moving quick-footed in the kitchen. She stops, and I picture her sliding onto a seat at the counter, reaching for a banana, drinking a mug of coffee.

My reflection stares back at me in the mirror as I smooth down my hair and fit my lips around the words I need to say: *I'm sorry.*

When I get downstairs, Lucy is right where I thought she'd be, sitting at the counter, mug in hand.

"Lucy," I try.

Lucy whips her head around, and even though there's a smile on her face, it falls as soon as she sees me. "What?" she asks.

"We need to talk."

"Not really," she says. "We don't *need* to do anything."

"Lucy," I say. "Everything that happened was a mistake. I was an idiot, and I want to say I'm sorry."

"You *should* be sorry," she says, pointing her milk-covered spoon in my direction, splashing a stray Cheerio on the floor.

"I am. That's what I'm trying to say. I talked to Ethan and—"

"Oh, you talked to Ethan? Well, how nice. Isn't that lovely."

I blink, trying to stop the stinging in my eyes. "What I'm trying to tell you is that I wish it never happened. I was totally misguided, and I'll do anything for you to forgive me."

"I don't have to forgive you for anything," Lucy says. "You *kissed* Ethan, Millie."

Behind me, someone gasps, and I spin around, horrified to see that Frankie is standing right there, wearing her bunny-print pajamas, dark circles under her eyes. She's holding a mini whiteboard, the kind you might stick on a wall above a desk.

"Frankie," I say. "It's not . . ."

"Not what it sounds like?" Lucy asks. "Yes, it is. Millie kissed Ethan after we broke up. Didn't even give it twenty-four hours. Not even twenty-four *minutes*."

"It was a mistake! I don't know how else I can say this—I regret the whole thing. I thought I loved him. I thought he liked me back. I thought . . ."

"You thought *wrong*," Lucy says, "because you didn't think about how this would affect me. You only thought about yourself." She looks over my shoulder and lifts her chin. "Right, Frankie?"

Frankie's eyes pinball back and forth, like she's trying to decide which side might benefit her, which sister to back. But in an instant, she flips the whiteboard around, revealing a complicated web of names and places and little scribbles all connected to one another.

"What the hell is this?" Lucy asks. "Did you go all psycho meme on us?"

"Worse," Frankie says. "I think I solved Billy's murder."

THE PARTY

3:45 A.M.

"Me?" Billy managed. "What are you *doing here?" He blinked and saw his father clearly. He wore seafaring pajamas, a long-sleeve navy set with white piping. Utterly dorky, but Billy couldn't help but feel a rush of emotion because, he remembered, they now had something in common besides their DNA. Billy was about to join the ranks of fatherhood.*

"Your mother and I had a disagreement," he said, taking Billy's drink from him and downing it.

"Again?" Billy asked, leaning back against the pillows.

"I told her I didn't want Olivia here. After what her parents did . . ."

"What did they do?"

Billy's dad looked at him with reluctance, like he wasn't sure how to answer the question, but then he sat down next to Billy. "Your aunt and uncle have used us many times over the years."

Billy nodded, but he didn't understand. Olivia's parents were enigmas to him, and he didn't really care about figuring them out.

"Dropping her off like she's a dog. They think this plan in Switzerland is going to fix everything. Absolute idiots."

"What are you talking about?"

Billy's father waved his hand and then refocused on Billy. "Did you take the tender here?"

"Yeah."

"Stupid thing to do this late at night. You could have been killed."

"I needed to be here."

"What you need is to sober up. You're a man now, William. The world won't be as kind to you off this island." He paused, looking out at the water. "We've made you soft."

Billy pushed himself to sit. "That's not my fault."

His father grunted in response.

"Besides. I'm about to show you I can handle a lot more than you think."

"How's that?"

"Erica's pregnant." He couldn't help it. He smiled. The news filled him with a strange sense of pleasure. A little kid running around with his face, Erica's hair. Her spunky sense of adventure. She would come around. He knew she would. Billy looked to his father, expecting to see shock or maybe even joy, but all he saw was rage.

When he spoke, his voice was tight. "She's going to get rid of it, isn't she?"

"I hope not. Dad, this could be amazing. We could live—"

But before he could finish, he felt a sharp pop of pain at the back of his head, a rattling inside his brain, and a shock so deep, he froze.

"We did not raise you to become a teenage father."

"Did you just hit me?" Billy stood, backing away from his father.

His dad's hands were clasped behind his neck, and he was pacing now, shaking his head. "You have no idea what it's like to be tethered to someone you barely know. You will give up your freedom. Your life.

Your will. Just because you made a stupid fucking mistake when you were a kid."

Billy looked at his dad and saw a mix of pain and fury and, horrifically, recognition. Billy had always known his mother was twenty-two when she had him, a young mom. She prided herself on that, whispering that all of his friends' mothers looked ancient compared to her. His father was older by ten years, and the story went that they met because his maternal grandfather was Reid's boss at the real estate development firm. Billy assumed it had been love at first sight, that his grandfather groomed his father to take over the business, and it had all been kismet. Sure, his parents fought all the time. But there had to have been brighter days in the past.

What if, Billy wondered, there was a darker truth? What if he never knew his parents at all?

"You didn't want to be with Mom?" he asked.

Billy's dad didn't answer the question. Instead, he only replied, "I won't watch you ruin your life." Billy could sense the rest of that sentence lingering in the air. Like I did mine.

And suddenly, Billy was filled with his own simmering fury. He didn't ask to be born into this world. To come from two people who hated each other. To never know what it's like to live in a house with two adults who cooked together and had inside jokes. He wasn't like Ethan or Lucy, whose parents modeled sickeningly perfect relationships. He had been made different, and he was overwhelmed by the injustice of it. By anger at the people who caused it.

"Go to bed, William. We'll talk about it in the morning."

His father stood and started to walk away from him, his hand on the railing that led to the cabins below. But Billy wouldn't let him leave. Not now.

"Dad?" As his father turned around, a wave curled up under the boat, causing Billy to stumble forward, out of control of his limbs, and in a breathless moment, he found himself midair. The last thing he heard was the sound of his skull cracking against his father's, slicing through the night like a thunderbolt.

FRANKIE

I finally get all three of us into my room by telling Lucy that she doesn't even have to *look* at Millie if she doesn't want to, and while I can't believe Millie actually made out with Ethan, there is simply no time to dwell on that. Not when the answers are right *here*.

Once we're all inside, I shut the door and push my desk chair up under the doorknob.

"No one's going to come in here," Lucy says, annoyed.

"You think you know everything," Millie says under her breath.

"Shut it, you two. You can fight it out later." I lay my whiteboard on the bed and take a step back. It must look crazy to the two of them—all red lines and names and scribbled sentences—but to me, it makes perfect sense.

"You've gone full murder doc," Lucy says, which causes Millie to snort. Lucy shoots her a dirty look, and Millie covers her mouth with her hand. Getting them on the same page is going to be a nightmare.

"Okay," I say. "Here's my theory."

But before I start talking, Lucy murmurs, "I can hear you breathing. You're too close to me."

"I am not," Millie says, scooting farther away on the bed.

"You sound like a dying raccoon."

"You don't even know what that sounds like."

"It sounds like *you*."

"Guys," I say, tapping the whiteboard with the end of my marker. "Come on."

They stare at me for a beat until Lucy's phone buzzes. She glances down and the corners of her mouth turn upward into a smile.

"What?" I ask.

"Nothing," she says, and I roll my eyes.

"Can I please get back to my theory?" I ask. Millie leans back on her palms, her face blank, like she's positive I'm not going to say anything important. She'll see. I take a deep breath and turn back to the whiteboard. "So, we know Erica's pregnant. Right?"

Lucy folds her arms in front of her chest and cocks her head at me. "She's fine, by the way. Not that you asked."

"Obviously I'm worried about her," I say, even though Lucy's right. I've barely thought about Erica in all this, as shameful as that sounds. "But you said Billy and Erica got into a fight after she told him, right?"

"Yeah, but . . ."

"Hold on! Let me finish." I roll my shoulders back, gathering confidence for my big reveal. "I got to thinking that something might be on the boat that could help us figure out what happened, so I took the boys' kayak—"

"You went to the boat?" Lucy says, her voice a hiss. "Are you trying to get yourself killed?"

"It doesn't matter, because guess who was on the boat when I got there."

Lucy leans forward, suddenly interested. "Mr. Godwin?"

I drop my arms by my side. "What? How did you know that?"

"I had the same theory," Lucy says, tucking a curl behind her ear. "Erica and I wondered if he was on that boat, but I asked Olivia and she's positive that he didn't hurt Billy. Apparently, the cops were able to prove he was at home."

"You talked to Olivia about this?" I ask.

Lucy's cheeks flush, and she tilts her chin up, ignoring the question. "Anyway, clearly his version of being in the doghouse with Billy's mom is sleeping on the *Sea Witch*. So, what? He was there when you got there?"

"Well, you kind of stole my thunder, but yeah. He was." I take a deep breath, readying the words. "I overheard him talking to someone on the phone, and he said, 'If you'd let me sleep at home that night, he'd still be alive.'"

They're both quiet for a moment, the words settling in like I knew they would.

"That's . . ." Millie comes up blank, but Lucy stands and starts pacing around the room.

"What did he tell the cops?" Lucy asks.

"I don't know. I'm not an actual detective," I say.

"I think I'm going to be sick," Millie says.

Lucy shakes her head. "This doesn't make any sense."

"But it's the *truth*," I say. "Billy's dad killed him. I don't know how, but he did."

Lucy shakes her head. "Olivia said he didn't."

"So?" Millie asks.

She looks up at me, her jaw set. "Olivia wouldn't lie to me. Not now."

Millie glances at me so quickly I barely catch her eye. But when I do, I know we're both thinking the same thing: *Yes, she would.*

MILLIE

"What do we do now?" I keep my gaze on Frankie, who's pacing around the room.

"Nothing," Lucy says, exasperated. "We let the people in charge figure it out."

Frankie taps her chin with her finger then shakes her head once. "No."

"No?" Lucy's eyes narrow, her frustration obvious.

"No," Frankie says again. "Someone sent me that note, which means I was onto something. And if it's not Erica, then it's someone else."

"What note?" I lean forward, confused.

Frankie reaches into her pocket and pulls out a folded piece of paper, creased and soft. The words are stark against the white: *Stop looking, Frankie, or someone will get hurt.*

"I'm not about to be intimidated by some stupid anonymous threat." Frankie scoffs. "All this means is that someone *did* something, and I'm close to finding out. I'm not going to stop."

"Unbelievable." Lucy throws up her hands.

"She's right." My voice is small, but I clutch the paper in both hands, suddenly so aware that despite the fact that someone threatened Frankie, that can only mean one thing: There's a darkness out there, one that no one has uncovered. "We have to keep going."

"But—" Lucy sputters.

"Girls!" Mom's voice rings out from the first floor. "It's time for the tennis tournament." No one says anything for a beat, and Mom calls again. "Girls?"

"Coming!" we say in unison.

"This is actually perfect," Frankie says. "Everyone will be there." She turns to Lucy. "You can talk to Olivia again and see if she lied—"

"She didn't lie."

"And you," Frankie says, pointing to me, "can talk to Trevor. Maybe see if he has any idea who sent me this note."

"Okay." I nod slowly. "And what are you going to do?"

"Me? I'm going to try to sneak around and see if Mr. Godwin does anything suspicious."

"But what if he saw you on the boat?" I ask, fear pricking the back of my neck.

Frankie shakes her head. "I'll keep Alex with me. Besides, there will be a million people there. It's not like he can hurt me in broad daylight at the Club."

"Okay." I nod, determined. "So that's the plan, right? Are we all in?" I dare to look at Lucy, who has her arms crossed over her chest, her eyes narrowed in a glare.

"Are we?" Frankie asks.

Lucy doesn't look at either of us, but she springs to her feet and moves to the door. "Fine," she says. "I'm in."

LUCY

By the time we get to the Club for the tennis tournament, all I want to do is run in the opposite direction. "Come on, girls," Mom says. "Keep up and stay close." We follow her toward the tennis courts, where bleachers are set up along the perimeter so everyone can watch their neighbors try to cream each other in straight sets.

"Remember," Mom says as she adjusts her visor, "no going off alone, okay?"

"Yes, Mom," Frankie says, annoyed.

The last thing I want to do is stick around my family—especially *Millie*, who keeps looking at me with a mixture of puppy dog eyes and desperation. Part of me feels guilty for still having all of this anger, especially since I kissed Olivia, but I can't seem to let it go. Every time I look at her, I picture her with Ethan, whether it's fair or not. Anyway, it doesn't matter, since apparently I'm "tasked" with talking to Olivia, which is what I was going to do anyway.

I glance around the welcome area and spot Olivia hanging at the back edge of the circle talking to Erica. A buzzing swarms my chest, and as if she senses my gaze, Olivia lifts her eyes, and they meet mine. She lifts a hand and waves. The smile breaks out on my face easily, and I relax, taking a step forward but not before Frankie elbows me in the side.

"I thought you guys dropped out when you broke up?" she asks.

"What are you talking about?"

Frankie thrusts her finger forward at a piece of paper hanging on the bulletin board. At the top of the page, big print says *18–25 Mixed Doubles*.

"You and Ethan are on court three. Playing Dylan and his older sister."

"You've got to be kidding me." I spin around, looking for Ethan, and sure enough, he's jogging toward me, a resigned look on his face.

"Ah, man," he says, approaching. "Guess I forgot to take us off the bracket." He's wearing tennis whites, a sweatband cinched around his forehead.

"Oh yeah? Sure looks that way." I cross my arms over my chest, furious.

Ethan glances down at his getup. "I thought I was playing singles."

"Unbelievable." I start to storm away toward the clubhouse, desperate for Olivia not to see me like this, ugly and rotten.

"What's the big deal?" Ethan's trailing behind me now, his voice sharp at the edge. "I thought we were cool."

I've stomped so far that we're now away from the crowd, closer to the beach, and I spin around to see his stupid face. "Cool?" I ask. *"Cool?"* I shake my head, unable to find the words to tell him how deeply *not* cool we are.

"Well, yeah. I mean . . . I see the way you look at Olivia. Didn't take you long to move on." His mouth is pursed, like he's practiced that line over and over in the mirror, like he was waiting for a chance to deploy it.

"Me kissing Olivia is not the same as you kissing Millie."

"Oh my god, so you did it?" He presses his palms to the top of his head. "Once again. Lucy the hypocrite!"

I ball my hands into fists by my side. *Shit.* I did not mean to admit that to him now, but how can he not see that what he did is *so* much worse?

I shake my head and look up to the clouds, furious. "You kissed my *sister.*"

"And you kissed your ex, who you were probably hung up on the entire time we dated."

"No, I wasn't! I loved *you*, Ethan. And I always will in some way. But right now, I'm pissed as hell at you."

Ethan blinks, stunned, and the tips of his ears turn red. "I loved you, too," he says.

"That doesn't mean we can or should be together," I say. "You know that, right?"

Ethan wipes his arm across his face. The ire inside me softens but doesn't dissipate, and as I look at him, I realize I'm not mad at him. Not really. Because he didn't choose this. I did. And the person I'm really mad at is the person who could have avoided all of this pain, who could have told Ethan the truth earlier. I'm only mad at myself.

"I'm sorry," I say. "Maybe we both need some space. It was stupid to think we could be friends."

"Lucy," Ethan calls, but I turn on my heel and start walking as quickly as I can to the pergola around the side of the clubhouse, forcing myself to keep going, to not look back and see where he is or what he's doing. Everything swirling in my chest is a frustrating mix of contradictions. I don't want to be with Ethan. I *know* that. But the idea of him with Millie, of him with *anyone*, is more painful that I imagined.

Under a pergola covered in wisteria, I drop onto a bench and rest my forehead on my knees. My hands make fists, and I force myself to breathe in and out, to focus on the distant sound of waves crashing and tennis balls thwacking, which is why I don't hear the footsteps coming up behind me.

"Hey." I lift my head and see Olivia walking toward me in a tennis dress and sneakers, her smile wide. But when she sees my blotchy complexion, the tears in my eyes, her mouth falls and she sits down beside me, touching her fingers to my shoulder. "Are you okay?"

To my horror, I whimper, and Olivia wraps an arm around my back and pulls me to her. She smells of lilac and sunscreen, of summer.

"Gonna take that as a no," she says softly into my hair, which only causes me to cry harder. "Is this about Ethan?" she asks.

I nod, pressing my teeth into my bottom lip. "But," I start, "not because I want him back."

Olivia nods slowly. "It's okay to feel sad for something you don't want." She keeps her arm steady around me, running her fingers up and down my back.

"He kissed Millie. Or Millie kissed him. Or they kissed each other. I don't know. That's what's bothering me."

Olivia twists her face into a grimace. "Oof. That's kinda gross."

"It is, right?"

"Definitely." She pauses. "But is that all? A one-time kiss?"

"You're saying a one-time kiss doesn't mean anything?" I raise an eyebrow at her, and she lets out a laugh.

"Touché." Olivia leans back on her elbows and looks toward the water, the tiny waves rolling toward us. "I think it's normal to be freaked out. And that you still care for Ethan."

I open my mouth to protest, but she holds up her hand.

"Come on. Don't deny it. It's not a bad thing. That's how relationships are. They don't end abruptly, or start that way either. And our job as people who want to love, who want to feel that kind of tether toward another person, is to accept that the people we like aren't ours to keep or control or put in tiny boxes."

I take in her words, watching her mouth set into a straight line. It's not a smile nor a frown, just a neutral, placid look of understanding.

"When did you become a fortune cookie?" I ask.

"I'm just saying that nothing will take away the time you guys had together. Just like nothing will take away what *we* had." A small smile forms on her lips. "What we could have."

The edge of her arm grazes mine, and I lean into her, testing how close I can get before she pulls away. But she doesn't. She stays still.

"What are you saying?" I ask, my voice quiet.

Olivia reaches her fingers up to graze my cheek. "All I mean is if I do this," Olivia whispers, tilting her head slightly, so close I can feel her lips hovering in the space above mine, "it doesn't change anything about your past or mine. It can just be a kiss." She pauses.

The freedom in that statement is overwhelming. I don't know what I want from the future, from her, but I do know that it feels good to lean forward and close the space between us and press my mouth to hers so gently, she's a feather, a fine piece of linen, a slick of ice. I don't want to think about Ethan or Millie or anything else besides the rush of air and warmth filling my lungs. The promise that life is a steady drumbeat, moving me forward—only forward—and that every action does not need to symbolize some great betrayal, movement, change.

A kiss can just be a kiss.

And maybe that means I can learn to forgive Ethan and Millie.

MILLIE

We've been at the tennis tournament for nearly twenty minutes, and I still haven't approached Trevor, who's standing only a few feet in front of me, talking to some kids from our class. The courage I summoned at home has dissipated now that we're actually here, surrounded by all our friends and neighbors, people who clearly don't want to be thinking about Billy's death.

Mr. and Mrs. Godwin are here, sitting front-row center in the bleachers near the over-forty-five men's singles tournament, clapping politely with each point, nodding as people come talk to them, pay their respects. Part of me wonders if Mr. Godwin would *really* hurt his own son.

"Okay, so what you're going to do is this," Frankie says, sidling up next to me. She's got a box of popcorn and is munching loudly next to me near the back of the crowd. "Ask Trevor if he thinks Erica could have left me a threatening note. Play the pity-friend card. *We never hang out anymore.*" Frankie pouts and makes puppy dog eyes before flashing back to her normal self. "Works every time."

"You're ridiculous."

"And you're a wimp. Come on. We need to know if she left it."

"What are you going to do?" I ask, eyeing the Godwins.

Frankie flinches for a moment. "I'm thinking about it," she says slowly. "But you go first." She elbows me in the side, and I stumble forward, knocking into Trevor's shoulder.

He spins around and looks genuinely happy to see me. "Millie, hey."

"Hi," I say. "Do you . . ." I look back at Frankie, whose eyes are wide as she nods vigorously. "Can we take a walk?"

Trevor shrugs. "Sure. Let's go." He waves at the kids he's talking to, and we leave the crowd, heading toward the boardwalk.

"I feel like we haven't hung out one-on-one in a bajillion years," he says.

"Well, whose fault is that?" The words slip out, and I recognize a cruel tinge I can't take back.

"I've been busy," he says, bristling. "So have you."

"With Erica?"

Trevor turns to me slowly, his mouth parted. "Sure, but it wasn't like you were hanging around waiting for me to hit you up. You've been spending so much time with Ethan this summer. Must be nice, since you like him, right?" He must see the shock on my face, because he leans in, an admission on his lips. "C'mon, Mill. I've known you had feelings for him for a long, long time."

I tense all over, and for a moment, I can't breathe. Having your crush—your *love*—exposed to everyone in your life is like being gutted from the inside out, hung from a meat hook, and asking those around you to come bid on your flank, your ribs, your stomach.

"It's *fine*, Millie," Trevor says, waving a hand in front of his face. "I got over it."

"Over it?"

Hie eyebrows shoot up. "You didn't know?"

"Know what?"

Trevor's cheeks flush, and he brings one hand up to the back of his neck, rubbing quickly. "I thought you and I . . . I figured one day . . ."

"You liked *me*?" The idea is so shocking I stop walking.

"I mean, yeah. Of course."

"I had no idea."

One corner of Trevor's mouth lifts up. "That's okay. Erica showed interest, and I figured why not, you know? Lost a little hope here." He motions to the space between us.

"God, I'm an idiot." I squeeze my eyes closed.

"Nah," he said. "I get it. I'm used to being in Ethan's shadow. And it's okay. I'm over it. Really."

"If it makes you feel better, he and I never should have happened," I say. But when I say the words, I realize based on his confused expression that Trevor might not know what I mean.

"What are you talking about?"

If I'm going to ask him to be honest with me, then the first thing I have to do is be honest with him. "I kissed him. A few days ago. Right after the breakup."

"Holy shit."

"It was a total mistake."

"Uh, yeah. No shit. That's fucked up."

But right as he speaks, I realize that, actually, it *wasn't* a mistake to kiss Ethan. "I'm glad it happened, because if it didn't, I would still be wondering *what if.* Now it's like I've flushed him from my system. I can move on."

And what I don't say is this: I can finally figure out who I am, who I'm *going* to be, without the longing that's been lining my core for so many years, the wistful notion that one day, Ethan and I might find each other and have it mean something. Now that the dream doesn't exist, I can let myself look beyond the bounds of Pelican Island Road. Of our tiny slice of the world. It's like kissing him has set me free.

Trevor winces. "Still weird as hell." But then he softens. "You could have told me. We could have talked about it."

"Oh really?"

"Well, yeah. We tell each other everything."

"Trevor," I say. "That's not true."

"Fair."

"Are you okay?" I ask. "About Erica and Billy, I mean. This can't be easy for you. Were you mad when she told you?"

"She didn't tell me. Billy did, the night he died."

"He did?"

Trevor pauses, his shoulders tense around his ears. Then he suddenly backs away, his hands outstretched, waving back and forth. "I gotta go."

"Wait." My mind is moving quickly, trying to put the timeline in place. "When did Billy tell you? At the party? Later?" I'm desperate now, pleading, and I don't know why, if I even want to know the answer. "You can tell me. I'm your friend, Trevor."

"You haven't been my friend all summer, Millie," he says, his words suddenly acidic and clipped. "Not when I really could have used one."

"I'm sorry," I say, tears stinging behind my eyes. "I'm so sorry."

"It's too late," he says. "Things are already so broken. And with

Billy . . . He's not coming back." Trevor's voice breaks. "Sometimes I can't forgive myself even though I know we didn't . . . It wasn't. . . ."

Ice runs through my veins. "What are you saying, Trevor? What do you mean?"

Trevor wipes his hands over his face and shakes his head. "I've got to go." I reach for him, but he's already gone, turning the corner away from me.

I crouch down and try to catch my breath, but it feels like Trevor's knocked all the air out of my lungs, like he's holding my throat in a choke hold. Because as I replay Trevor's words in my head, I worry that what he's just said, what he just revealed, is that all along we were looking for answers in the wrong places. This whole time, the answer about what happened to Billy has been kept safe with Trevor.

THE PARTY

4:00 A.M.

Billy pressed his fingers to his temple, and when he brought them down, he saw blood, tiny specks coating his skin like paint. He looked up at his father and saw a gash right above his left eyebrow, small but visible.

"Jesus, Billy," his dad said, pressing his palm to his forehead. He stormed away and returned a few moments later with the first aid kit, pulling out alcohol swabs and Band-Aids. "Sit."

Billy did as instructed and let his father patch him up. "I'm sorry, Dad," Billy said.

His dad nodded once as he unfurled the bandage, tapping it lightly in place over Billy's cut. "I know," he said.

They were quiet for a moment, the water rippling below them.

His father looked down at the tender tied to the ladder. "Let's go back, okay? We can figure this out on dry land tomorrow."

Billy looked up at the stars. The last place he wanted to be was home, where the reality of what was happening would actually set in, where tomorrow would bring stern talking-tos and tears from his mother, a conversation with Erica's parents. No. Billy wanted one more night of peace, one more night of pretending that everything would be as it was in his mind. "Can I stay here tonight?" he asked, looking up at the stars.

Billy's dad pursed his lips but then sighed. "Okay," he said, glancing at his watch. "It's almost morning, and I have a call with London soon. I'll have Olivia come pick you up in the tender at dawn, okay?"

"You don't want to stay here, too?"

His dad shook his head. "My alarm's going off in an hour anyway."

They both stood, and Billy's dad paused for a moment, looking at his son. There was so much unsaid between them. No I love you. *No* I'm proud of you. *But Billy's dad rested a hand on his shoulder and patted him once. "It will work out."*

Billy's mouth dropped open. It was the closest his father had ever come to comfort, to outward emotion, and Billy wanted to savor the moment. He was quiet as he watched his dad drive the tender back toward shore and suddenly, he realized he was all alone.

Billy stretched his neck up to the sky, looking for the Big Dipper. He and Ethan learned about the constellations when they were kids, and he liked to think they could chart the sea just by looking up. Not that he ever tried.

But once Billy started thinking about Ethan, he couldn't help but let his mind wander to Trevor. That dumb kid who was screwing Erica in the dunes behind his house. How was that okay? How was that right? Billy wanted to set that kid straight, especially now that there was going to be a baby in the picture.

He reached for his phone and was pleased to see it still had battery. His fingers moved clumsily over the screen, but he got his text out through that disappearing message app they all used. Get your ass to the Sea Witch, *he wrote.* We need to talk.

Billy tossed his phone back onto the couch. He wasn't sure if the kid would show, how he'd get here, anyway. But he had to do it. Had to prove to Trevor that he was tough. That Erica would choose him in the end.

Billy closed his eyes, rocked gently with the water. It was so calm here. Now he was having second thoughts. Did he really want to deal with Trevor tonight? He was suddenly so, so tired.

He didn't know how long he slept, could barely keep track of time, but he was woken up by the sound of water churning, the dipping of paddles as they pushed through water.

"Hello?" Billy called, his voice hoarse. But no one answered. He pushed himself to sit up and swiveled to face the ladder. Damn. The kid came.

Trevor was climbing aboard, just like Billy suspected, but behind him, Billy was surprised to see another face, someone who had betrayed Billy by not telling him the truth. Someone Billy didn't want to see at all: Ethan.

FRANKIE

"Yo, Earth to Frankie?" Alex waves his hand in front of my face, wiggling his eyebrows until I blink and focus on him.

"Sorry, what did you say?"

"I *said*, how pissed do you think Ethan's going to be now that Lucy pulled out of the tournament?"

I glance around the bleachers and see Ethan sitting next to Dylan, holding a sno-cone. "Uh, it's probably fine. Bigger fish to fry."

"What does that mean?"

"Look. I know you didn't want to be involved in my little investigation or whatever, but . . ."

"But what?"

I pause, pursing my lips. "We have this theory that Mr. Godwin did it."

Alex tenses beside me and leans in. "Frankie, we've been through this. It's not your job to solve a murder."

"I know," I say, "but what if he's dangerous and no one knows?"

Alex stands quickly. "I'm gonna get a hot dog. Do you want anything?"

I snap my attention to Alex, and can't help but feel like he's hiding something. "You always run away when I ask you stuff like this. Can you just wait a sec?"

"Stop looking, Frankie," Alex says. "Or someone will get hurt."

Alex walks away quickly, and as he hurries, the words replay in my mind. The same words written in blocky letters on that piece of paper. The note that was left beside me while I slept in the backyard. I clench my fists by my side. Alex was right behind the hedge that day, right where I left him after we fought in the pool.

What if . . .

"Frankie!"

I spin around and see Millie rushing up from the boardwalk, her eyes wild as she looks all around her. I get up from my seat and push through the bleachers, stepping over handbags and soda cans until I finally break free into the aisle and bolt down onto the grass.

"Are you okay?" I ask, but Millie barely seems to register my presence. "What did Trevor say? Did he say Erica wrote the note?" *Please*, I plead. *Please let it be Erica.*

Millie spins around to me. "We can't talk here. Come on." She grabs my hand and pulls me to the parking lot, away from everyone, from the din of the party and the thwacking of tennis balls. When we're finally alone, she stops and turns to me, her cheeks flushed.

"I think Trevor may have done something to Billy."

"What? Why?" I glance back to Alex, standing at the snack hut, my heart beating fast inside my chest.

Millie tells me everything Trevor just revealed, staring at me with her eyes wide, curls springing from the crown of her head, and finally, when she's done speaking, her brows narrow, and she nods once. "Find Lucy. Get Alex. We all need to meet at their pool house. Now."

Millie walks off to the car, leaving me alone. I know she's right. We need to get them all in one place and ask them the questions we've been avoiding all summer. Well, *avoiding* isn't the right word. It's just that we never thought we had to ask them. Never thought they would have the answers.

I dash off a text to Lucy—meet at your car. NOW—and as I walk back to Alex, my stomach flips.

"Guess what," Alex says, bounding over to me, back to his usual cheerful self.

"What?" I eye his face, the same face I've known my entire life. The one that has always been on my side. But those words. That note. It's like everything clicks inside my brain, and I know, all of a sudden, that he wrote it.

"Rishi's down to get ice cream tomorrow."

"Wow," I say, picking my words carefully. He can't know I suspect him. "Hey, do you think you, Ethan, and Trevor can meet us at the pool house? Now?"

Alex cocks his head. "Why?"

"Because . . ." I don't know how to finish the sentence. But there's a thrumming in my heart, and I pull at a truth, something Millie would say. "The six of us haven't been together all week. We skipped cards after Shabbat last Friday, and this tournament's boring as hell. Ethan already won his match, and . . . I think Trevor's pissed at Millie, but maybe you can work some magic? Get everyone there?"

"I don't know, Frankie."

"Alex," I say, gripping his hands. "Please. For me."

He hesitates, glancing at Ethan standing by the sidelines watching a match, his cheeks damp with sweat. "I'll see what I can do."

I grab him in a quick hug and he holds me tight, too, like we know it means something, like there's a whole conversation happening between us.

And for a moment, I get why Millie was so choked up in the beginning of the summer, how she couldn't bear that our lives might no longer look the same when it came time for Ethan and Lucy to leave. Now that so much has happened, all I want is for the six of us to be together like we were in June, for us all to know where we stand with one another, for our secrets to be spilled before us. After knowing each other our entire lives, it's the least we can do.

I rush to the parking lot and hop in the passenger seat of Lucy's car, while Millie climbs in the back. "They'll meet us there," I say, and Lucy starts the engine. We drive the rest of the way in silence.

Sure enough, a few moments after we pull into the Silvers' driveway, Ethan parks next to Lucy, and the boys spill out of his car. Trevor's shoulders are slumped, and he won't make eye contact with anyone as he shuffles forward, and Alex brings up the rear. In silence, we walk around the side of Four Pelican Island Road and file into the pool house, one by one, until Ethan shuts the door behind me.

No one offers to get snacks from the pantry or cans of seltzer from the refrigerator. No one even sits down, and instead we sneak looks at one another, us girls on one side of the room, the boys on the other. No one wants to say the first word, to draw the first sword. But this is my investigation. Right when I'm about to take charge, it's Trevor who takes the first swing.

"If you're going to accuse us of something, do it," Trevor says.

"I'm not accusing you of anything," Millie says.

Alex's face gets pale, and for a moment, I wonder if he's going to be sick.

"Everyone has kept secrets this summer," I say, looking from one face to the next, stopping on the space between Trevor and Ethan. "Millie, you kissed Ethan. Lucy, you got into Penn. I learned about Trevor and Erica." Trevor shakes his head quickly like he's trying to get rid of a memory. "But you three have been keeping secrets, too. Haven't you?"

Millie and Lucy move closer behind me, almost like they're soldiers by my side, and I'm emboldened by their support.

"No one here hurt Billy, okay? That's not what happened." Ethan moves in front of his brother. "It wasn't only Trevor on that boat—"

But Trevor cuts him off. "Stop it, Ethan."

Millie's face scrunches in frustration. "You were there? Trevor, what happened?"

"We didn't *do* anything!" Trevor calls. "None of this was our fault. None of it."

"Then be honest," Lucy says, her voice harsh.

The air inside the pool house shifts as the boys look at one another, a silent conversation in motion, until finally Ethan speaks, as if for the group. "Fine," he says. "I'll tell you what happened. And you'll realize we're telling the truth."

THE PARTY

4:30 A.M.

"I wasn't going to let him come alone in the middle of the night," Ethan said, stepping closer. "You wanted to talk to him, so here I am."

Billy shook his head. "Unbelievable."

"Why am I here?" Trevor asked.

"I want you to stay away from Erica," Billy said, trying to keep his voice firm.

"That's really not up to you."

"I get a say!" Billy said. He was screaming now. He couldn't help it. "If she's going to be the mother of my child, I get a fucking say."

"What?" Trevor said, stepping closer.

"Billy . . ." Ethan started. "What are you talking about?"

"She's pregnant, and it's mine, and we're going to have a life together. You're just a placeholder. You're nothing."

"Dude, calm down," Ethan said. "I don't think that we should—"

Trevor threw a thumb over his shoulder, pointing toward the water. "We're leaving."

"Fine!" Billy called. "Get out of here! Just know that tomorrow, Erica is going to come running back to me."

Trevor was shaking as he climbed over the edge of the boat, and Billy was pleased. He should be shaking. He should be terrified.

"This couldn't have waited until morning?" Ethan asked.

Billy stared at his best friend. It was so obvious he had known about Trevor and Erica and hadn't told him, had kept his brother's secret. If he was ever going to draw a line in the sand and say I choose you, *he'd done it now, and he'd picked his brother. Billy should have known. Though they had been loyal to each other their entire lives, it wasn't like that loyalty had ever been tested. Not like this. But now that it had been, Billy would never trust him again.*

"Get out of here," Billy said. "Just go."

"I'm pissed as hell at you right now, but I'm not a monster. Do you want a ride home? It's almost morning," Ethan asked.

Billy gave him the middle finger. "Fuck you. Olivia's going to pick me up."

Ethan paused but then headed over the ladder, following his brother. Billy shuffled to the side of the boat and was surprised to see at the base of the ladder, bobbing in the water, the Silver boys' kayak. Trevor sat with his back hunched over, and Ethan scooted in beside him. But there was also a third person. Someone whose hood stayed up, whose face turned away. Without saying a word, the three of them dipped their paddles into the water and started inching away from the boat.

"That's right. Leave!"

They heard him. Billy knew *they heard him, but they didn't stop. Didn't turn around.*

"All you Silvers are assholes!" Billy called, leaning further over the ladder until . . .

All of a sudden, the water that was once beneath him was now above him, and all he could see was the blackness of the Sound before he crashed right into it, water filling his ears, his lungs, his throat.

Billy pushed to the surface, gasping for air, flailing around as he looked for the Silver boys on that stupid rinky-dink kayak. He saw them, so close, but none of them turned around, and in the distance, the boys got smaller and smaller, farther away.

After all this, *he had fallen into the Sound. How dumb was he? Billy started breaststroking to the ladder. He was an excellent swimmer, and the only reason why he wasn't a lifeguard was because he refused to take a drug test. But why wasn't the ladder getting closer? Suddenly, his mouth was full of salt water, and he gurgled, spitting it out just in time to get another mouthful.*

The current was strong, and Billy was exhausted all the way down to his bones. The water was freezing and salty, like a shock to his system every time he swallowed a gulp. And he was swallowing many, many gulps. Soon he felt like he was drinking the sea, like if only he could reach the bottom of the glass, he would be able to stand up straight in the dirt, in the sand, and scream at the top of his lungs that he had won. He had beat the Sound. Who else could say that?!

Except Billy could not drink the sea.

He could not reach the bottom of the glass.

He would not stand up on dry land and scream or claim victory.

Instead, he was going. And then he was gone.

MILLIE

"So, you left him there," Frankie says, her mouth open. "You left him in the water, and he drowned?"

Ethan slumps down on the couch like he's exhausted from telling the story. "No! That's not what happened. I swear. We didn't . . ."

"Who was the third person in the kayak?" Frankie asks, cutting him off, though we all know the answer. Everyone's gaze flits to Alex, who's been pacing behind the couches this whole time. "Alex," she says. "It was you?"

I press the heel of my palm to my forehead. "I feel like I'm going to be sick," I say, but no one's listening to me. They're all zeroed in on Alex, who has stopped moving and is now looking around the room like he's trying to find an escape hatch.

"Say it." I surprise myself with how loud my voice is, how furious I am at all of them for keeping something like this from us, for doing it in the first place. "If we're really free of secrets, if we really want to tell each other everything, we need to know every single detail."

"Damn, Millie," Frankie says, almost impressed, then turns back to Alex, pain on her face, like every word she says is excruciating. "But she's right. We need to know. *I* need to know."

"I was there," Alex says, his voice a whisper. "But we didn't leave him for dead." His voice is panicked now, rising. "I hated Billy for what he did to me, but I swear. We didn't. That's not what happened."

"He jumped," Trevor said. "I know he did. I heard a splash, and I turned around, and Alex swore he saw him jump, too. Right?"

Alex nods. "It looked like he cannonballed in, and he was right next to the ladder. I thought he would climb back up and be fine. We've all jumped into that water a million times."

"But he didn't," I say. "He drowned. He had scrapes and bruises all over his body." I turn to Ethan. "You think he jumped?"

Ethan covers his face with his hands, and when he speaks, his words are muffled. "That's what it looked like to us." He looks up, his cheeks stained with tears. "I swear."

"Then why didn't you tell anyone?" Frankie asks, disbelief in her voice.

"I did!" Ethan said. "I told your dad."

"What?" I ask, my voice high.

"After the police questioned us. I told your dad what we saw, and he told me not to say anything. He said that if I did, they might charge us with involuntary manslaughter for not going after him."

My mouth drops open, a mix of fear and disgust swirling in my brain.

"We were terrified," Alex says. "What if Hampton didn't believe us and thought we pushed him? What if she found out about the catfishing and determined I had motive? We *all* had motive!"

"Is that why you wrote me that note?" Frankie says, her voice small. "It was you, wasn't it, Alex?"

Alex drops his head but mumbles a yes. "I just wanted you to stop looking."

"We thought that he would climb back up, and we'd talk about everything in the morning," Ethan says. "But when I saw him out in the water, tried to save him . . ." He swallows, his face pale. "I didn't want any of us to get in trouble. I'm supposed to keep them safe. I'm supposed to protect them." Ethan's voice cracks on the final word before he breaks down, sobs coming out of his throat like eruptions from a volcano.

For a moment, all of us are quiet, listening to Ethan wail. All of it's a shock, a moment of overwhelm, and sheer terror rushes through my body.

These boys may not have killed Billy with their bare hands. May not have held his head underwater. But they left him there to die. Each of their actions led to this moment, and all summer, they let everyone on Pelican Island believe a killer was roaming free, lying in wait, looking to strike again.

The weight of the realization is staggering.

I glance at Lucy, who hasn't said a single thing since we got here, who listened as they spoke and didn't nod her head or say a word. Only stood there with a blank expression.

My hands shake at my sides, and I lick my lips, looking at Lucy. *We need to leave.*

She says nothing, only spins around and walks right out the door.

LUCY

I can barely remember the bike ride over to French Moor Drive or how I found myself heading through the Godwins' gate. All I know is that I couldn't be around those boys, couldn't stand to look at them after what they'd said.

But it's not for the reasons they might think. It's not only because they didn't save Billy when they could have. It's because I couldn't ignore one tiny detail in their story—that Olivia was supposed to come back for Billy.

My brain is foggy, like I can't form complete thoughts as I pedal through the backyard to Olivia's pool house. I stop and stagger off my bike, knocking on the door.

"Olivia," I call. "It's me, Lucy." A figure moves inside, and the din of a television squawks in the background. In a moment the door opens and Olivia's leaning against it in a white tank top and jean cutoff shorts, her blond hair spilling over her shoulders. "Hey," she says, smiling, but in an instant, her face falls, and she stands up straighter. "Are you okay?"

I don't know how to answer that question other than by stepping inside the pool house and pressing my lips to Olivia's. All I want to do is remember this feeling once more, feel the warmth of her body close to mine, a reminder that this felt good and right, even if I'm about to blow it all up.

A deep well of desire fills my stomach, but Olivia steps away and folds her bottom lip inside her mouth. "Wow," she says. "As much as I want that right now, I feel like something's going on?"

"Billy . . ." I start, trying to find the words. But how do you accuse someone of something so ghastly? How do you ask the simple question *Where were you*?

Olivia sits down next to me on the couch, holding my hand in hers. "What about him?"

"Did they ever release a cause of death?" I ask.

Olivia wrinkles her nose. "Actually," she says, leaning down to retrieve her laptop from under the couch. "Hampton just sent us the autopsy report."

"Really?"

Olivia nods. "They're going to share it with the press tomorrow," she says, tapping open her email. She pulls up a file, scooching over so I can see it. "Drowning," she says, pointing to a line on the document that says as much. Then she scrolls to another document with the word *Toxicology* in big letters at the top. "He had Xanax and amphetamines in his system," she says. "They're calling it an accident."

"An accident," I repeat.

"That's what Hampton said." Olivia sets the computer down. "Can you believe that? After a freaking manhunt all summer, they're declaring it an accident. He must have fallen overboard and been too messed up to get himself back on the boat. Uncle Reid and Aunt Sally are devastated. I think in some ways it's easier to think your son was murdered by someone else than to think he did this to himself."

"Wow." My throat is sandy, and I think of the Silver boys, of what they did and *didn't* do, if they would be held liable for their inaction.

"They're going to close the case tomorrow," Olivia says. "That's it."

"And all those wounds?"

"From his fight with Justin, I guess." She shakes her head. "It's awful," Olivia says, running a hand through her hair. Then she stops and looks at me, her fingers still pushing through her waves. "I was supposed to get him."

"What?" I lean in toward her, my chest pounding. *She's going to tell me.*

"Uncle Reid asked me to take the tender out and pick him up once it was light out."

"And you did?"

"Yep. I was already awake, so I went out around five. Climbed aboard the *Sea Witch* looking for him and everything. But he wasn't there. I figured someone else picked him up. Or . . . I don't know. I never assumed *this*." She rests a hand on her heart. "I feel like I could have saved him if I'd gone earlier."

"How could you have known?" I place a hand on her shoulder, ashamed that there's a bubble of relief expanding in my chest. Olivia had nothing to do with this. She was only trying to help.

"I told Hampton, but she told me to keep quiet during the investigation while they ruled everything out. Otherwise, I would have mentioned it sooner." Olivia sighs. "Anyway, can I get you some water or something? You look like you're going to faint."

"An Advil would be amazing. I feel like I'm about to get a serious headache."

"Coming right up." Olivia scoots down the hallway to her bedroom.

I lean forward and rest my head in my hands, looking down at the mirrored coffee table in the middle of the room. In it, I can see my reflection—my pink lips, now puffy, and my hair, all frizzy and out of place. I hadn't worn makeup today, and for the first time, I realize that I look so different than I did only a few weeks ago, when I was preparing to graduate, when I was still with Ethan, when our futures were planned together.

So much has changed since then, and while I don't want it any other way, my reflection shocks me. I didn't expect to look so changed, so free, and it makes me wonder if the shift I've gone through inside my body and brain is noticeable to those around me. Because despite what had happened, I've never felt more like myself than I do in this exact moment. I've never been more certain of myself, of what I want, *who* I want, and that feeling is intoxicating.

"Hold on," Olivia says from the bedroom, her voice muffled. "I know I have some here somewhere."

"All good." I shift my gaze to Olivia's laptop, still open beside me. Billy's files from the detective are bright on her screen, and I pick up the computer, studying the documents. Right there on the paper—*drowning, Xanax, amphetamines.*

Maybe the boys couldn't have helped him. Maybe by the time they reached him, he would have already been gone. The truth I have to believe is this: Billy did it to himself.

A notification blinks in the top right corner of the screen, and before I can think better of it, I tap it open, revealing an email from someone named Elora Tanner, Esq. I try not to read it. Really, I do. But my eyes scan the screen and there's nothing I can do to stop myself.

Dear Olivia,

After much back-and-forth, William Godwin's trust has been transferred into your name. Thank you for your patience. None of us expected Sally and Reid to push back on the clause, but we are pleased for you to move forward without litigation.

I glance up at the hallway and see Olivia's still ducked inside her bedroom, humming, totally unaware of what I've found.

I scroll down and see more details dated from the past month—logistics about the trust, when she can access funds—until I get to a message dated a week after Billy died, when Olivia's parents wrote:

We hate to bring this up, but is there a timeline in place for William's funds to be transferred into Olivia's name?

Sally had responded only three minutes later:

I cannot believe you are asking such a crass question right now. Our lawyer will be in touch.

Something grips my stomach—a prickle of suspicion, of doubt—and I type the lawyer's name into Olivia's email, searching for old messages. One pops up from months before and I tap it, my eyes moving over the screen furtively.

From: Elora Tanner, Esq.
To: Olivia Godwin

Dear Olivia,

In answer to your question: Now that you are both eighteen, if something were to happen to your cousin William, your grandfather stated that his trust would be transferred to you. And if something happened to you, your trust would be transferred to him. Please let me know if you need additional counsel.

"Ah, found it!" Olivia calls.

I slam the laptop shut and sit back, suddenly aware of every hair on the back of my neck.

"Here we go." Olivia plops down beside me on the couch. She opens up her fist containing two white pills. "Take them." I glance down at them, then back at her, smiling and encouraging. "Go on."

I take the pills from her palm, and when I speak next, I choose my words carefully. "Did you know that Billy's trust would go to you? If he died?"

"No," Olivia says. "It was a total surprise."

A lie.

"Crazy, right?"

"Crazy," I echo.

"You know what?" I say, standing. "I feel okay, actually. I'm gonna head home."

"You sure?"

"Mm-hmm. It's been a day."

"Do you want to hang out tomorrow after work?"

I pause, taking in Olivia's striking face, her high cheekbones and her freckled shoulders. It would be so easy to say yes and spend the rest of the summer burying myself in my desire, in possibilities. But the answer is obvious. "I think I need to be on my own for a while," I say. "But I'll see you at the office?"

Olivia's mouth drops open, but I don't stay to look at her.

I don't want to know if she planned all this months ago. I don't want to know if those emails have meaning, or if she simply needed an answer to a question. I'm not Frankie, and I don't want to know if Billy's accident was a murder after all. Maybe I can convince myself that no one is responsible for his death except the boat, the current, the power of the Sound.

Maybe it *was* all an accident. Maybe that's the truth that matters most.

I walk out the door and hop on my bike, every pedal taking me farther away from her, from French Moor Drive, and closer to home, to the house full of the people who look at me like I make them whole. *My* people.

THE PARTY

5:00 A.M.

"Billy? Billy, where are you? Your dad's going to kill me." Olivia's voice was loud and clear, a siren in the night as she puttered closer and closer on the tender. Billy gasped for air as he smacked at the water around him, trying to breathe. He had no concept of time. Couldn't possibly tell how long he had been treading, how long he had been drowning. His limbs were numb, like they were disconnected from his body, and his teeth were chattering so loud, he thought the entire island could hear him. But still, he found a way to raise his hand, to wave his fingers, to be his own white flag, desperate for help.

"Hello!" Olivia climbed aboard the Sea Witch, *was stomping around all mad. Billy could see her, though she looked like a doll, so far away at the mercy of the sea. It was light out now, the sun coming up over the horizon. Was it possible she didn't see his arm waving?*

Olivia headed downstairs to the cabins. She'd come upstairs soon, walk around a little bit, and realize he wasn't there, that he needed help and was in the FUCKING WATER. Wouldn't she?

A moment later, Olivia popped back up on the deck, shaking her head. "You know I inherit your trust if you die!" Olivia called jokingly. She clucked her tongue and climbed back down on the ladder, hopping into the tender.

Surely, she would see him now. Except . . .

Except Billy was farther away than he thought. Already drifting, a speck in the sea. Why the hell had his parents thought to moor here *and not closer to other boats, where he could have grabbed onto their tow lines? Their buoys?*

"I'm leaving," Olivia said, her voice crystal clear. "Last chance." She revved the engine, took one last look around.

"Liv!" Billy called as loudly as he could, desperate, a plea, a prayer.

Olivia cocked her head like she heard something, and turned toward him. But then she waved her hand in the air as if annoyed and headed home.

Six weeks later

After Detective Hampton officially declared that Billy died from accidental drowning aided by a pretty hefty dose of Xanax and amphetamines, it only took a few days before the report was published online. Hampton found that the kinds of wounds Billy sustained weren't enough to knock him unconscious once he fell in the water, that everything that transpired beforehand had amounted to a standard number of cuts and bruises that come with getting beat up by one of your buddies, by knocking heads with your father by accident.

That didn't stop the Pelican Island Police Department from going after Justin for assaulting an officer, for putting him under house arrest while his lawyer works out a plea deal. Or the Godwins from searching far and wide for someone to blame for their child's death. Or Mr. Gold from keeping the Silver boys' secret. From never telling his wife nor his daughters, even though the girls knew every detail.

It was Lucy who urged her sisters to stop focusing on *them*—the world outside their home—and to focus on repairing *us*, the three girls who had the same chins, the same curls, the same piercing eyes.

It was Lucy who asked, on the final Friday night of the summer, if they could watch the stars blink above, just the three of them, huddled under one blanket after Shabbat dinner. And it was Millie who realized then that her sister had forgiven her for kissing Ethan.

Together, they pulled the fabric over their knees and looked up at the dark, inky sky. It was one of those perfect cool summer nights where the breeze from the ocean can make your heart beat faster, feel more powerful, and the smell of briny shellfish and long-burning charcoal lingers in the air.

Millie didn't even miss the cards. Nor the boys next door. Though they hadn't played games with them in weeks, not since they had learned what happened.

This Friday night, Frankie was the one to rest her head on her knees and study her sisters, try to remember tiny details she could stash away like hidden candy. The way Millie's mouth puckered when she thought really hard. The well-drawn arc of Lucy's eyeliner. The softness of their hands as they tickled her back. She was the baby, after all, and tonight she wanted to embrace that. To remember what it felt like to know that your sisters would keep you safe.

Lucy glanced back at the archway that connected their backyard to the Silvers'. There was no movement, no hint of life. Perhaps the boys were together, in the pool house or on their own stretch of sand, but Lucy didn't mind not knowing. It was better this way.

For eighteen years, their families had been intertwined, and with that closeness came secrets that unfurled like leaves on a bird-of-paradise, inviting the girls to take a peek at what the boys had been hiding. Since that night in the pool house, all the secrets had been put on display, and the girls stepped back from them, marveled at them, let them go. They said they would move on. But that didn't mean they could forgive. Only that they welcomed the future because they could not reshape the past.

"I think we need a toast," Lucy said. Her voice broke, and Millie noticed with satisfaction that she had grown more sentimental as her departure for Penn inched closer. Lucy popped a small bottle of champagne, the liquid spilling onto the sand.

"What are we celebrating?" Frankie asked, her eyes greedy as she reached for the bottle.

The tall seagrass swayed in the night, the rustling another reminder that summer was coming to a close. Soon there would be no more thwacking of tennis balls against the courts at the Club, no seagulls fighting for hot dog buns under the jagged rocks. No more melting ice cream from Scoop DeVille.

But even after the leaves changed color and the temperatures dropped and the birds flew south for winter, the three Gold girls would have this: the comfort of what it felt like to sit limb-to-limb with the people who *knew* you, who shared your flesh and blood and even after a summer of secrets would still say, *I choose you. I love you.*

"Us," Millie said. "We're celebrating us."

ACKNOWLEDGMENTS

Thank you to Alyssa Reuben for everything. Always. Forever! An agent who can move mountains, you are my north star in this industry.

Thank you endlessly to Rūta Rimas and Simone Roberts-Payne, two editors without whom I could not have written this book or found these sisters' voices. I am so lucky to work with you.

Elyse Marshall, six books in and I still smile when I see your name in my inbox. You are the publicist of my dreams.

Thank you to Jordy Moses and Theresa Evangelista, who designed this beautiful cover, an image that makes me swoon.

There is no better team than the one at Penguin Young Readers and Putnam Young Readers, led by the indomitable Jen Loja and Jen Klonsky. Thank you to the folks who work tirelessly behind the scenes when it comes to production, distribution, marketing, and everything in between: Rebecca Aidlin, Sola Akinlana, Katie Bircher, Jaleesa Davis, Alex Garber, Natalie Melius, Astrid Rojas, Shannon Spann, Marinda Valenti, Felicity Vallence, and the entire sales team.

Sanjana Seelam and Olivia Burgher, thank you for continuing to bring my work to wider audiences and for always supporting my wild, wild what-ifs. James Munro, thank you for championing my YA novels abroad.

The assistants at WME are workhorses, cheerleaders, and excellent at their jobs. Liza Mullett, this counts double for you.

To the readers and booksellers who continue to pick up and shout about my books, thank you for sticking around and coming along for another ride. I hope you enjoy this one.

I gain so much strength and support from my adoring and devoted family: Mom, Dad, Halley, Ben, Luke, Charlotte, and James.

And to Maxwell, what a year. What a life. I love you madly.

BE SURE TO READ ALL OF JESSICA GOODMAN'S PAGE-TURNING THRILLERS!

"Seductive and slick."

—JESSICA KNOLL, *NEW YORK TIMES* BESTSELLING AUTHOR

"Completely consuming."

—MEGAN MIRANDA, *NEW YORK TIMES* BESTSELLING AUTHOR

"Goodman is a YA thriller genius."

—JORDYN TAYLOR, AWARD-WINNING AUTHOR

"An incisive and exciting must-read author."

—COURTNEY SUMMERS, *NEW YORK TIMES* BESTSELLING AUTHOR

"Nervy, intense, and expertly crafted."

—KATHLEEN GLASGOW, *NEW YORK TIMES* BESTSELLING AUTHOR

"Razor-sharp."

—TIFFANY D. JACKSON, *NEW YORK TIMES* BESTSELLING AUTHOR

"Unputdownable."

—DIANA URBAN, BESTSELLING AUTHOR

"Jessica Goodman keeps getting better with every book."

—KARA THOMAS, AUTHOR OF *THE CHEERLEADERS*

"Smart and twisty."

—JOELLE WELLINGTON, AUTHOR OF *THEIR VICIOUS GAMES*

"An absolute thrill ride."

—NATALIE D. RICHARDS, *NEW YORK TIMES* BESTSELLING AUTHOR

"Utterly impossible to put down."

—SLOAN HARLOW, *NEW YORK TIMES* BESTSELLING AUTHOR

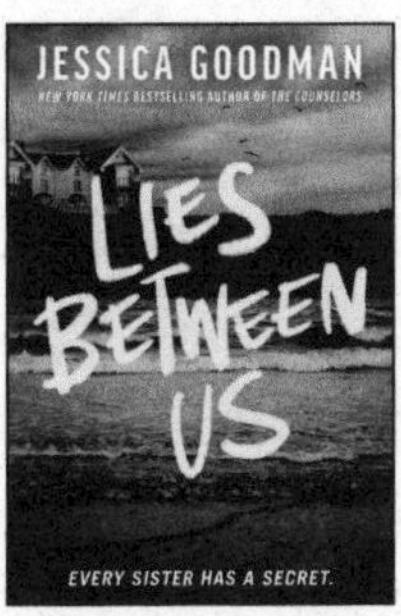